BEARE PARTS

Richard A. Dominico

PublishAmerica
Baltimore

© 2003 by Richard A. Dominico.
All rights reserved. No part of this book may be reproduced in any form without written permission from the publishers, except by a reviewer who may quote brief passages in a review to be printed in a newspaper or magazine.

First printing

ISBN: 1-59286-478-3
PUBLISHED BY PUBLISHAMERICA BOOK PUBLISHERS
www.publishamerica.com
Baltimore

Printed in the United States of America

For Christine

Nothing in this work is meant to be read as anything other than fiction. Any resemblance to any persons living or dead is pure coincidence.

Chapter One
New Beginnings? Or Old Haunts?

Old cottages have a certain charm, call it a history, which is missing in most of the penis extensions which replace them. At least that was the opinion of this man who entered a particular older cottage one fine evening in late spring. His appreciation for such vintage buildings was evident in the way he disturbed nothing and quietly observed where his best vantage point might lie. Of course, the nature of his work required that he touch nothing. And he always did his work meticulously. He wondered momentarily whether his intended might enjoy surprises. He chuckled to himself. After all, there was no need to reject the humour in his night's work.

What did he see? Typically, an entrance way which was hardly spacious and brought one immediately into the kitchen. A bathroom, what appeared to be two bedrooms, a living room into which the kitchen flowed, with picture window framing the beautiful lake in sunset. Reddish orange light at the end of mirror like water stretching for miles into the distance. Very nice, very comfortable, very inviting, thought the intruder.

He decided upon the master bedroom, behind the door. But standing there, he became bored, and realized, too, that perhaps his friend, the occupant, might not enter this bedroom for some time, after coming home. No, that wouldn't do. Reconsidering, he went back to the entrance way, and stood for a moment. Then he realized that the light of the sunset was leaving, and the entrance way, like the rest of the interior was dimming. The shadows became more pronounced. Perfect. There will be no mistake this time. He had had enough of this Lakeshore Drive.

He wasn't long in this position when the headlights showed a vehicle parking across the road. Wonderful. "I can be on my way to Toronto even sooner than I had thought, and before I know it, my busy weekend hat trick will be a fait accompli."

Across the street the car doors had slammed. First the driver's door, and then the back seat door, whence the driver had retrieved what looked to be a dark coloured briefcase and an armful of books and some kind of large manila envelope bursting with its contents. Great. His arms will be full. How convenient thought Jean-Guy, standing silently at the edge of the entrance way, his posterior resting against the back of the kitchen counter.

But, whoa, what is this? He spotted another vehicle cruising slowly to a stop at the edge of the now quiet street but somewhat back of where the occupant had parked his car across the street. As the occupant now found his opportunity, arms full, to begin his crossing of the thoroughfare, he had taken no notice of the other car coming quietly to a halt not all that far from him. But Jean-Guy noticed the second car. And Jean-Guy also knew immediately what was going on. His intended was being tailed. Damn it. He had not counted on this. What the hell was all this about?

No time for answers now. Too late for any change in plans. He would be swift and efficient as always. He didn't need much time. And he was effective as usual.

As the cottager entered the building, his back to his visitor, his arms full, shutting the door with his foot, for the first time he noticed the car and someone inside parked almost across the street. There was a momentary shudder inside him then because of what had happened on that street some months before. And he thought immediately of Wally and Gerry–which one should he call first?

But this shudder was as of nothing to the violent lurch his body suddenly made as the knife entered his back, not once, but again and again, as the figure behind him, Norman Bates-like, stabbed and stabbed, blood spouting all over the place, before bolting out the door, and running away toward his own hidden vehicle.

All the surprised observer across the street saw was someone running like a deer in the shadows. He considered chasing him but opted instead to run first into the cottage to see what had befallen his charge.

* * *

BEARE PARTS

Marriage over. Dad dead. New job. Which item could he have predicted five years ago. One? None? And what would his life look like five years from now? Who the hell knew? John Lennon knew–life happens while you're making other plans.

This was his interior monologue as he came to the split–the divorce of one major highway into two–and it was not an unexpected split. Unlike his marriage. Like so many things happening without warning. As if anyone could prepare for life's big curves.

His hands on the steering wheel, his eyes on the highway signs, his mind picking away at the scabs of recent memory. His life a puzzle he could never get used to.

How many times had he said this to himself? It still seemed profound to him. And painful, too. That's the way it goes with insight, always a price you didn't know you were paying until you got the insight. His life had surprised him since he was a kid, not just the last five years. He had never really been in control. Planning was a waste of time. Control was an illusion. Picturing any kind of future a sham exercise. In retrospect, a cruel and unusual punishment.

So why plan? Live in the present only. Screw the future.... Yeah, but here's the rub...just try to live like this. Not so easy. Especially when the present is the shits.

The Camry carried him northwards, speeding gracefully across the lanes , steering him straight toward... what? Home? This small city, still home, after 30 years in the huge metropolis? Hardly. There was no more home. Not with Dad dead. Louise not dead but gone, the pain just the same, as far as his gut was concerned? It's a son of a bitch when there isn't any more home anywhere! The world's a colder place, like Toronto to a Sunday morning kid moving there from the boonies.

And typically, an article on divorce had said, the husband was usually the main cause of the breakdown. And so she had also said on more than one occasion. This, of course, was before they had found civility in the interests of the children, after the split. A civility certainly not intended to satisfy the lawyers who profited from acrimony, but not from matrimony.

One town after another. Halfway. Reading the odd bumper sticker: Vegetarian, an Indian word for lousy hunter. That might have been funny once upon a time. But right now he was not into laughing. He was on his way to a new job.

Imagine. My old high school, not goofing off in the locker room, hiding away from phys ed, smoke in hand. Now I'll either be teaching or looking for the same hideaways, police-man like. They don't teach you that part about teaching in the education faculties; there are no courses in lunch room supervision, handling the sandwich-throwing kid you have never taught, or the two guys exchanging punches, making work for dentists.

And now he would be obligated to eye-measure the length of the skirt from the floor.

"Excuse me, son. Let me see the label on the back of that tie. It doesn't appear to be a McTavish tie. You will have to go to the office for permission to wear that tie." Would that be a Catholic "fuck-you" under the barely audible breath?

Nor did they teach you how to endure willingly the monthly staff meetings, listening to aging clerics read their mimeo-graphed directives on how the school will be run, or else.

Teaching literature. That's what he thought he was getting into 25 years ago. He did not willingly choose police work. Like his buddy did. Hall duty. Bus duty. Arguing with kids you hadn't taught, didn't really know. Kids who did not respect you because they had not had you in class yet, had not seen that you were a genuine guy who cared, who knew his stuff, who could even make some of the poems, some of the stories, touch their own lives.

No, no, no… to these kids on the asphalt outside on some March school day at 3.30 in the afternoon, you were simply one of "them", the administration, one of the prick class, out to harass them, make their adolescent lives even more self conscious, more difficult.

"As if," one kid was overheard complaining all those years ago, "being short, having unwanted pimples, lacking athletic ability, missing school smarts were not pain enough… as if more were required in the way of Lenten harassment – now we have to have this prick bothering us. Just because we are not standing where we should be to let the bus pick us up, or because we want to shove each other into the snow right now, to wear off the boredom of afternoon classes taught by an old cleric who hasn't had a hard-on since Judas tried to throw the hand to Mary Magdalene."

And what really pisses me off, he thought to himself, are the principals who see themselves as social workers, the special ed types, the counselor-principals, the ones who coddle the kids, the ones who are not much into letting kids live by the reality of consequences. Well, he'd left one behind. What would the new one be like to work for?

Still, what else was there? Marriage over. Kids with her. A chance to go back – yes, you CAN go back, desperate he was to believe this right now – as if in starting all over at the beginning he could undo what had transpired. No, never win her back. He had accepted that. Or so he kept telling himself.

So, teaching at the old high school was kind of a new beginning. Golf with the guys, the old guys he grew up with, the best friends after all, with him through these last 10 months of agony. They would continue to support him, if not at one drinking hole after school on Friday, then at another. Some of them there at this emotional place before him. Strange how women laugh at male bonding. But what the hell, they're jealous, making movies themselves now about female bonding, telling jokes about each other's men. What next? A female version of macho, that other thing they like to rail about?

John's thoughts raced on... Wives always resented their juvenile husbands getting together, sharing laughs about the old times, the screw-ups which never seemed so funny then but were indeed hilarious today, a kind of cement for friendships which, like good wine, gets better with aging. And when the ladies leave, it's what remains, "what we began with, each other, no broads, Saturday night, a case of 24, or a bottle of scotch now that we've all prospered... So this is prosperity," he thought, holding back tears as he whizzed past the highway motel where murder had once been committed, and opted to skip breakfast.

Driving on this Sunday morning. And they've already gone to the 9.30 Eucharist. Or is she just now rousing them from their slumbers, enticing them to the 11 o'clock service, with hot chocolate in bed, snuggles, giggles. Or tears when Debbie says, "I miss Daddy, Mom."

Yeah. I miss you, too. How can a thirteen-year-old be so heartbreaking in her absence and such a pain in the butt when you're marking papers? It's not surprising. Her older sister has the same power. Nancy at 17 years of age, a beauty. Our daughter, too. Eucharist. Communion. Stop it. I don't need these thoughts now. What am I, a fucking cry baby who can't live with consequences?

Another small town. And piss at the next. And gas at the one after that. And bypass the next. Through this one and that one. And finally, Mom. The guys. Great first semester. Two Grade 12 English classes and one Grade 11 Religion. What? He'd never taught religion in his life. Didn't hardly go to church any more, except once in a while to set a good example for the girls...

Just don't think about it being Sunday morning, late, and you are not at Church with Louise and the girls. It's not all right with the world and may never be again. Just don't think about it. Go to your new-to-you cottage on the lake, there's furniture there, a bed, a place to mark papers–oh joy–drink with the guys, cry yourself to sleep at nights.

"What a poor excuse for a bypass," John thought to himself. It's just a busy downtown street these days, but he had to take it to get to his exit. And then five minutes from Mom's.

And he began to pass the landmarks of his growing up here in Beach Bay: Aunt Lucy's Restaurant where Connolly had broken the pinball machine from shaking the shit out of it once too often trying to get a free game and old Mrs. Gavotsny, Dirty Mary they had called her, calling him up one day, totally surprising him, asking, "Con-ly, when you going to pay?"

And going by the hangout with the fountain in front where one day... Dimaggio's Deli...

"Hi guys!" was all Grimman said as he came across the street from having parked his car in front of the private Catholic girls' school across the street, when, completely on impulse, at the suggestion of John, the rest of the guys ran across the street, grabbed Grimman, and tore his pants off, throwing them into the fountain for sheer hellery. Grimman getting back into his car in his undershorts, as they guys returned to their pop cases to await the next afternoon adventure in front of Dimaggio's.

The same hangout where on another day they had turned a bicycle upside down, stuck cannon firecrackers into one end of the handlebars, and a small rock into the other side, attempting to hit the private school. Great distance if the rock made it.

Where on so many Friday and Saturday nights they had taken up the collections, like good little Catholics and Protestants. Either three or four guys to a case of 24 which they would drink before going to the dances. Hoping to pick up the girls but inevitably ending up eating pizza together, no girls, but laughing just the same.

Drinking the beer up at the sand pits, or on the edge of high snow-banked highways rarely used by any one on winter evenings, graduating eventually to rented motel rooms. The one particular Sunday night he could never forget when they came to get him because they had somehow managed a whole keg of draft beer from some bootlegger. Up at the sandpit, standing there while no one knew how to open the keg properly. It blowing straight up into the cold night air, from the car trunk, to their complete horror and surprise, four guys running around holding paper cups up trying to catch a glass of draft raining down from the night sky. After a third of a cup each, they drove him home, twenty dollars poorer.

And then there was the house. And the hug, quick and healing. No more tears now. Just teasing. "I thought you said you'd be here by ten?"

"It is 10, Mom , but just not here. It's 12.00 here but I prefer to go by Mountain time. Alberta time. I hate flat land, Mom. I like mountains. Better scenery. Besides I gain two hours."

"You are crazy. No wonders Louise... Oh, I'm so sorry. I didn't mean that…"

"It's okay, Mom. I know you didn't. But let's change the subject, anyway, shall we?

"What's that delicious aroma? Your meatballs! The famous Emma Coliani meatballs, with her equally famous sauce?"

"As if you didn't know, Giovanni! You spoiled thing, you!"

"Hey, Mom. I haven't heard my Christian name since…" and his voice was about to break when she hugged him, remembering how he had told her before that when Louise was angry with him and he with her, they would resort to their full Christian names; otherwise it was always the inevitable nicknames they had for each other, or even John, but rarely Giovanni.

It's hard to escape memory… an invincible enemy. Better to make it your friend. Live a life without regrets. Impossible. Born fucking loser. Stop it. Stop it. Brain. I want to rip you out by times.

"You want to eat in the dining room, John?"

"No, Ma, the kitchen's fine. No trouble, please. I am glad you cooked pasta though. And glad I did not stop for breaks on the highway. Now I can pig out, like always."

And the twinge of guilt about his weight. Especially now. He knew that if he were to enter the meat market again, to go on the golf holidays, the ski trips with the guys, he would have to lose this paunch. Bad enough a lot of the hair had already gone. But now the weight would have to go, too. And he was scared. It wasn't his desire to date again; but he was frightened of the impending loneliness of February nights in this town. Felt them before, he had. He hadn't been able to lose weight while married. Would necessity birth a new resolve? A new strength of character? Why hadn't this damned necessity helped him to change before, to save his marriage? The meat market. Did he really want to get back into it?

He had heard the guys talking all these last few years about the great pursuits. The women available. And while he had found it interesting, he had never wanted to get back into the game. No. He wanted to stay home and relax. Screw the chase. But, hey, you gotta do it or stay home lonely. Loneliness vs solitude. Mature people were supposed to be able to relish the latter, eschew the former. To John, lately, the distinction was like the one between constructive and destructive criticism, bullshit. Both are destructive. Both are cruel, and leading to despair.

Yeah, sure, after too many meetings, some time at home alone was good. Quiet time. Down time. But only when you knew she was in the next room. Or, if gone to see her parents, home soon. Ready at the slightest invitation to share a cup of tea. A laugh. And long, long ago, before the kids, even a romp in the sack. Saying things, promising things you cannot believe you said so earnestly then, and now you're split forever. "Fuck you, life," he thought. And stick faith and trust up your arse, too, while you're at it, he wanted to scream. But he'd done that already one night after a half bottle of Johnny Walker Red. Or was it Teacher's Highland Cream?

"John, are you gonna eat with me, or go to sleep daydreaming?"

"Oh, sorry, Ma. I guess I suck as a guest today, huh?"

"Guest? What guest? I didn't know I was carrying a guest for nine months 51 years ago. Nor would I have spent all that money on a guest for the 20 years you lived under this roof."

"Ma, you never told me. You spent money on my youth? I thought I was the only one who wasted money on my youth!"

"Wasted – you wasted the money. Your father – God rest his soul – and I – we spent it on bringing you up to be a good man. Come to think of it, maybe it was wasted," she laughed. "But seriously, my son, you are a good man. No matter what!" she blurted this out quickly, almost too quickly, so that it revealed what she had seen, the quick glistening of his eyes, with the joke that had gone wrong again.

"Thanks, Mom. Here I get the best food, and I get you, too, still believing in me."

And then, to change the subject. "Mom. How'd it go at the doctor's this week?"

"Oh, no big deal. He wants me to get a mammogram. Apparently there's some kind of shadow which could be nothing more than that benign stuff that has showed up before."

"Are you worried, Mom?"

"Who has energy for worry these days? Or should I say, I only have so much energy, and right now most of it is going into your account."

"Mom, I'll be okay. Honest. Yeah, I know, you don't believe me, any more than I believe that you aren't worried about that mammogram. But, I'll be fine."

"Yes, for every door which closes, a new one opens. Isn't that what I keep telling myself? So, while you and Louise are no more, maybe another person will come into your life and protect you from the loneliness I have been experiencing since we lost your father. You are still young, after all." Suddenly, and without invitation, there were now tears in her eyes. For herself? For Louise? For John? He didn't know. Nor could he deal with them. So they went unacknowledged by either of them.

"I don't even want to think about all of that right now. I just want to get settled and get into this new teaching job. And try to be happy being home again. It is going to be strange being on the other side of things at that school this time."

"Yes, God knows you caused a few of those teachers no little grief when you were one of the students there."

"But everyone has to have a boyhood or a girlhood. I enjoyed mine and I am tried of feeling guilty about it, Ma."

"When do you folks begin up there?'

"September 4, right after Labour Day, as usual."

"Are you looking forward to it? I mean, really?"

"Yes, actually I am. Well, a little bit anyway. It will be something to see whether I can recognize old friends' faces in the countenances of their offspring. And teaching senior English is okay. Religion I am not too sure about. In fact, I am a little uptight about that. A lot will depend upon how many idiot staff meetings we have to attend. And on how supportive the administration is. This Principal is another non-creative entity, the only kind which gets promoted these days, another I-promise-not-to-rock-the-boat-and-to-be-seen-at-church-every-single-Sunday kind of fellow. Not the type to stand up for his staff."

"Will all of these changes in the papers make it harder for teachers, easier for parents to control the curriculum, John?"

"That's what some of us are worrying about, but what the hell, let's wait to see what unfolds. As you just said, there only so much energy for worrying these days, Mom, and I have pretty well used up mine as well. Besides, maybe school councils can't be any worse than some of the trustees we've met over the years.

"Anyway, Mom, I have to get over to the new pad and see whether the landlord fixed the water pressure. I think I also have to cut the grass now that I am the tenant. Maybe I'll even relax with the sunset on the lake tonight."

John left for his new accommodations, anxious that if anything, the sunset would be a downer experienced alone.

But he got through his first night on the lakeshore and his second and third as well. Until September 4, 9.00 a.m. came, and his first meeting with all 83 students, his charges for the first semester. Fifty-one Grade 12s, and thirty-two Grade 11s.

How many would develop under his tutelage into lovers of great books? How many would go on to study literature seriously at university? One or two, perhaps. It had been his experience that not many did, but yet you had to teach them as if all were going on to major in literature. He knew that this was a problem with being a high school English teacher, that English ought to be about helping them succeed with the English they would need in all of their subjects, with the kinds of writing they would need in science and geography, not just in literature classes.

Yet there was very little cooperation between teachers of various subjects; such an approach would have been in the best interests of all of the kids. He also knew enough that even when he did teach students who could major in literature, the keeners, the bright ones, most of them would go on in other fields, for they were good at everything. And job potential was more important to their parents than the study of the arts.

Sometimes, it was the quiet student at the back of the room in Grade 12 who would suddenly announce one day on a return visit that s/he had gone on to major in English at university and was now in fourth year and would there possibly be an English teaching position back at the old alma matter? And John could hardly remember teaching that student, so quiet had the student been while in his class. And certainly this one had never shown any inclination toward a major in English.

Still, he loved introducing young minds to D.H. Lawrence's take on the necessary tension in heterosexual relationships, on the need for a power balance between people supposedly in love with each other. He could see the shock of recognition on their young faces. He also loved watching them react to Marlow's, "No, I don't like work. I like what's in the work, a chance to get to know yourself."

John knew that ultimately, the most important curriculum these kids would ever study was their own selves. He knew how important it was that the literature touched them in their very cores, where they lived life, to see them realize that they were not after all alone in what seriously bothered them, to have them discover sometimes for the first time, that yes, maybe there was something important to this school business.

John was convinced when he told his Dad that day following his decision to leave law school that teaching was important work. Yeah, he knew that law was more prestigious. Medicine even more so. Yeah, so what, fixing elbows was more important than molding minds. C'est la vie, he had thought. Perhaps anyone *could* teach, in a way that not everyone could doctor, but let them try it then.

He was confident in his choice of profession. John the rabbi. Just like Jesus. He laughed to himself. Some Jesus!

"Mr. Coliani, may I ask a question of a somewhat politically incorrect sort. I mean given the nature of this school, sir."

"I have come to expect nothing less from you, Bruno." Laughter from most of the students.

"Well, sir, it's only this. In *Portrait of the Artist as a Young Man*, there is this anti-Catholic feeling. You know, Stephen goes through a religious phase, is badly scared by the possibility of hell fire, and eternal damnation, during his high school retreat. And yet ultimately he ends up leaving not only Ireland, but also his Catholicism. He is liberated, as it were, from most of his past. And Joyce seems to make of this whole rejection a positive thing. And yet here we are, sir, studying all of this in a Catholic high school. And you could be accused of contaminating our young minds. We may have to ask our parent to buy you some hemlock, Sir."

"Ah, it does my heart good to see you have remembered something from your course in ancient Greek lit, Bruno. I will have to commend Miss Decaro. And I am flattered to have you compare me to Socrates. But, in truth, Bruno, I am sure the analogy does indeed limp greatly, particularly with the presumption of minds in this classroom." More laughter.

"Now to take advantage, Bruno, of what is really a fine question… Do you remember in *Sons and Lovers*, Bruno, where Clara Dawes, I believe, also speaks about breaking out, starting her life anew, do you remember what Paul Morel says to her?"

"I do, Sir." This from Diane, ever ready with the answer.

"And what does Morel say to Clara Dawes, Diane?'

"Morel says something like, 'You'll find my dear, that you are always stepping over the things you think you have put behind you.'"

"As ususal, a very fine answer, Diane."

From the back of the room, "Not fair, Sir, she has a bloody photographic mind."

"Out of turn, young man."

He deliberately ignored the, "… and a nice set of tits to go with it," John thought he had heard under someone's breath from another corner of the room. He did not know what Diane would make of the comment had she heard it. He strongly doubted that she would find the comment flattering. But he ignored what he thought he had heard. No sense making trouble he could avoid.

"So, my good friend, Bruno. What does Morel's answer to Clara Dawes have to do with Daedalus' throwing off the traces of his entire past, on his way to becoming the smithy of his own soul, as he puts it?"

"Ah, another trick question, is it, Sir?"

"Not at all, Bruno. Think about it." And that damned bell again, just when he had them going somewhere, to a place they needed to go, a place where the real limits to liberation are exposed. You had to at least recognize the height of the walls before you began trying to scale them, John thought to himself as he gathered his notes and thought of the sandwiches he suddenly wanted to tuck into.

"Thanks, sir, for allowing me to ask that question, and for not being upset with me."

"Bruno, that's the very kind of question which has to be asked. Maybe we can pursue the discussion next time."

John wondered if Bruno would make the connection on his own between Clara Dawes' inability to escape her past and Joyce's writing about his past for the rest of his life, no matter Stephen's intention at the end of *Portrait*.

The afternoons were short in this semester's timetable and so it seemed to John almost unbelievably soon when he found himself in the watering hole eyeballing that first draft which Wally slid over to him.

"Thanks, Wally, does this mean you're buying all evening?"

"Eat shit, Collie. And get your money onto the table. Fuckin' teachers always cheap."

"Now, now, Wally. Easy. I just got here. I must be eased into such polite conversation. How goes the real estate market? Sell any mansions this week?"

"You really know how to ruin a Friday evening, Collie."

"That good, huh?"

"The son of a bitch doesn't work at it. He's either at the golf club or, he is at the golf club." From Horney.

"Fuck you, you jealous prick."

Horney: "Wally wouldn't know if the market's good or bad. Only whether Arnie made any money in the pro shop this year. Or whether dues are going up this spring. Or whether Heather's having a sell off in the pro shop."

"So, things are normal here. Everyone's sharp as the butt end of a saw log as usual."

"Well, listen to 'teach' here, newly returned, and declaiming against our local wit," laughed Wally.

The three of them looked up in time to see Buns and Bonnie approaching their table. John with more interest than either Wally or Horney. It was the first time he had seen the two of them since his return. Bonnie had been Louise's best friend when they were all first married. Louise had been in touch with Bonnie when making her decision to let John stay on his own without much effort to get him to come home. Somehow seeing her hurt him somewhere deep inside, as if memory was at it again.

"So, the best of Dimaggio's Deli has once again graced these premises on this late October afternoon. What's the matter, teach, no football game after four today?"

"Not today, Buns. How goes it with you?" He said nothing to Bonnie and it was slightly embarrassing that he did not, could not, greet her personally.

"I am a very happy man today. I bought some BCE Inc at $63 in September and it is at $70.50 as we speak. Maybe there will be a retirement for me after all." Someone said something about having to work for a living before you could retire. Someone else reminded the speaker that Buns did not have to work… he was a thief, that is, a lawyer, which Buns ignored.

"Are you still screwing around in the market after what you've been through, Buns," asked Horney. "I'da thought you'd learned your lesson by now."

"Me too!" quipped Bonnie. She was the brave one first: "John, it's nice to see you home again. But I am sorry about what's happened."

"Thanks. Are you teaching Grade Five again?" John and Bonnie had attended the faculty of education together way back in 1969. Buns was a family lawyer doing very well. John wondered whether Louise had asked Buns initially to represent her in the divorce action he didn't want to think about. He was grateful that if Louise had asked Buns, he had declined the work. It would have made this even more awkward. Instead, she had chosen thank God, a totally incompetent firm with connections to her Anglican Church. John didn't know who was more slippery, the law firm, or the Anglican priest who had recommended the firm to her. The closest this priest ever came to agape was during his frequent drunken lunches invariably paid for by whichever wealthy parishioner he was sucking up to on any particular day. The ultimate sleaze in white collar and rotting teeth. A man of God indeed.

After too many moments of awkward silence, they were rescued by the arrival of another couple whom John didn't know, but who were clearly intending to meet Buns and Bonnie for a beer at the tavern. The four of them moved away to their own table, with the usual we'll-have-to-get-together-soon.

"She still looks good, doesn't she?"

"Horney, a snake looks good to you. And come to think of it, not a bad association, aye Collie?"

"Enough, Wally."

John remembered telling Wally what he thought of Bonnie's role in their break-up. He still resented Bonnie's apparent advice to Louise, that if it was over, it was over, and time to move on. John hadn't quite seen it that way, and had wished that Louise would have come and begged him to come home but she didn't. Louise's perception had seemed to coincide more exactly with Bonnie's. John inwardly hoped that one day Bonnie would walk in the same moccasins he was now wearing, that one of her old friends would say exactly the same to Buns, that if it's over, it's over, and let her drink from the same cup which was now his. Oh shit, what's the sense in revenge, he wondered.

As John began to slink visibly into a place his friends could not follow, Wally grabbed him by the metaphorical collar with, "So, what do you think of our Junior A possibilities this year, John. I hear you watched them practice the other night."

"Yeah, we had the ice at four, so I hung around after for a while and took a gander. Where the hell did they get that animal on defence, that Ostrowski kid, number 4 I think?"

"Ahh, you noticed him, huh? A few guys in the league are going to know the feel of the boards with that sucker on defence this year. He's only 15 for cryin' out loud." Wally loved to go to the games. Never missed a home game. Was their biggest fan. Had played himself but not beyond Junior B, and that a long time ago.

"We picked him up from St. Kits but he comes originally from Foleyet."

"Where the hell is Foleyet?" asked Horney.

"Big university town west of Timmins," said John. "You've heard of F.U.?"

"You're as bad as when you left here," laughed Wally. "Bartender, mon ami, another round and make sure Collie here digs deeply, the cheap prick. All you teachers are cheap pricks. Every real estate agent in this province hates to deal with fuckin' teachers."

"You are just jealous, my good man, that as teachers we know the value of a dollar and are not wont to waste what God has provided us for our hard work. Unlike you crooked bastards, who never work, but instead, always trying to screw some little old lady out of her home-based pension."

"You got it wrong, Collie, you dog-fucker. It's Horney over there who's the crook. Don't you know that all car salesmen would screw their own grandmothers."

"Yeah, call me again, you prick, when you want to borrow another half-ton, for your stupid moose hunt."

"Now. Now, Horney, be nice to your old buddies. And above all, be honest. You fucking guys are all crooks, or you wouldn't be flogging cars. I don't know what's worse, your way over-priced new ones with the built-in obsolescence, the ones which lose 25 per cent when we drive them off your dealer's lot, or the used clunkers everyone tried to get rid of because they were bought from you in the first place and are known to be a pile of expensive shit."

"So how come you keep coming in and crying for a good deal, you weasel. If you so dislike our fine product?"

"Because I like to give to charity, especially to the mentally disabled. And the brain damage injury also helps," Wally laughed.

"Well. With the latter, I couldn't agree more," from Horney.

"Listen. Don't make fun of my brain damage, Horney. Not you of all guys. I seem to remember you taking a Thanksgiving turkey out of someone's fridge one weekend at one of our boyhood socials. Filling the damn thing with beer, then making sure that everyone at the place had a throw of it, either up or down the stairs, and from one room to another, till the damn thing looked like a Bangladesh pigeon."

"Yeah, and as I remember, he put the damn thing back in the fridge and the unknowing family ate the damn turkey on Thanksgiving Monday."

"And were none the wiser," laughed Horney.

"You were a crazy bastard. I mean are," Wally said.

"Fuck you, Wally. Didn't you, at that same party, throw a whole pie into that kid's face, whose only sin was merely to have knocked at the door? What the fuck was his name anyway? I remember you opening the door, and letting fly. The kid didn't know what hit him. Speaking of crazy bastards!"

And their threesome grew to four (Jimmy-Jones), to five (Knockers), to six (Ham), to seven (Or-val), and with each expansion, another round, to a number approximating 15 people at three tables now pulled together, till Collie didn't notice that some were leaving to go home for supper, new ones were coming from other tables, and the laughter got merrier, the jokes more raucous, the insults louder, and the pain lesser. Till,

At about 8 o'clock, Wally, whose voice got louder with each new round, yelled, "So who's going for pasta?"

"You fucking pig! Look at your gut. You don't need more food. You need a diet."

"And you would need a lobotomy if there were a brain to sever."

But eventually, after still three more rounds, about six of the hard core made it to Sorrento's for whatever. Once inside, John was sorry that he had kept up to Wally and Horney, as now the floor seemed not quite level. At the urinal, he knew the walls were also skew. Nonetheless, he did not say no to the red wine Wally was pouring into his glass. And David, the proprietor's oldest son, was addressing him:

"John, my son loves your English class. Little bugger came home the other day and said he wanted a briefcase. Knapsack's not good enough for him now. A reader of books he says he is now. What the hell you saying to those kids in class these days?"

"Dave, Collie's not saying anything to them. He's giving out free safes – in a Catholic high school no less, and paid for by our hard earned tax dollars – and that's why they like going to class. Your son probably wants the briefcase to transport the safes to market. He's going to be a filthy entrepreneur like his old man."

David: " How come you still hang around with these bums, John?"

"I was just asking myself the same thing, David. Anyway, glad to hear that Bruno is enjoying the class. Actually, I enjoy having him in class."

"Watch it, Dave, he's a teacher. He'll be trying to get a free pizza out of you. He's been going to the washroom all fucking night at the pub when time came to buy a round."

"You're lying, dickhead."

And so it went like it went most Friday evenings, a lot of draft, a lot of laughter, a lot of old buddies. And then home, bed, wake Saturday morning, self lacerating again, too much beer, too much wine, not-going-to-do-that again, shit-I-shouldna-drove-home-again, now it's marking time, and I have a headache, damn it. Coffee. Pop. Hunger about 11. And all day Saturday till around 3 in the afternoon, four hours of marking and about 12 papers marked out of 51. And then the phone.

"No, Mom, not tonight for supper but tomorrow for sure, okay?"

A run, a shower. And then Wally's for supper and maybe the hockey game on TV. A wonderful life. But it was at least comfortable to be with friends on a Saturday night. At first it was not so comforting because Wally's wife Brenda reminded John that Louise was absent from these Saturday night get togethers. But Brenda tended not to watch the hockey games and did her own thing, leaving Wally and John alone in the family room to curse the refereeing, shout obscenities at the dirty play of whichever team was battling the Leafs, and enjoy the beer, which rarely changed from Blue, Saturday after

Saturday.

How long had John Coliani known Wally Misener? That six-foot-two, white haired, thin son of a bitch whose laugh was infectious, whose kindness legendary. From high school days when they smoked together in the locker room at the Catholic high school, when they were supposed to be outside doing self-directed phys ed, or at least in the gym competing while the priest-teacher read his office. Wally always had money for smokes, John rarely. Thus something bad, in and of itself, smoking, had left John with something good – a lifelong friendship. And John could see that Wally felt the same way about their friendship.

Wally had been delighted with John's decision to come home. John just wished it could have been sooner and with Louise and the kids, but enough of that regret for tonight. This he thought while trying to get deeply involved with the second period, the Leafs losing 4-2 to Chicago.

Since Grade 10, Wally had been John's closest friend, sticking by him especially in these last two years, the hardest of John's life to date. When they graduated together from the high school, they had gone on to different lives, John to university and Wally to the police college, eventually becoming one of the force's finest. He lasted as a police officer for 20 years and then suddenly one day packed it in, went away to study for his real estate licence and became a top salesman. People loved Wally Misener and most of his success in real estate was owing to the great many referrals he got.

Wally followed up after he sold your house, or helped you find a new one. He dropped by. Brought gifts, calendars, letter openers – his latest gizmo a mouse pad with his name and phone number on it, and his slogan, "I want to be your only real estate agent – for life." Corney but effective. He had done well at real estate ever since he got into it. He never missed police work. It had left a bad taste in his mouth, especially since the Falwell case, which broke Wally's heart. As a cop, Wally had spent a great deal of his professional time working on this mystery disappearance. He had believed very strongly that the Falwells had been abducted. He did not buy the drowning hypothesis. Like so many others, Wally figured the bodies would have to have floated up to the surface at some time that spring of 1957 or at least by the following Fall.

Wally suspected foul play from day one but he could never produce the evidence to prove to his superiors that the case had to be kept open, no matter the cost, until the criminals were found. The police, he had argued passionately, were obligated to bring closure to the case.

But he was eventually pulled off the case, and given other cases to solve. He had lasted for a few more years but he never got over the Falwell mystery. It haunted him continuously.

Since becoming a real estate salesman, Wally had given up on solving the thing. Did he experience guilt and shame because of his apparent failure? It appeared that he had himself brought the case to some kind of emotional closure, in the way that he refused to be brought into discussion about it any more. But appearances were deceiving, John knew, and John could not help suspect that deep down inside Wally there was still a very large file not yet closed on the missing Falwells.

Once Wally had been used to talking to anyone about the case during the years when he was a policeman, always on the lookout for something someone might say to him which would give him a hint, a clue, a lead, something to go on which might lead him down some avenue of investigation that would prove fruitful.

No, Wally did not seem very interested in the Falwell disappearance any more. Nor did he see any of his old police colleagues much any more. But then, Wally was so damn busy with his clients, he hardly had any time for himself any longer. Even though Horney teased Wally about the amount of golf Wally played, about his hunting trips, in actual fact, Wally really did not play that much golf. He did go up to the clubhouse for lunches and late afternoon beer fests but John believed that Wally real did this because of the real estate contacts Wally acquired by his presence at the golf club.

And as far as hunting was concerned, Wally talked more hunting than he actually hunted. He was not merely a gun hunter. Wally was also an avid bow hunter who loved to talk about hunting moose and deer with his recurve bow. But he loved the talking about it more than he apparently loved the actual hunting because he hardly went any more. Thanksgiving weekend was sacred to Wally each year because he did go hunting then but that was about it.

Everyone loved Wally so much that he was forever getting invitations from one group of hunters or another, but although he often said yes, he always backed out at the last minute, claiming a huge deal would go down the tubes if he wasn't in town at that time. He would also claim that his clients depended upon him and he just had to be there to serve them or they would go to someone else. And that just couldn't happen in Wally's code: not to be there for a client was simply unthinkable.

Yes, Wally worked hard to be the top real estate salesman in John's home town. And people respected him for that. When he was given a listing, he more than any other salesman, would sell that house if it could be sold at the price the vendor had to get. Most Sundays he was doing open houses somewhere or other, and John would often get telephone calls from Wally while Wally was bored at some open house, waiting for some prospective buyer to show up in the middle of a huge snowstorm.

John loved these calls, as he loved being on holidays back home just so he could get up in the morning and go with Wally to their favourite greasy spoon for ham and eggs. It was at this time that John and Wally would dream together about one trip or another that both of them were going to take, to tour some picturesque golf courses in one place or another. These trips, of course, never came to fruition because John would be teaching when Wally could get time off, and because Wally would not take time off in any season.

"Wally," John said one day, "you gotta be putting in more hours at this job than you did even as a policeman."

"For sure," Wally had answered. "But now my income reflects those extra hours, John. It's the old story, put the carrot before the horse and he is going to run like hell. I am part horse I guess. Moreover, once you get into the President's club as the number one

BEARE PARTS

salesman for your brokerage, you don't want to slip to number two or three. I know I don't. I think that much of my business comes to me because people hear that I get good results when I list houses. If I were not known as the most successful salesman, I wouldn't get the listings I get. And I am getting addicted to the money I have been making these last few years.

"Mind you, John, when I see what goes out in expenses – promotion, advertising, cars, that kind of thing – sometimes I wonder if I really am doing that well financially. But I am on this treadmill and I don't seem to want, or even to know how, to get off."

"Wally, with you and real estate, I think it's more than the money. I believe you just love people."

"True enough. I do enjoy working with folks. I can't imagine myself earning a living in a way that does not involve working with others a lot. I get real satisfaction when people buy the house of their dreams and I am the one who helped to close the deal. That's why I drop by on their moving days, and bring them the potted plants and the congratulations. I get as much satisfaction out of being there to see how excited they are, as I get repeat business just by following up like that."

Brenda walked into the family room and asked if either of these two armchair hockey players wanted popcorn. She offered to make it. "I'm in," John said.

Wally laughed. "Brenda, don't be offering too much. The son of a bitch'll be back next week, too."

Brenda laughed and said, "Yeah, you're right Wally. I have not been taken dancing on a Saturday night since John moved back here. But then come to think of it, Wally, the way you dance, sitting at the table telling jokes and getting inebriated, I'm better at home on Saturday nights anyway. Here I can have a drink or two myself, without getting to be the designated driver every Saturday."

"You're such a martyr, Brenda. I offered to be the designated driver many a Saturday night."

"Name once," came the quick retort.

"As I was saying, John, yeah, I do enjoy real estate."

Brenda left the room to make the popcorn and John got distracted from what Wally was mumbling as he remembered the courtship of Wally and Brenda, how stormy, how on-and-off- again their romance had been. John thought that Wally and Brenda had gone out for at least three years before they married back in the late sixties. Some time after John and Louise. There's that name again.

Brenda had left high school after Grade 12. She had not bothered with Grade 13, but instead went to a community college and took some kind of computer information technology course in the infancy days of computers. It had been a real good move because Bell Telephone had scooped her up and employed her immediately on main frame computers. Over the years Brenda had gotten more and more computer literate and now occupied a very senior position with Bell and had a great many employees for whom she was responsible. She had been promoted many times over the years and her salary was enormous. Thus, the beautiful home on Three Mile Bay where she and Wally lived childless.

John had often talked to Wally about children but he had known a long time ago, because Wally had told hm, that Wally and Brenda would never have their own children owing to some female complication which John never quite understood. Brenda and Wally had talked to John and Louise about the possibility of adopting one day but somehow it had never happened. And John had always thought this was a kind of tragedy since Brenda and Wally were so good with John and Louise's two daughters. Uncle Wally and Aunt Brenda were two of Nancy and Debbie's favorites. And Wally and Brenda never came to Toronto to see the girls without the usual bag of gifts for them.

Life is funny that way, mused John. The very people who would seem to be the most natural of parents do not have them sometimes. He knew of other folks in the same predicament, although most of the ones he knew had in fact adopted children. John also knew, however, as a teacher, how difficult it had been for so many parents of adopted children. Try as so many of them did to make the child feel like a natural child in the family, it often did not turn out that way and the drop out statistics showed far too many adopted children in their numbers. Adopted children ended up all too often as street kids, kids in trouble with the law. And John had known some of these parents and they were good people who did try very hard to love these children as their very own.

It was heart breaking to discover some adolescent suddenly missing from one's class, and then to discover that it was someone John had thought had been making good progress in school, who was now said to have run away from home and was living on the street, completely estranged from the only parents he or she had ever known, even if they were adoptive parents. When John knew the parents, it had been even harder to accept. More than once, John had been called in to mediate with sets of parents and their adopted kids, both before and after the running away. Rarely had John felt successful but he had developed something of a reputation for being able to help both sides talk to each other without screaming insults and hurts that would never go away. But to John, these things had a certain depressing inevitability to them.

He just knew that this kid would never come home again. And most of the time his feelings of apprehension turned out to be right on the money. So it was that John had no real difficulty accepting that Wally and Brenda had not after all adopted any children. John figured that his two good friends were therefore spared a great deal of emotional agony down the road. Besides, he thought, although feeling selfish for thinking it, there's more of their love for Nancy and Debbie, and then he'd put the thought out of his mind every time it surfaced there unbidden.

Brenda come into the room with the popcorn just as the Leafs got penalized late in the third period and Wally was yelling obscenities, both at the penalized player and at the referee. "Glad to hear that you are enjoying the game, Wally," laughed Brenda as she tried to snuggle down on his lap.

"Ah, these bloody Leafs! Why do I bother caring about them? They tie the bloody game up and then take a stupid penalty with three minutes to go in the game."

"Wally, you gotta have faith, man. They're going to do it yet." This from John.

"You fucking Torontonians are all the same, John. You can't accept the truth about these bushwhackers. They are as useless as tits on a bull. I don't know who's worse, the players or the management. Bunch of overpaid crybabies. Maybe I should listen to Horney and start cheering for the Habs. Now there's a hockey team, John. Consistently a contender no matter how many rookies they have on the roster. They come to play, not to jerk off at center ice."

"Such language tonight, Wally."

"Sorry Babe, but these assholes bug me. I get upset every time I watch them screw up, over and over again."

"Hey Wally, there's three minutes left."

"Yeah and two of them are shorthanded minutes."

Wally's anger proved justified, Chicago scored on a power play and won 5 to 4. The three of them finished the popcorn and Brenda also made decaffeinated coffee which they enjoyed while listening to Brenda's new Narrada CD. What a gal, thought John, as he drove home to his little cottage. How lucky that Wally was. And tears came again to his eyes in a wave of self pity.

Chapter Two
House of Horrors

The staff at the high school where he had taught in Toronto held degrees from all over Canada, and even from outside of Canada. The degrees of the teachers, however, at this Catholic high school where John was now teaching seemed to come more from a smaller group of Ontario universities, many of them with Catholic colleges on campus. It followed of necessity that many of the teachers had already known each other from university days. Staff room banter tended to be of the teasing kind. People knew each other. John was pleased by this, and felt a kind of family atmosphere at lunch time.

He himself knew some of these teachers not only because they were old Beach Bayites, but because he had met them at his Catholic College when he had been at university. Adjustment to this staff was therefore easy.

It came as a great shock to John that one particular staffer did not seem to fit in. A real loner. Barry McDevitt by name. It was rumored that the guy had once taught mathematics but now he served as the A-V technician for the whole school and was not much spoken of by anyone including students. It was difficult to see how a guy could be so inconspicuous in a small school such as this. But there he was, a largely unknown entity pushing audio visual carts through the hallways. Perhaps he was so much a part of the visual scenery that no one, neither students nor staff, even noticed him. His continuous silence added to his non-existence.

This was not exactly the case in the staff room, however. Not that McDevitt was discussed by his colleagues. No. That was not it. It was more the business of his never being present in the staff room. Where did this guy eat his lunch? Where did he hang around in his spare time? Surely no staffer was so disciplined as to never goof off at some time. In fact, many teachers coffee'd away their prep time, opting to do the work at home in the evenings, in the comfort of their own homes. Most teachers just accepted the nightly reality of marking and preparation.

John was puzzled by McDevitt. He was a mystery. What was the guy doing on a Catholic high school staff if he didn't want anything to do with anyone? What did the guy make of the concept of community? The administration had evidently long ago given up trying to help him fit in. There had been overtures which had evidently gone awry. Instead of help, the overtures were perceived as interference and McDevitt had gone to his union for assistance. What began as an attempt to help the guy ended badly in the polarization of McDevitt on the one side, and ultimately the administration and the local school board on the other.

John had heard that at least initially, his union had defended McDevitt, had paid for a lawyer when the school tried finally to get rid of him. Apparently, the court ruled in McDevitt's favour, stating that refusal to fit into a staff is not grounds enough to fire an employee, does not constitute any kind of just cause. The board and the school were unable to convince the court of the need to fit in within a Catholic community. While McDevitt did not attend Church, for some reason the board chose not to pursue this fact as a grounds for dismissal, his lapsed Catholicism.

To make matters even stranger, there were rumours about McDevitt in the neighbourhood in which he lived, apparently alone. The house was at the end of a long street which dead-ended where the bush began. Children in the neighbourhood took no pleasure in the rumours. It was not as if the place had a haunted aspect, something to add spice on a Hallowe'en Eve. The rumours were not so much rumours, as they were feelings about the place. Difficult to articulate. The place was different from the Old Pest House, where the impecunious lived during the great Depression. The only similarity with the Pest House was the degree of shabbiness about the place.

But it did remind one of the Radley place in *To Kill a Mockingbird*. People avoided it. It might even be said that they avoided talking about it. As if everyone would have preferred that it simply not be there.

BEARE PARTS

This feeling was picked up by John soon upon his return to Beach Bay. It was elaborated upon by things he had heard around the school, so that by December he was au courant on how the school community and the neighbourhood felt about Barry McDevitt and his house on Wycliffe Road. But that didn't mean he knew much, for no one really did, so much of a mystery was this guy.

Thus it was really awkward for John that night in the basement of the restaurant, the House of Chan, that Tuesday evening, when John normally never went out, because it was a school night and too damn cold in late January to be out and about. It was cold enough on such nights even in the cottage John now called home, even with the old fireplace roaring, which John suspected merely drained the place of heat, without putting a heck of lot of it back into the tiny premises. The fireplace made the living room look comfortable but it required a Mary Maxim sweater to survive. A typical January evening in Beach Bay.

This particular night, John stayed quite late at school, first helping a student revise a paper, after an irate parent had demanded that John not simply grade the paper, but give the youngster another shot at writing it, despite the fact that John had to chase the young man for ten days to get him even to submit the essay. Being an accommodating kind of teacher, even though he resented the parent's assumption that John was out to get the kid, when the very opposite was true and had been evidenced all year in the breaks given, John had agreed to help the boy after school, with an attempt at revision.

And after that tutoring that evening, it was photocopy time. Not many left in the building at 5 p.m. So John had spent an hour photocopying and collating material he needed for his next week's classes. With only one working photocopier available to staff, a teacher had to use every opportunity when the machine was free, or this teacher did without. And the purchase of multiple copies of the material was simply expensively out of the question.

At 6 p.m. John decided he still wasn't ready to go home so he went into the library and began making notes from the Critical Edition of a couple of novels he had assigned as possible works for independent study units for his Grade 12s. These were novels he had read a long time ago but hardly remembered, and he also wanted to review them. And as often happens, a novel one has read at another point in life, sometimes becomes much more interesting upon a return visit to its themes. John could not put down Paton's *Cry, the Beloved Country*. It not only came back to him; it spoke to him in new ways, especially now with all of the changes in South Africa. It was 7.30 before he realized that now he was, in fact, very hungry, so he packed up his things and left the school for the evening.

On the way to his car, he decided that he wasn't going to cook. He hankered after something quick. And he wanted Chinese. And that's what he got at the House of Chan, egg rolls, egg drop soup, sweet and sour chicken, the works... including the fortune cookie which told him that good fortune would soon be his. Following coffee, it now being 8.45, he decided not to chance the trip home without a visit downstairs to the men's room.

But on reaching the men's room door, he discovered the out-of-order sign. Since no one else was in the restaurant upstairs on this cold evening, John said to hell with it and went into the women's washroom, where he chose a stall with some degree of cleanliness, wiped off the seat with a paper hand towel, and sat down to do his business.

Just before he was to rip off the toilet tissue to finish up, he heard what he thought were voices coming from the men's washroom next door which had been posted as out-of-order. The voices got louder and the tones indicated accusations of some sort. Both voices were male, and one was definitely Chinese. Worrying that it would look awkward for him to be found in a women's washroom when there was now nothing wrong with the men's washroom, John wondered whether to wipe and get out quickly, or whether to sit tight and wait for the voices to get out of the basement. He opted for the latter. A definite mistake, for now the argument went on for at least 20 minutes, and John had no choice or so he thought, but to wait it out.

When finally the acrimony stopped and a door slammed, John

was relieved to hear footsteps going upward. He finished, rinsed his hands with haste, and left the women's washroom and stepped squarely into the face of Barry McDevitt who was striding as if propelled with a force that would not be stopped. McDevitt merely glanced at John, then seemed as if to withhold a gasp, and bounded up the stairs. When John reached the top of the stairs, McDevitt was nowhere to be seen, but the Chinese Proprietor was staring at John's back as he left the restaurant and John could almost feel two little holes boring into the backs of his shoulders.

John reached his car, turned the engine over, and was grateful that he had only been inside for an hour and a half, for the Camry groaned even then with the effect of the minus 30 already this early in the January night. John drove all the way to his cottage not really knowing which emotion to focus on, his embarrassment at being seen by a fellow employee coming out of a women's washroom in the basement of a Chinese restaurant, his discomfort at being seen as a prying, albeit unwilling, witness to a heated argument, or his absolute surprise at seeing McDevitt in these circumstances. In fact, it was the first time John had ever heard McDevitt's voice, let alone see him outside the halls of the school. John knew not what to make of anything he had witnessed.

He got into the cottage, checked to see that the oil space heater was running – it sometimes stopped for its own reasons, which necessitated late calls to a landlord who seemed to get off on this as a customary response, "So, what have you done now?" John often fantasized shouting back something like, "I deliberately screwed up such and such so that I could have this wonderful opportunity to call you, as I so enjoy our little telephone calls and I really have nothing better to do, you fucking moron." At such times, there was a great deal to be said for owning one's own place.

Luckily, on this particular night, the heater was working, and John then went to the fireplace, put in kindling and lit the newspaper. In ten minutes he had a fire crackling away, in front of which he now sat with a cup of herbal tea, apple and spice, his favourite, and contemplated what had gone on after supper in the Chinese restaurant.

After an hour of this, he picked up the day's newspaper and fell asleep reading the sports pages.

When the phone rang at 11 it was a gronked out John who sleepily answered, having dropped the phone first, with "Hello?"

"John, it's Louise."

And then John was suddenly, completely, excitedly, awake. But frightened. How should he respond went through his mind. "Will it do to let her see how excited I am." All of this faster than any computer chip.

"Hi. Are you okay? Are the kids okay? Is anything wrong?"

"Everything's fine, John."

And his heart dropped to hear that. He did not want everything to be fine. He wanted her to cry. He wanted her to say she missed him, even that the kids missed him. To be missed. To be loved. His heart would not leave him alone.

"I called because I am apprehensive about a letter my lawyer felt he had to write to your lawyer. And he did it without saying in it what I wanted him to say. Another one of his own compositions, John, and I don't want you hurt by its tone or by its language. We both agreed last July to be civil with each other and, for my part, John I want it to continue that way between us. But my lawyer says that when one of your payments is late, we must react quickly and definitively, so that in any future court action, we can show our letter stating that we warned you about late payments from day one. I'm sure, John, that there was a reason for the 15-day lateness of the payment for January 1. But the mortgage company came after me and I had to tell the lawyer. Sorry."

"What happened, Lou, was that I switched from the bank to a trust company, because it has Saturday morning hours which are more convenient to me up here. Then the school board could not process my payroll deposit change to the trust company in time for the January 1st payday, so the money went no where, not even to my old bank account, as I had issued a written request not to send it to the bank any more. Because we didn't begin school for the first few days in January, I didn't get around to getting the whole thing fixed up as fast as I might have, and so part of it was my own damn fault. At any rate, it took a couple of weeks to get the whole thing straightened out and there shouldn't be any more problems from this point on. I am sorry for my part in this and for the trouble you seemed to have had."

"John, really, I know you are trying to get us the money as fast as you can. And I explained that to Arnold but he always seems to know better how to handle your lawyer than I do, or so he says. You know the tune, John. We have already spoken about it and I don't have to tell you any more. I just wanted you to know that this was not my idea, this letter I am sure you will be getting a copy of. How's everything else?"

"Louise, I don't know how to answer that. And maybe I will just say that I hope all is well with you and the girls and leave it go at that. Are they at all excited about coming up here for March Break to see me?"

"John, you know they are dying to go up there. Is your Mother going to be there or will she be in Florida?"

"Here this year. She hates the exchange on the dollar and is not going down after all."

"Good. The girls really want to see her. Oh hell, John, just a sec, there's another call coming through."

John waited until Louise came back on to say that she had to take this call and that she was sorry and had to run for now. He thanked her for calling and they hung up. His heart just dropped right out of him, as if free falling down an elevator shaft. He sat down and wondered for how long it had been this way, another call, something, anything, interrupting their life together. Not that it was only her corporate legal career which was to blame. No, he was way more honest than that.

She worked nights, weekends. He marked papers or played golf. She took more courses. He went south to Myrtle with the guys for golf holidays. She went to conferences and he on canoe trips. When did all this separate activity start anyway? It was certainly not predictable that night he first noticed her at Rugantino's on Yonge

Street, eating a slice of pizza, all those many years ago. Wasn't it 1968? He in fourth year Honours English and she in first year law at Toronto. Nor could he have foreseen how it would all wash out that night they drank draft together and laughed themselves silly at the old Bay Bloor. Shit. She sounded like she'd be a perfect bow partner for his canoe, eagerly talking about wanting to try a trip some day.

But it didn't work out that way. At first, it was the most intense courtship, the kind that every young man feels is totally unique, with a perfect partner. Teasing. Laughter. Clowning around all of the time. After their third date, back at Rugantino's, but this time just the two of them, he never doubted that she was the woman for him. And it wasn't just the red wine that night. It actually was how they liked all of the same things, or so he thought. Time would later show how wrong they were about their mutual tastes. It certainly did not come out that night that he would spend the next 25 years trying to move North and she would be just as equally determined not to leave Bay Street where her identity would become increasingly anchored.

They married in the summer of 1969, celebrated at the Old Mill, honeymooned in New York City, doing the Broadway thing, Radio City Music Hall, Empire State Building – they could have been as happy doing Guelph, Ontario – hot as hell in July, and came back to Toronto to an apartment in the Married Students' Quarters so that he could begin the M.A./Ph.D. program. It turned out that the M.A. was enough for him. He then attended the Faculty of Education while she continued with law school. John had already been teaching almost two years when Louise, finished with articling and bar ads, joined her Bay Street firm, specializing in corporate work, where she would make a specialty practice out of corporate mergers.

That Louise had a law degree often made John wish he had finished his Ph.D. He sometimes felt the stinging judgments of others who wondered how a woman with such prestige, a lawyer, could stay enchanted with a mere high school teacher. Or was this inferiority merely inside himself, and not truly in the judgments of others? In truth, he could not much abide graduate school and saw it as a major epiphany that day, walking into a class given by "Nory" Frye, when he overheard one grad telling another about the some guy he knew who had actually read another student's thesis. As if no one ever read any one else's thesis. And John wondered suddenly, yeah, why the hell do we slave over these damn things, to what end, for whose benefit? We are indeed like parasites here in grad school, existing on government and university grants, writing things no one really gives a shit about. This is a contribution to society? This is making a difference?

And then Louise, who had to live each day with John's generalized anger about being in graduate school, one day showed him that passage from Margaret Atwood's *The Edible Woman*, where Duncan rails away in a laundromat about the futility of being a graduate student in English, to Marian who thinks graduate school must be exciting. John read not only the passage over again but the whole novel, dropping everything else he was doing at the time. The shock of recognition would not allow him to do otherwise. It was shortly after that John went over to the Faculty of Education and applied for the next September. And gave up the Canada Council grant which every one said he would never get for the first year of a Ph.D.; these same people freaked when he then gave it up to go to a teacher's college.

Memory cut deeply into John now as he remembered the intensity of their love for each other, the fun they had, the certitude that this was indeed a match made in heaven. So why did he stop going to Church somewhere around that time? If things were so idyllic, then why give up on God? And he knew why. It was not that she was an Anglican and he a Catholic. That had nothing to do with it. He had gone to church on Sundays all alone through most of his days at university. Had even gone to a couple of things at the Newman Club, liked the priests and their sermons, enjoyed Father Bellweather in class – it wasn't as if he needed Louise to accompany him on Sunday mornings when she went off to the Anglican service.

No, he simply lost his faith, and perhaps in not working at it by going to Church on Sundays, things went from bad to worse, until he found himself collecting bits of evidence here and there to bolster his increasing atheism. His reading lead him to all kinds of reasons to be angry with the church. His study of the limitations of finite human language lead him to the conclusion that theology was doomed *a priori* in its attempt to describe the infinite. His reading of scriptural exegesis made him doubt the authenticity of the Gospels when he read how the politics of the early church influenced the editing of these gospels. He sickened at the possibility that Roman Catholicism was merely the more powerful of the early Christian sects, the one which won out in the ensuing struggle for dominance and made sure to destroy all the competition and their more heretical views. He wondered about Faith being just a result of the family one was born into. John figured he could just as easily have been born a convinced and committed Muslim.

And while studying literature in a Catholic College, he took some philosophy courses. Initially he was impressed with Jacques Maritain's visits to the campus. He fell in love with the fine precision of Thomas Aquinas' argumentative explanations. It was the later courses in the history of philosophy which did in his compete respect for Thomas, although he never completely abandoned this admiration. Nor was it Descartes who challenged his Faith. But slowly, the materialistic philosophers chipped away at his belief in things like prime matter and substantial form, the hylomorphic theory upon which the Catholic dogma of transubstantiation was based. If this was nonsense, John, thought, then is the miracle of the Eucharist also nonsense?

So many things combined to make going to Church harder and harder until John stopped altogether. So that both Nancy and Debbie were baptized in the Anglican Church. Louise had not been adamant about that until she saw that they were not about to be baptized in any church whatsoever. That's when she put her foot down and said, "Look, John, I don't care whether you are going to your own church or not at this point. That's your affair. But these are my daughters, too, and I want them baptized as Christians. I want them to get instruction in Christianity. So if you are giving up on all things Catholic, then fine. But they are going to be baptized."

BEARE PARTS

So a double christening had followed a few Sundays later, at Louise's Church, with double godparents – John couldn't even remember who they all were now; he only remembered that Wally had declined the offer as he, too, was not going to church in those days but was now – and he remembered that his own mother had gotten smashed on the punch, a very rare and very funny thing, when she told Louise first that the punch did not have much booze in it and later told her that she could not feel her ears any longer. Louise never forgot that and often teased John's mother about it. They always had, and still did have, a perfect mother-in-law-daughter-in-law relationship. Which only made the whole damn split even harder on John.

By this time John and Louise were long out of their first and even out of their second apartment, a nice apartment in the Don Mills area. They eventually bought their dream house – the fighting would see Louise give it another name some day – in the west end, a modest side split close to where John was teaching secondary English. Louise was happy with her proximity to the Bloor subway; she hated driving to work, preferred reading novels or legal briefs on her way to the office.

They enjoyed the house together. The landscaping was shared responsibility at first: he took pains with the lawn and she coddled the flower beds. They both agreed that there was no shrub as pretty as a Colorado Blue and together bought and planted five of them on the front lawn. The back yard got a fence and a couple of less expensive trees, one a red maple, another of their mutual favourites, and for Mother's Day one year he got her a beautiful flowering crab, and had it professionally planted and in place for that May morning. Nancy was only four then.

He became a barbecue fanatic, she enjoying every minute of it. Late Saturday afternoons, after the lawn was cut and she was looking for a shower to get the black loam from her hands, he would open the red wine, light up the grill, and relax on the deck with the Saturday paper till she joined him. And they would laugh at Nancy falling down the slope on the lawn, getting back up and chasing whatever took her fancy on the lawn.

One day, dangerously, it was a skunk which Louise saw luckily just in time, John with his head buried in the sport pages, and Nancy in hot pursuit of the backyard kitty with the nice white stripe. John could still hear Louise's shout of pure terror, as he damn near threw the paper over his head in an attempt to see what had happened. The only unfortunate result was Nancy's tears after she had been stopped dead in her tracks by her mother's shout. The "kitty" meanwhile managed to escape safely under the fence and into the neighbour's yard whose dog was happily inside. John never saw "Kitty" again though he regularly saw holes in his lawn on some mornings, and knew who had been to call.

So what the hell had happened, he frequently asked himself somewhere at this point in these ruminations. Was it because he rediscovered golf? Did golf put an end to these happy Saturday afternoons, and just as happy Sundays? What the hell else was he to do on those summer days when he was finished summer school teaching, sick of marking, and she was working, before the kids were born? Why not whack the ball around? He was not afraid of its addictive potential. He had played as a teenager and could take the game or leave it, at least he could then. But now in his 40s, he was really getting into it, and not just because he was missing Louise at the house. In fact, after the kids were born, if they weren't in some kind of summer program, he would get a babysitter so he could go to the links and bond with earth, sky and buddy. Rarely with ball. He never got that good.

And just as golf seemed to consume John, so did career lock its grip on Louise. Canoe trips were not to be for the both of them. Louise had a back problem and a total aversion to all little flying creatures who like to bite human flesh. John got a couple of annual trips in, when Louise went home with the girls to her parents' cottage in Haliburton. And as John got older, he found himself going only once a year with the guys into Algonquin Park. He did not hunt, although he did like to fish, but really there wasn't the time for everything. When he did go with the guys to someone's cottage, the fishing rods rarely came out of the trunk. Only the beer, the scotch and the cards.

In the winter, for a few years, John and Louise shared an interest in cross country skiing, which died for a few years when the girls were really young. Tobogganing replaced the skiing, but when the girls got to the right age, skiing came back into their lives, and one Christmas everybody got a new package and there was even talk about a family trip to Vermont for March Break. But Louise could not get the time off, and they sent the girls to Florida to see both sets of parents while John when to the Carolinas with the guys to try the links again. These separate March Breaks became the pattern as Louise was less and less in charge of when she could take time off, and it was usually when John could not, because of the nature of the school year. It got to the point where only the statutory holidays were common time off, and these days they spent with the children, although sometimes not together. Rarely was there any time for just the two of them. The usual pattern with young marriages on their way to self destruction.

As in so many marriages gone sour, excitement had been replaced by boredom, by indifference. Sometimes hostility and acrimony reared their heads and took a very real bite out of the self esteem of both John and Nancy, both as spouses and as parents.

"Money! Is that all there is to our marriage these days?"

"John, you just don't want to face facts, financial or otherwise."

"Fact number one: My wife loves money more than me and always has. Fact number two: She doesn't want me to look after the books so she does them herself and then complains that she has too much to do in this marriage."

"John, I do not want to look after our finances. Only my own. I can't deal any more with how you spend your own money."

"Yes, I am such a spendthrift. And I do not know how to handle money. That I suggested we buy this house when you didn't want to because, as you then said, we wouldn't be able to carry it; that it's now doubled in value…"

"But at what price, John? Look at how the damned house has caused us to do without so often. How many times we have fought over money because there's just not enough to do what has to be done, what we sometimes want to do."

"We haven't done so badly, Louise. You just don't have a perspective broad enough to celebrate what we have accomplished financially. You are so damned anxious about money all the time that you cannot think straight about money. You're always worried and you aren't happy unless you have me worried too."

"John, it wasn't just buying this house. You were never satisfied with the house. You had to have the landscaping done to perfection as soon as we moved into the damn thing when we barely had enough money to close the stupid deal."

"For crying out loud. I did most of the bloody work myself during that first summer after we moved in. Precious little recognition I got for it too."

"Yes, and the Visa bill that Fall was in the $6,000 range as I recall. And then there was the rec room downstairs. No, you could not live with it being unfinished. You needed your TV room to have the guys over. So next it was the materials for that and I don't care if you did most of the work yourself. It still cost money we didn't have. Here we couldn't pay off the $6,000 on our Visa and yet you went on charging for materials for the downstairs."

"Louise, you are always bitching about the way I spend money. You wouldn't be happy even if I never spent any and we saved it all. You would worry then about how we are protecting what we have in the bank. You never seem able to enjoy the damn stuff."

"And you want to enjoy it before we have even made it, John. Credit is your worst enemy."

"Yeah, we are so badly off, Louise. I mean, for shit's sake, let's look at the whole picture."

"Agreed. How come most other couples have no mortgage by this time in their marriage? How come we still owe money on this damned house?"

"Because we have enjoyed our lives along the way, Louise."

"On what I ask you? Holidays? You mean your stupid March Break holidays golfing with the guys?"

"That was your choice, Louise, a long time ago when you decided you could not take time off with the girls and me to go away in March. Your partners frowned upon being away in March I think you said."

"So I am going to be blamed for the demands of my job again. You never could accept my career could you, John?"

"Your career is not the problem, Louise. It's your attitude as to what's important, me and the girls, or your damned career. And the choices you make all the time give us the answers, don't they? But Louise, the real issue here is not your career but our marriage and money. It's not that I wanted this house, that I wanted to spend money on the outside or on the inside, that I take holidays to get away from this house of horrors at times… it's that you don't want to spend any money, on anything."

"Nonsense, John. It's that I want to pay off existing debt before taking on any new debt. It's that I can be content with what I have before I have to go and spend more when we can't afford to spend more. It's that I don't want the aggravation of having more monthly bills to worry about. You just go golfing and don't worry about the expenses like I do."

"Here we go again, with the golf bullshit, Louise. You have your career and I am not supposed to complain when you work nights and even weekends, when you can't take family holidays with me and the girls. But when I go golfing to occupy myself, this is wrong. My golf is not important like your fucking career."

"And here's another problem, John. You and your language. The M.A. in English is sure hard to spot when you use that kind of English."

"And you know how to rile me by bringing up my use of language when I am upset. When you can't win the argument, you think, get him upset, make him lose it, so he looks like an ass in mine and in his own eyes. Isn't that your strategy in most of our fights, Louise?

"You are never goddamned satisfied are you, Louise, Haven't been since early in our marriage. I gotta wonder why you ever said yes to my proposal. You wanted separate bank accounts, we got separate bank accounts. You arranged it so that I could never have school holidays when you could take yours, so we have had separate vacations for a long time now. And you keep mouthing bullshit platitudes about the value of family togetherness, but mostly when I am going golfing and you don't want me to go. You are so much in control of this damned arrangement but it's never enough.

"You wanted a more perfect marriage you said, so we went to counseling with, as it turned out, some asshole whose own marriage had failed and I had to go once a week for six fucking weeks and share my weaknesses as a husband, as a parent with this prick, whom you in your wisdom thought was going to help us.

"You can never celebrate what we have together, either financially or even emotionally. Yeah, our marriage, our relationship is not perfect. It never was, yet we agreed to spend the rest of our lives together. We fought when we went out together. We fought after we married. But still, we had good times, too. Both before and after we married. No relationship, for Christ's sake, is ever perfect. Where the hell are you coming from on this, that we have to measure up to some kind of perfect marriage? Who the hell has this kind of marriage, and who even cares? This is what we have and it's good enough for me if we could just stop fighting all the time about money and other things that won't matter a tinker's damn in 20 years."

"Can I talk now? You raise your voice, you yell, and you mistake this for winning our arguments, John, but you don't win. You just yell louder than me, and I refuse to enter into this kind of emotional tirade, with you."

"What's next, Louise, the ususal slur on my Italian heritage now? And how we are hot blooded as a race?"

"No slur, John, but I would like to have the floor for a while, to get a word or two in myself, if that's all right.

"John, just think about how you have made most of the decisions about the money which comes into this house..."

"Oh shit, here it comes, you make so much more than I do…"

"John, let me speak now, and I rarely bring that fact up. It's in your mind, it's your inferiority here which makes you think about how much more I make. And in your guilt, because you spend most of the money. Cars, how many new ones did I ever decide to buy, John? Yes, I take the TTC to work, I know, and you've told me that you look after the cars and so you know better when to trade, etc., etc. But John, I could always have been more content with an economical car, one on which we didn't lose all that damned depreciation as soon as you brought it home. I have no trouble with seeing a car as a means to get somewhere. I just don't get off on the damn things like you always did. It must me a man thing.

"Nor did I need those weekend trips to Buffalo, to Collingwood, wherever, that we didn't have the money for, but you insisted and I went along every time until the girls came along. And your wardrobe, John, is as good as any of the lawyers I work with on Bay Street. And I know you have said that some of your students never see this kind of wardrobe at home and you are trying to show them another way a man can dress. You have a reason for every time you overspend our money, even if I don't agree with these reasons.

"And every wedding for every one of your relatives necessitated a gift which I would buy only for a sister or brother. But you spent three to five hundred on wedding gifts for nieces and nephews when we couldn't afford it, John. And we fought about that, too, and you always had your way."

"Yes, Louise, you were only happy when we spent the money on insurance policies, as if you were more ready to celebrate my death than to enjoy our lives together."

"No, John. It's just that I don't believe, as you seem to, that enjoyment comes only with the spending of money we don't have."

"Louise, do you even believe in enjoying life any more? Your religion lately seems to have you convinced that this life is merely a vale of tears and we will only be happy in the next life."

"John, there was a time, when I married you, that you, too, had faith in an after life. So don't you dare make fun of my faith now just because you have lost yours."

"And now it's sermon time again, right, Louise. Faith is a gift from god, but we have to use the gift before it takes root, right? Isn't that what that jerk of a clergyman told you?"

"John, does it help your self esteem to put others down? To degrade them with your juvenile names for them, when they have given much of their lives for what they believe in?"

"The only thing that Anglican clergyman of yours believes in is a free lunch Louise. That and the wisdom of socializing with the wealthiest of his parishioners."

"Enough, John, this is going nowhere as usual and I do not want to get farther into the place where the name of the game is simply to see who can hurt the other the most. And you are entering there now by making fun of my religion again. A Catholic always feels so superior to an Anglican, even a lapsed Catholic with a regular hangover."

"And who's going for the throat now, Louise?"

"So it's just my drinking that's the problem, right Louise? You, of course, never provoke any of the harsh words between us? You are always guiltless?"

"Well, John, you're the one who started to curse and swear in the restaurant last night."

For a second John wanted to ask just what he did say and do last night but he was too ashamed to admit to her that he did not remember the whole evening. It often happened that way to him now. Go out to a pub on Friday evenings and get blasted on draft beer with colleagues. Louise joins them. A group of the diehards go to the restaurant after and then the wine does John in. Saturday morning and he hopes like hell that he hasn't embarrassed himself too much the night before.

The depression Saturday mornings was always fierce. Why, he would ask himself, over and over again, can't I drink reasonably like other guys? The morning after the night before, alcohol deprivation got physiologically worse for John with age. Many a morning he'd swear that that was it. No more booze. But the resolution would always last just as long as the hangover.

At one point he had quit drinking altogether for an entire year. That was after a particularly bad night when Louise was so embarrassed by his drunkenness that she had taken a cab home. That was the night he had picked a fight with the host of the evening. A lawyer in Louise's office, with a big home in a wealthy country setting. And John had opted to walk home after being asked to leave the premises, Louise having gone in the cab by this time. While he sincerely meant the apology proffered next evening, he never felt forgiven. Nor did he ever go again to any of her staff functions. Too ashamed.

This was not the husband he had wanted to become. Nor the parent, nor the teacher. Most of the time he could drink and get blasted and be funny and have fun. There were these times, however, when he simply drank too much and hostility seemed to take over his personality. Bottled up rage he did not himself even know he was harboring way down deep inside, just waiting for a chance to get out in any big night with booze.

And if he did not pick a fight with Louise, it was with someone else. God only knew how he did not get the beans kicked out of him at these times. At least seven to ten of these incidents scarred the 25 years of their marriage, and he could barely bring himself to remember any of them, so painful were the memories. And thus it was that he would swear off the booze for varying lengths of time, but eventually concluding that there wasn't much of a social life without booze for him.

"I don't feel like dancing, Louise. Can't I just sit and chat at the table? Many men dislike dancing."

"But you used to like dancing, John."

"Yeah, and I used to drink too."

"So, no alcohol, no dancing, huh?"

"I'm sorry, Lou, It's just that I feel so self-conscious up there while you are kicking up your heels. You are such a good dancer, and everyone watches us dance. And when I'm sober, I feel shy. As if I can't stand being stared at. I know they're watching you dance,

Louise, not me, but I'm being noticed just because I'm up there with you."

"Oh, John, it's in your head, silly. After all, they're your own relatives at these weddings. What's the big deal? It's supposed to be a happy occasion. Didn't you always say how much you liked Zorba the Greek because of his ability to express his emotions thorough his dancing?"

"Yes, but he, too, drank wine. It's a great relaxer, Louise."

"I don't know what to say, John. It's not for me to tell you to drink or not to drink. I am certainly not ready to give up my social drinking. Or is that what you really want, so I will stop bugging you to dance with me?"

"No, it's not Lou, honest. I would appreciate it, however, if you would try to understand me. I have always used booze to help me relax at these events, whether with family or with strangers. Dancing does not come easy to me without a drink or two or three.

"After I've had a few drinks, I can dance freely with abandon. I can even tell jokes then. And, yes, I admit that there are times that I can tell jokes, and even be the life of the party when I am not drinking, but I have to be in the mood. And I also admit that I am moody. I can't help the moods. But if I am feeling uptight, or shy, or pensive, it's tough to find any social grace inside myself."

"John, this is not the guy I married. The fellow who wooed me used to meet my relatives and within a few minutes had even My Uncle Bert coming out of himself. And I don't even think he spoke to his own children!"

"Admitted, Lou, I have had some moments when for reasons I do not understand, maybe because I felt better about who I am, that I was able to relax and draw people out. To make them laugh even. But I don't know, lately, I can't seem to do this."

"You have been drinking so long, John, so much, that maybe you're just out of practice. Maybe you just have to learn again to socialize without alcohol. You can do it, John. I know you can."

And at these times her belief in him would really help. For he *had* lost confidence in himself, especially if these conversations took place when he was badly hung. But if they talked in anger the next morning after he had been really drunk, and couldn't remember much after a certain point from the night before, it was really bad for John. He wanted to crawl out of sight. He wanted life to be over. He was afraid even to remember what had happened the night before, afraid what he might find out about the evening. He would be very relieved if he discovered that he had done nothing very much, that Louise had simply driven him home and he had gone to bed. One of his problems was that he rarely got sick to his stomach. He would just keep on drinking until he was just another guy who embarrassed himself and all those around him. Others were lucky, he told himself; they would get violently sick to their stomachs, and then maybe embarrass themselves in this way, but at least they wouldn't have their behaviour to apologize for in the mornings.

Funny how he still had so many friends, so many people who themselves drank too much and therefore didn't really hold it against him. He figured that he must just naturally gravitate toward people for whom alcohol was something to be abused and fuck the guilt over it. So many people overindulged that it wasn't hard to find such friends. John had often said that most people were more alcohol dependent than they wanted to admit.

He was convinced from his own struggles to abstain at certain functions that he wasn't the only one finding temperance so difficult; he knew that others, if they would try to go out of an evening and not drink at all, would find it just as tough. He never understood designated driver types. How the hell did they do it? In fact, John thought society in general had a problem with alcohol. It was like tobacco in some ways. It generated a lot of money in taxes. It provided a lot of people with pleasure, with release from anxiety and care. So that a majority of people simply refused to deal with their dependency.

Alcohol enjoyment was more than socially acceptable. In fact, rare was the social occasion when there wasn't booze. People remembered derisively any dry weddings they had attended. And at one dinner party John had tried to point out how dependent society was on booze and was quickly shot down, as if the problem was strictly his own and told he should stop trying to moralize and project his own private problem with alcohol onto everyone else.

John had a certain sympathy for the youngsters he taught who were on to the hypocrisy of adult society and couldn't understand why marijuana was not decriminalized like that royal commission had recommended in the 70s.

But he himself had his own guilt to deal with. Moreover, he had a wife who did not overdrink very often and was always embarrassed when John did overdrink, though most times she suffered this abuse in silence and did not even embarrass him in the morning by referring to the night before. Unless, it was one of those bad nights.

Like the time he told his mother-in-law to fuck off and leave the raising of his children to him and to his wife. It had been the double christening on a Sunday afternoon and John had been the bartender at the outdoor lawn party which followed the church ceremony. His in-laws had a great backyard and so wanted to have the party at their place. John had given in, provided he and Louise could pay for the libations at the bar. Unfortunately, Reverend Shithead, who had baptized their daughters, was also a guest.

And John had gone out of his way to get the bastard shit faced, pouring the clergyman drink after drink and downing shots with the reverend to get him to overdrink. It had worked; the clergyman spilled his dinner all over his own lap and had also leaned too heavily on one of the tables, putting his hand right into the strawberry shortcake, which left him quite a sight on this fine June Sunday afternoon. But John's uncontrolled laughter had later turned to anger when his mother-in-law was giving hell to Nancy, then about four years of age, for helping herself to more milk at the table and spilling it.

"Nancy, don't just think you can take what you want, child. You have to ask for more of something."

Nancy began to cry, unused to having her Grandma discipline her. John happened to see all of this and came over and picked Nancy up, and wiped the milk from her blouse and the tears from her cheek. He said nothing until Louise's Mother said,

"They really do have to be taught to ask for things."

"Why, is there a shortage of milk or something? Should we have offered to pay for the fucking milk, too, as well as the booze?" It was too late; he couldn't take it back now. But his anger had been coming for a while now. His mother-in-law was always telling Louise how to respond or react to everything Nancy did. And John figured that they had had their chance as parents and now it was his and Louise's turn, without interference from in-laws. He said as much to Louise on many an occasion, but never before in front of his mother-in-law, before whom he merely swallowed it.

"Have you had a little too much to drink, dear?" This from Louise. And that pushed him even further over the edge.

"Why, because I don't want your mother raising our children?"

"John, please don't embarrass me here."

"Fuck you."

When Louise's mother-in-law heard these words she gasped, and then followed with, "In 30 years of marriage your father has never spoken like this to me, Louise."

"And that's part of the fucking problem. He should have told you to fuck off a long time ago. And since he seems incapable of same, fuck off for both of us."

John then stormed home on foot to await the inevitable moment to arrive when he would simply have to apologize yet again for his drunken anger. Which he did do, after the ususal groveling with Louise, the ususal self loathing, the usual wish that he could deal more effectively with his drinking. It was only very recently that he had begun to enjoy the memory of the Reverend Shithead with his hand all covered in strawberries and whipping cream, his black clerical slacks looking like some genetically deformed zebra, his while collar now mostly unbuttoned and one end of it trying hard to escape the disgrace to the cloth by running up into his nostril which it could not of course enter no matter how hard it tried.

"So you see, doctor, it's not been a marriage made in heaven. I wanted it to be precisely that. But I found out soon enough that you don't change a person after you marry him. I ought to have known he would never give up the guys, this damn male bonding thing. But then I'm not sure whether it's the guys which always take him away from the family or the golf itself.

"Funny, I thought that men tended to hang their identity on what they did for a living. Not John. Golf was where he drew his energy, or spent it all. Maybe he didn't have energy enough for courting me after we had been married for a while because he always spent it all on the golf course.

"Oh, I'd argue with him about it, especially after our first was born. When all of a sudden I realized that here was this little baby, Nancy, completely dependent on me for her very existence, for food, emotional sustenance, diapers, etc., John wasn't there beside me. He did try getting up with me in the middle of the night to feed her but with breast feeding, he could not do a heck of a lot. I tried to tell him that his presence beside me in the middle of the night was of value to me, but he soon dropped the effort anyway. And soon I was up by myself in the night, trying to do what is supposed to come naturally to all mothers. Well, it didn't always come naturally to me. In fact, there were times in those nights, and even on the long afternoons of my maternity leave, that I wondered whether I was really cut out for motherhood. And it wasn't something I could talk to John about, even if he had been there beside me.

"You have to know this, Doctor, to be fair to John, I talked him into having children in the first place. I think he was prepared to be married without children. Whether he would have always had this desire I do not know because by the fifth year of our marriage he could see that I really wanted children badly and just seemed to look the other way when I stopped all birth control precautions.

"Nor was he upset when I told him that I was pregnant. In fact, he was supportive and down right enthusiastic. I began to wonder what had happened inside of John to change his attitude so drastically. He went from arguing vehemently about not giving up our freedom as a couple, completely threw away his devotion to the views of Malthus on overpopulation of the planet, and suddenly was refinishing a crib he got from one of his buddies.

"I could not believe the energy he suddenly had for the nursery we now needed. And what a good job he did. Helping me choose the change table, the wallpaper, the curtains – he had time for all of these details. And he was really very supportive throughout my first ever pregnancy. Nor could any father have been happier when Nancy was finally born, something like four weeks after my due date.

"No father took more pleasure in passing out the cigars. Come to think of it, he was equally happy when Debbie was born. It's just that when I found myself home alone with first one, and then two, children to look after, and he was out with his buddies, golfing, fishing, whatever, I resented his absences.

"Why I feel so damn guilty about ending up having an affair with someone who had time for my loneliness, someone who wasn't even married, I don't know. But God knows, I certainly feel guilty about the damn thing. Obviously I wish it had never happened, that John and I could have gotten help from somewhere, patched up our relationship, or at least reaffirmed our mutual desire to make our marriage work, come hell or high water, but it happened. It's long over, but it did happen. And John was devastated as I told you last session.

"Larry and I have no interest in each other whatsoever any more, that is, I certainly don't. And I think that he's onto another relationship these days. I don't hear from him at all now that he's on his own. I am not even sure we would ever have slept together had circumstances not fallen together as they did that weekend in Vancouver. But there we were, too much to drink for one of the few times in my life, lonely, both of us, separate rooms in the Mr. Sport Hotel, and we made the mistake of his coming to my room for one last drink and to laugh at Saturday Night Live together. And suddenly we were in the sack, couldn't get enough of kissing each other. There hadn't even been that much flirting between us. Hell, he was right out of law school, and hadn't even been practising that long. And we both went to that weekend conference in Vancouver, never expecting such a thing to happen. I am certain that I did not expect to end up in his arms in a Vancouver hotel room.

"But a weekend fling is as much adultery as a two-year affair in John's mind, and in my own. It ought not to have happened. And it did. And John couldn't handle it. So he left and got an apartment when he found out what had happened. I never told him, that's for sure, though part of me really wished I could have told him, and been forgiven by him. I know as sure as I am sitting here that I could have promised and executed the promise, never to have such a thing happen again. John did not deserve this. No matter how often I missed him on the golf course, he didn't deserve this,

"I try to tell myself that it wasn't totally my fault. I was after all that lonely at the time. I had not experienced any great desire for me from John. And I know enough about my sexuality now to know that I need to be loved as much as anyone. And when Larry confessed in that room to wanting me for as long as he had known me, I simply couldn't handle rejecting him. I wanted him, too. I am sure that I enjoyed the love-making as much as Larry did. I don't think I came with that much intensity for a long time in our marriage bed. Even now it sends shivers down my spine remembering, until the guilt takes over. And the realization that I am not married any more, that I have a 17 and a 13-year-old who miss their father. And I miss him, too. But there you have it, Doctor, I ought to have considered all of this before that weekend in Vancouver.

"In fact, perhaps it *is* time to take another look at the total impact of my career on our marriage. John certainly tried to get me to do exactly that, in more than one of our fights. But I wouldn't listen. It seemed to me that he was just jealous that he hadn't the drive to go to law school when he considered it himself. Now I have a career and no husband. The other day I got to remembering our courtship, how eager I was for every one of our dates, how little doubt I had when he proposed in that restaurant. I knew very soon in our relationship that I would marry John. It might have been during our third date that I knew I was very much in love with this guy.

"And when I remember these things I get overwhelmingly sad, like, what the hell happened? How did we go from being helplessly in love with each other – all of those plans we made before and after we married. We could just sit or walk and plan and we enjoyed each other's company so much. Do all people who split up feel this way? Are we all stunned by the changes in attitude toward the ones we so used to love? What the hell gives in this vale of tears? One day you're madly in love, the next you are split up, a single parent, wanting like hell to undo some things you have done, and knowing they can't be undone. That you have passed over into a place from which there is no escape. Hotel California – but here with us, drugs aren't the problem. It's the bloody mistakes we have made, choices we have exercised, relationships we have messed up beyond all efforts at repair.

"To this day, I would like to tell John to his face, 'Honey, I am so sorry. Yeah, I know I have always blamed you for pushing me into Larry's arms that weekend in Vancouver. But deep down inside where I am very vulnerable, in a place I do not, can not let your lawyer see, I am guilty, John, not so much of having an affair but of not working at our marriage as much as I ought to. Yeah, I know that I can blame you for the same thing. But I want to focus on my part in the tragedy, not on your role. I cannot be held responsible for your doings. But, damn it, so that I can live with myself again, I have to take the blame for whatever I did or did not do. And I didn't work hard enough at loving you.' But somehow I can't say all of this to John. My lawyer would kill me, for one thing."

"We both promised to work at loving each other forever when we married, but then I guess I didn't live out the promise. I got all tied up in my law practice, proving to the men in our office that I could bill just as highly as any one of them. Win cases as difficult as any they might win. Attract big buck corporate clients lining up to pay as successfully as any other lawyer in our office. I tried so hard to be one of the guys, I think I forgot that it was also okay to be a woman, that I didn't even have to try to be one of the guys. I am a woman, damn it, and not a man, and I am so ashamed that I forgot this and wasted so much energy trying to be a man.

"Why can't a woman succeed in the world of work on her own

terms? What kind of a liberation is it when really all we are doing is giving up our femininity for a bastardized manhood that is not natural in any way, shape or form? So what if I can compete with men? If I could do it strictly as a woman, and I am not even sure of the value in that, maybe that would be one thing. But to give up being female in order to win the respect of men in a law office, I've had enough of it, thank you very much.

"Shit, there were times I was really worried about the girls and I was afraid to talk about that in the office. I did not want my partners to see that I could easily cry with anxiety if Nancy or Debbie were in hospital or even just sick with a virus at home. I did not want them to think less of me because I cared deeply about my maternity. I did not want them to see that it was important for me to be a good wife. In fact, I played down the importance of my marriage, offering to go to any conference whatsoever, no matter if it were a weekend, particularly before the girls were born. What the hell, I said, John has no trouble going fishing with the guys, spending all Saturday at his golf club, why shouldn't I go to weekend conferences?

"I am rambling now, am I not, and I just now see that our hour is about done, and I have to get to an appointment at the office so, Doctor Stroud, I am out of here until next time. Okay?"

The effort to get up was automatic, and Louise was hardly conscious of the Doctor's presence in the room, nor of his walking her to the door of his office as she made the required gestures that go with the saying of goodbyes both to the Doctor and to his receptionist. On the way down in the elevator, whether there were others in the elevator she would not be able to say if asked today.

She was thinking again about what had gone wrong. What she ought to have done to prevent the slide into break-up. How guilty she felt about their daughters having no father now to make them laugh, to tease them to bed at night, to read them stories, to show them manhood with all of its warts and wonders. For a girl growing up has an advantage in living with a male in the house. There would be less of a shock when she dated and married if she knew a little at least of what to expect from the opposite sex. Yes, there was some truth to men being from Mars. And Venetians did have to make some adjustments for men's easily bruised egos.

Louise was glad that her father showed her what it was like to be male. Her only brother had helped, too, even if in their younger years he was a bully who used the force of his personality to assert his dominance over her and ticked her off so often. It wasn't like that now with her brother; she truly loved him and thanked God he was able to be there periodically since John had left. Frank could never be to his nieces what John was, but at least Frank was around some times and Nancy and Debbie could relate to a male.

Louise didn't harbor anything but gratitude for Frank these days. Moreover, she had long ago told Frank where to go and had achieved a certain equality in their relationship. He hadn't tried to bully her since the time she threw the shovel at him to let him know that her anger, too, was a force to reckon with. His shin regularly reminded him not to risk the anger of such a sister.

It had all been over who should do what part of the shoveling and when. An argument had begun in the driveway and Frank had pushed Louise hard into a snowbank to assert his power. She simply stood up and threw the shovel hard at him. Luckily, he was standing far enough away that she caught him on the shin and not on the head. When he fell to the asphalt in pain, she had second thoughts about her decisive response. But recover he did and he also stopped bullying her after that and, more importantly, she herself recovered two things: her self respect, and the beginnings of a brand new relationship with her only brother.

As she got into her car in the underground parking lot, she wondered now if this standing up to Frank that day had anything to do with her repeatedly standing up to John in their marriage. And now she saw again that growing up with males had its importance and here she was again, back at feeling guilty for depriving Nancy and Debbie of opportunities to relate to the most important of males in their young lives, their father.

These thoughts preoccupied her all the way back to the office and she was still lost in thought when the receptionist was telling her that clients were waiting for her in the waiting room, more than a little irritated for having been kept waiting. Finally, Louise snapped out of it and said, "What was that, Anna?"

"That you are late is one thing, Louise, but that you haven't heard what I have been saying to you is another. McDonald is upset at being stood up, as he calls it. He angrily muttered something about lawyers believing that only their time was important. I think he has cooled down a little bit now, since I got him a coffee and chatted with him about that new housing development he's responsible for. I told him that I really liked the models, and especially the interior decorating. Shit, I only saw one of the models, but I was trying to divert him when I saw that you were going to be late, Lou."

"Thanks, Anna, you're a trooper, and that's why I love you. Let's see if I can undo some of McDonald's anger now. Bring him into my office as soon as I go to the john, will you?"

Chapter Three
Cottage Life

It was about 1.30 a.m. when John Coliani came close to becoming a hit and run statistic. His driveway was on the other side of the road from where his rented cottage stood. The cottage was on lakefront but in order to achieve that, the builder all those years ago had to settle for a driveway across the road from the place. It was not that big a deal when the cottage was initially built. It had become something of an inconvenience in the ensuing years, however, as Lakeshore Drive became a rather busy thoroughfare with so many people turning cottages into permanent homes just to be on the lake. But it was this very drawback to the place that make it a little more affordable for John. The landlord couldn't get full pop with a driveway across a busy street.

As John stepped onto Lakeshore Drive his life once again proved that some habits can be very dangerous. Force of habit did not allow John to look very hard for oncoming traffic. He might have noticed the car accelerating as it neared his entry onto the roadway. Then again, with its headlights off, maybe he would not have seen it. Whether the guy was a very poor driver became a question much asked by John in the next few weeks. For the guy missed John by only a few inches. Was this miss intentional, or just an error in judgment on the driver's part? Or did the driver lose his nerve at the very last minute?

The driver may have been a drunk. John remembered hearing the car start up, as he got out of his own car, or so he told the police later same that night. It was just after John had closed the car door and asked himself whether there had been anything in his own car that he had forgotten to bring with him into the cottage. He hated getting into the cottage, getting his overshoes off, his coat off, his teeth brushed for bed, and then realizing that the novel he was reading was in the car across the road. It meant a quick dash in his house coat more than once to the locked car in the cold.

As he closed his car door, he told police that he had noticed the noise of a car engine starting but had paid no attention to it other than wondering which of his neighbours was up so late. Probably someone working night shift. What he was very definite about was the horror of seeing this car coming straight at him at a distance of 20 to 30 feet with no lights on. It was the kind of feeling that could have made his bowel move. But when it was over, only the perspiration on his face was an instant witness to what had just happened. The trembling in his legs and the urge to vomit came shortly after, as he walked into the cottage, closed the door, locked it and phoned Wally. The police were at the cottage within 15 minutes to discover a well bolted door and a man with a very white complexion standing in the dim light trying to unlock this door.

The interview went on for at least an hour but John was too shocked to think much about the passing of time. Wally arrived just after the police and poured John a mighty scotch, to which he helped himself as well. Brenda had wanted to come as well, but Wally had said that it might not be a good idea, since John seemed so upset on the phone. In fact, Wally could hear panic mixed with anger and tears in John's voice. Wally knew how to get the police immediately aware of the seriousness of what had happened to his friend.

The police had no doubt about it either. Attempted murder was not hard to recognize. Not if John Coliani was telling the truth. And given his job, as a teacher in a Catholic High School, given his very close friendship with Wally Misener, a man still respected on the police force in Beach Bay, the investigating officers had no doubt about the truth of what they were hearing.

But the usual questions produced nothing very much in the way of answers for the police to go on. John had no enemies that he knew of, at least none that might want his life over with. Try as he might he could remember no one with whom he had even had an argument with since moving back to Beach Bay. But the police were not content with these answers. They knew very quickly that his marriage had recently broken up and that he was living alone in the Bay. They asked a great many questions about the split, looking for motives in someone affected by the split.

They asked about Louise, about her lawyer, about her father, about her brother, Frank. They probed and probed. Getting no where and finding it very strange that they were listening to a guy who seemed to love his wife and family still, even though they were split up, they went back to the people John worked with. One by one they asked him about his colleagues. And when John got to Barry McDevitt, they became very interested indeed.

"So, let me get this straight, you were in a woman's washroom because the men's was out of order, and you overheard two guys yelling at each other, one of whom had a Chinese accent. And when you came out of the washroom, you walked right into the face of this Barry McDevitt, a guy you work with, and he doesn't say anything to you but just runs up the stairs and out of your vision?"

"Yeah, that's about it. But you gotta understand. This guy doesn't talk to anyone that I can see... ever... He is a very quiet guy on the staff and just does his job without relating to anyone. He's almost a hermit and I don't know how he gets the job done without talking to people. But this same phenom puzzles a lot of us on the teaching staff."

The one police officer addressed the other: "Isn't McDevitt the loonie who lives alone down by the old pest house?"

"Yeah, that's the one. We had some trouble with him about 10 years ago. Remember he kicked some kid's ass who was on his property or something like that? The father of the kid was going to press charges and then he dropped the whole thing because there was a trespass issue involved."

"So tell me, John, what kind of a vehicle does this guy McDevitt drive?"

"Actually, I do know because I have seen him getting out of his vehicle and used to wonder why he never said hello when I first started to teach at the school. He drives a little navy blue truck, like a Ranger or a Mazda and it's got a lot of rust on it."

"That would make sense if it were a Ford," Wally said almost to himself, wishing Horney were here so that he could have heard the remark, and then realizing this was not the time for humor. The policeman just looked at Wally and smiled.

"And this car which came right at you tonight was not a truck?"

"No, it was definitely not a truck. It was big old car, like an old Olds or a big Chev Impala, but not a truck. I am sure of that. And it was dark colored."

And on the questions went, until the police said that that was all they were going to ask that night, but that a detective would be contacting John on Monday, or even the next day, and would want to talk at length with him. They left, after having been there for at least an hour and a half and Wally suggested that John come and sleep at his house but John declined, saying that now that it was three o'clock in the morning, he knew he would be able to sleep just fine in his own place and Wally said that, well, he would crash there, too, and so he did.

When the phone rang the next day at 11 o'clock in the morning it was a tired John Coliani who picked up the receiver: "Hello?"

"John, are you all right?" It was Louise.

At first John did not know how to respond until his brain processed what had happened the night before, who the face was staring at him from the couch, Wally, himself still wearing the look of, what's happening, man, all over his face.

"Louise! What on earth? How do you know what is going on? I don't understand. I just woke up."

"John, you were never that good in the mornings anyway. But really, are you okay?"

"Yes. Of course I'm okay. What do you mean?"

"Well, I heard from Brenda that someone tried to run you over last night, you big jerk." She sounded almost hurt now. As if she was aware that John was deliberately not telling her the intimate details of his life. Or maybe John was just hoping that she was hurt, that she cared.

"So, that's why you called. Brenda said something to you."

"John, for God's sake, man. You don't spend all those years with someone, someone who fathers your children, hear about someone trying to kill him, and then not get really, really worried about what you have just heard."

"Louise, listen to me. I am sorry this has upset you so much. I don't know what happened, honestly. And I just woke up so I am not thinking as straight as I would like to when you call. All I know for sure is that, after saying good night to Brenda and Wally, I drove home and got out of my car, and just as I was about to cross Lakeshore Drive, a car whizzed by me very fast and very close and kept going north I guess. But it seemed like the car had started up just as I closed my car door and took a run at me. But, I don't know. Maybe I am just imagining the whole damn thing. Maybe it was just coincidental timing. Maybe some guy had a fight with his significant other and jumped into his car and sped away and I just happened to be in the wrong place at the time, crossing a busy street to get to my cottage. I am not so sure it wasn't all a scare I had... but maybe a fright that was not really caused by malice, just careless driving on someone's part who happened to be very upset about something. Or maybe he was just drunk, I don't know. Anyway, it did scare me and I called Wally and he called the police and I guess Brenda called you. And here we are. Good morning."

"Good morning, John. But Brenda said that Wally did not come home, that he was very worried about you and what happened to you."

"Yeah, he's here in front of me now, looking up with the face like the east end of a monkey going west. Oh sorry, Wally."

"John, excuse me if I cannot change as quickly as you into the humor mode, but I am worried about you. Who would try to do this to you?"

"Louise, as I said, maybe *nobody* tried to do it to me. Maybe it was just a fluke occurrence, one that the police made a big deal out of because Wally called them, and he is still considered one of them, and I am his friend."

From the couch. "Don't be so presumptuous. But you might try a little more reality therapy. You idiot. Stop trying to whitewash a late night attempt on your life."

"I heard that John. Could I speak to Wally?"

"You most certainly may. But just don't believe anything he says." Handing the phone to Wally: "Louise would like to speak to you; do *not* alarm her."

"It appears that she already is or she wouldn't be asking to speak to me. Taking the phone from John. "Hello, Sweetheart."

"Wally, level with me please. What the hell is going on? What has John gotten himself into to that he does not want to tell me about? Or, should I call you later at home where we can talk better about this?"

"Louise, to my knowledge, nothing has gone on that would provoke anyone to try and run John down. That's the truth. I really am not sure either, that there was an actual attempt on his life. I only want what happened completely checked out, that's all. Call it my background. It may well be as John says, that it was a matter of simple bad timing. Sheer coincidence could in fact be the real explanation of what seemed to happen."

"Well, and why did you sleep over at John's then?"

"Louise, John and I are going to come out of the closet this week and you and Brenda will be the first to hear. Promise."

"Wally, for Christ's sake."

"Sorry. Actually, I stayed here because John was upset, and why wouldn't he be? But I asked him to sleep at our place and he said he was too tired so I crashed here on the couch. Actually, I thought I'd probably wake up in the early hours, make sure John was sleeping peacefully and head off home to Brenda, but I was rudely awakened by your phone call. I guess this couch was a pretty good sleep after all. I might try it out again if Brenda sentences me to the doghouse."

"Well, Wally, I would really appreciate it if you do want to talk some time, if you just gave me a call. I don't mean just about this incident but about, well, anything, about John even, and how he's getting along. Yeah, I know, I can talk to him myself, and I do. But... I don't know what I'm saying, except maybe, oh I don't know, I am so damn lonely, and so confused. Oh to hell with it. Put John back

BEARE PARTS

on, please."

Wally didn't say very much to this. His eyes looked as those of a man suddenly very surprised and he looked at John even more quizzically as he looked for John to hand him the phone. "She wants to talk to you again," Wally yelled to no one else in the room.

John came into the living room wearing an apron over clothes he had somehow put on very quickly. "What are you supposed to be, a short order chef?" queried Wally. "Louise wants to talk to you again."

"Wally, put the finishing touches on that pot of coffee I began, will you? That is, if you are capable, asshole."

"Hi again." This into the mouth piece.

"John, if you know more than you're telling me... please don't hold back on me. You... are... important to the kids... and... and to me." And then a dial tone followed the click on the phone line. John stood holding the phone and tears came into his eyes. He wanted to yell out, then why the hell are we going through all of this then? But he said nothing and just stared out the window at the wind rustling the surface of the lake newly cleared of its ice, and looking very, very cold, like his heart had felt after that car went by him last night. Like this cottage had felt on too many nights this past winter without Louise and the kids to share it with him. Enough. He caught himself. Wiped his eyes. This is the way it is. Stop with the fucking self pity he ordered himself.

Wally yelled. "Where's the sugar," and this snapped John back into Sunday, April, 1997. As did the sound of the car door slamming in the driveway.

When John looked out the window he did not recognize the fellow, but Wally would. The car was a small green Cavalier, nothing to look at, although John had admired the look of these Cavaliers at other times. Quite sporty looking they can be in some models, that is, until a look is taken at the thinness of the door panels. John had often thought he would not want to be side smashed in one of these little tin cans. But who was driving this drab little Cavalier, wondered John, as the fellow got out of car and took his time walking across the road and onto John's pathway.

Wally, having now come up behind John, also stared out of the window as the coffee dripped into the pot and gave the room an aroma that only morning coffee can give. "Oh! Look who it is."

"What? You know this guy? Come to think of it, I've seen him before myself. Long ago, when I was growing up here."

"Yeah, it's Gary Desfresnes of Beach Bay's finest. He's was in plain clothes when I was a cop in a cruiser citing traffic violations on Webster Street. Good guy, though. Solid. Honest. Hard working."

A knocking on the door and John went to open it. "Come on in. I'm John Coliani." Extending his hand.

"Hello there. I'm Detective Desfresnes." But the formality turned to a wide smile when he spotted Wally behind John. "I should have recognized that 4-wheel drive out there. How ya doin' Wally?"

"Couldn't be better, Gary. How's the coaching? Still enjoying those little guys and their baseball these days?"

"No, Wally. As much as I enjoyed the little league challenge, I had to give it up when I had heart bypass last year. I just try to do this job and take all the rest of the time for me and Lil these days. Got two years left and then, God willing, it's take the gratuity allowance, buy a small condo around Clearwater, and get the hell out of here every October until April at least, and if I have my way, until May, though Lil says she doesn't know if she can last till May down there."

"Your boy okay now?"

"Well, I guess you know he had to drop out of the bar ads course last year because he had colitis so bad they were talking a colostomy at one point. But he came home and worked back at his uncle's law firm again, same place he had articled, and is goin' to try bar ads again next year. He was three weeks in hospital with the bowel surgery and then he's back in again for another week with complications, after he'd been home for a month, but now things look like they are settlin' down for him. He eats regularly and his bowel seems to be tryin' to be normal. We are sure hopin' he's been through the worst of it. Kid's been in school so long he needs to get workin' regular and makin' a salary and enjoyin' himself a little. Beside, I'm runnin' outa money to support the guy though we're sure proud of him and

BEARE PARTS

all that.

"But enough of all that. I hear your friend, here," turning to John, "John is it? Actually, you look a little familiar to me. Saw you around here in the old days. Had a little scare last night?

"They called me in to work today and it was my day off. I was headin' for the cottage up at Timachi to see if the lake trout stayed over the winter, or if they smartened up and went south, too. Don't laugh, Wally. Judgin' by their fewer an' fewer numbers each spring, I gotta believe the sons o' bitches are goin' somewhere every winter."

Wally laughed. "Gary, you just ain't no hell of a fisherman. I always told you that."

They both laughed again. "So, John. I read the report at the station before I came down here this mornin' but I would really appreciate it if you could tell me what happened las' night and then I want to ask you some extra questions myself if you don't mind."

So, John went through the whole story again, and following that he answered Gary's questions, much the same questions as the two officers had asked John the night before. About whether he'd had altercations with anyone, and that kind of thing. And, of course, Detective Desfresnes wanted as much detail as possible about Barry McDevitt, which was kind of strange, given what Gary revealed to both Wally and to John toward the end of the interview that morning.

For it came out that Gary had been on the job and on this case long before he had arrived at John's cottage that morning. It turned out that he had begun at 7 o'clock that morning. Moreover, he had already done some checking on Barry McDevitt's whereabouts and had discovered that McDevitt was not in the Beach Bay area this weekend but was, in fact, in Toronto and his hotel reservation at a Toronto hotel had been checked and confirmed. He was a paying guest for two nights and the night clerk confirmed talking to McDevitt at around 11.30 when he had requested something from room service.

So much for appearances once again, thought John. You just can't rely on shit like that. "So, Mr. Desfresnes, where do we go from here? What if what I saw last night was just a fluke? A guy speeding down the road, upset about something, or just drunk, dark, doesn't see me, it's late, doesn't even know he's come so close to hitting me, keeps going and I am so scared I call Wally, instead of just counting my blessings and coming in and just going to bed?"

"Could be you're right, John. And it's nice to deal with a rational guy now and then. We all make mistakes, though some of the people I talk to, seem to think that doesn't apply to them. But, hey, sure what you say is possible. Guy might even have realized he damn near killed someone but was too scared to come back and check it out once he realized his mistake. Happens all the time. That's why we have too damn many of them hit and runs to check out. Any rate, I guess where we go from here kinda depends on what happens from here on in.

"Anything out of the ordinary pops up. You call me right away. I'm not there, you tell them at the station I said I wanna be called right away when you call. I'll tell them that myself, but you never know who's goin' to be on dispatch any given time. But, tell them to get me immediately at my own request; they'll usually respond no matter how rude they can be with the public. I know about their rudeness. But in truth they're too damn scared of the repercussions not to call us right away. They usually can get hold of me. I carry a cell phone up to the cottage and it sometimes even works. I'll also give you my pager number, though I gotta confess if I'm fishin', I don't wear the damn thing then.

"Wally, you got one of them cellular phones, too? Useless as tits on a bull. Damn thing rarely works. Shuts off in the middle of a conversation. Gotta stop the damn car on top of a hill to get it workin' and be sure of finishin' the conversation with anyone. I hate the damn thing. And I'm sorry I ever bought the piece of shit. Now, with these new deals, you get one for a loaner I hear, and you buy the package of service. A guy don't have to put up the bread to buy the damn phone itself. I was one of the early suckers, an bought my own phone. Fool that I am. I'd throw the damn thing into Lake Timachi except I like to have it in Lil's car when she goes out at nights in case the damn car lets her down somewhere and she needs help. Tow truck whatever. Can't afford to trade her little old Jetta in. And the damned glow plugs or somethin' else is always lettin' her down somewhere. But I sure hate these goddammed cell phones. Bloody world. There's always somethin' suckerin' us for our hard earned dollars. Right, Wally?"

"Gary, you old Tiger. You haven't changed a bit. And I don't think you should either. And by the way, I hate the damn things myself, but I gotta have it."

"Well, anyway, John, I sure hope your explanation holds water, this mornin'. And no one's tryin' to run you over after all. I gotta go now and look into some other things come up over the weekend which is why they called me in today. So, let's just agree that if anythin' comes up, you're on the blower to me right away. S'all I can do for now. Thanks for the coffee, John. And it was good to see you Wally. Let's do the lake trout thing again up at my cottage, just like we used to, for sure this spring or summer, Wally. Show you how to catcha fish."

Wally and John laughed their goodbyes to Gary, and he was gone into the Cavalier, and down Lakeshore Drive. "Told you he was a good guy, Coli." John smiled in agreement. He had liked Gary. And he had felt a little more relaxed now that he had coffee and had almost convinced himself that what happened last night had been a fluke.

"So, Gary's been a detective a long time now, Wally? How come he never went any higher if he's been in plain clothes so long, especially in a small town like the Bay?"

"You mean why he never got the Chief's job? Well, Gary is one of those guys who speaks his mind, and can't help doing it, even if he ever decided to overlook horseshit. But he'd never come to that decision. If someone's feeding him horseshit for breakfast and trying to call it scrambled eggs, even if everyone one of his colleagues is saying this is really good, while puking on the inside for fear of calling it horseshit to the cook's face, Gary's the kind of guy to stand up and call it what it is – horseshit. Much to his chickenshit colleagues' delight, when their only response is part fear, part awe, part gratitude. Though they never say thank you after the fact for fear of being associated with the unpromotable rebel. Gary's the kind of guy other guys go to and ask him to speak up for them. And Gary does. He can't abide nonsense, whether handed to him or to anyone else. He will speak up just as much for his colleagues as for himself. But then, he won't get the promotions either.

"Others who didn't speak up, and let Gary do the talking, they got the promotions. The guy who's Chief right now is a case in point. He went right over Gary's head to get that job and he isn't half the policeman Gary is. Doesn't have half the service in. I'm no great lover of the seniority bit, but in Gary's case, he's got merit plus seniority. This current Chief also hasn't half the smarts. But what he does have is this, he knows enough to keep his mouth shut, never back talks any one who might get his nose out of joint. I've seen Gary hang the phone up on politicians who were acting like assholes. Even if they were his bosses. I admired him for that. But his temper got in the way of his career.

"Guys who get promoted like today's Chief, they don't have tempers. They don't have balls and when you don't have balls you never feel any one stepping on them. They never have any ideas either. But they're not above borrowing ideas from those with the balls. They never solve one fucking problem, but they know who to buy the drinks for, how to barbecue a steak and who to invite to the barbecue. Gary tells his bosses, be they police or politician, that they are full of shit, has his own buddies to his barbecues, and prefers to wear a dirty t-shirt while cooking great steaks at his camp in Timachi. I love the guy. But I feel sorry for him, too. Because I've heard the hurt he feels when he doesn't get recognized for the work, and the results, he achieves. He's a damn good cop. The police services commission doesn't know the half of it. The Chief tells the commission what he wants them to know and if it doesn't serve his purposes to give more influence to a rebel like Gary, the Commission doesn't get the full report on the quality of such a guy, the full worth of such a cop.

"It's partly why I left police work, only partly, John, but it was a consideration. I saw what happened to guys like Gary, and not just in police work. In other walks of life, too. That's why I wanted to work for myself. Remax provided me with what I wanted. An opportunity to work for myself, to work hard and to be rewarded according to how hard I worked. Not according to whom I blew." He paused, a little exhausted but still convinced as to what he had said. Then he smiled. "Sorry. Tirade's over for today." Almost a little embarrassed now.

"But you're right, Wally. I know what you mean. Teaching isn't much different. You don't get anywhere by showing temper, by standing up for what you believe in. You don't challenge authorities, that's for sure. Guys who get promoted to principals are those who don't ever challenge anybody about anything.

"This guy, Des Dixon, wrote this book called *Future Schools*. He's right on the money when he says that boards of education don't ever pick creative people to be principals because they might rock the boat too much. In fact, creative principals are a rarity Dixon says. And I couldn't agree more. Boards want conservative, safe people in positions of authority. No vision. Dixon calls them Pretenders. I like that. Pretenders.

"And as for our teacher unions. They're unbelievable too. Every teacher is dealing with the effects of all these cutbacks in education. But not the folks who work in the union offices. And I can't stand this stupid seniority syndrome shit. I don't believe the unions when they say we can't come up with a system of ranking and paying teachers according to how well they do their job, teach kids. No, they say, the only fair way is to pay us for our qualifications and our experience. It's not how good you are, but how long you been here. No wonder the public hates teachers.

"My own union embarrasses me. I want to be paid for my teaching skills, not my seniority. And I don't want assholes in my profession who ought to be doing something else because they are ruining kids' education. In fact, some of the younger teachers today should be protected and the older ones sent to a happier hunting ground. Yeah, Wally, I hate the same things in teaching that I guess you had no use for in police work. But at least you found a way out. I don't think I can do anything else but teach. Good thing I still enjoy it. Still love the classroom and the action there. But I wouldn't want to be a Vice-Principal, dealing with discipline and that kind of shit all day. Or dealing with these new school councils. Trustees might have been out of it and had way too much power but I can't see how school councils are going to be any better. If they are allowed to be prescriptive rather than to play advisory roles, schools will be run by those untrained for the role. The rule of ignorance scares the hell out of me. Then maybe I will have to get out if it comes to that.

"But I seriously believe these school councils will go the way of most educational innovation, into the trash can, for the ususal reason, apathy. Education keeps suffering from do gooder politicians out to get votes, making changes that affect kids and teachers, and after kids and teachers have been bothered, harassed, the idea dies and things get back to their usual equilibrium, until the next crusader comes along, and interferes again with kids' educations. A lot of teachers are cynical and just ignore all of these changes. They've seen them before. And they know these changes will die out just like the last ones. I myself just get pissed right off at having to go to these board-wide professional development days to listen to some guru, who's surely promotion-bound, talk about one change or another. First of all, I get ticked off that someone at the board level has decided what my professional development needs are, and second, I am convinced whatever change we are going to hear about is dead in the water anyway. Been there, done that.

"Screw them all, Wally. How about a drink?"

"No, John, I gotta bugger off. John, have you ever thought about quitting and selling real estate like me?"

"Wally, it's true that in a classroom I am a salesman. In fact, given my unwillingness to be more disciplined with money, Louise once called me Willy Loman. But, no, I don't think I want to sell real estate. I do enjoy selling literature to students. Sometimes I wish I could have older clients, people who wanted to be there. With teaching, a great deal of the challenge is convincing them just to be there, not to become drop out statistics. A lot of kids don't want to be in school any more when I get them in Grade 10 or 11. I've often wondered if I would enjoy adults more, older folks who are in school because they really want to be."

"What's wrong with selling real estate? You're articulate, John, and I can see you doing really well at it. You'd win people's confidence and that counts in real estate? Not to mention that your income might double or triple, although your lifestyle would give up most of its free time, and you'd feel guilty as hell any time you took time off, like I do. Ever since I got to be a top real estate salesman, there's been pressure on me to stay at the top."

"Yes, Wally, I expect that you laugh at my two weeks holidays at Christmas, my week off in March, and then my two months off in the summer, but I chose this profession partly because of that time off. I need that kind of time off."

"Don't get defensive, John. I don't laugh at you. I envy you sometimes. I do laugh at the whiners in teaching who get the same holidays as you do, and who don't seem to work in the evenings as much as you do. Who don't seem to work at all out of their hours at school. And school hours aren't exactly crushing in their sheer weight. I know that much of your work as a teacher is at home marking preparing, et cetera. But some of these guys I see in the pub Friday after Friday, I don't think they do a hell of a lot at home, John."

"That's not for me to say, Wally, but I know I spend a lot of time at my career at home. And I don't have a problem with it. That's my profession. It's what I get paid to do. And it's why I think the union approach to my profession is stupid. So much of a teacher's effort has to be at home. But, as I said, I sometimes wonder if it would be more enjoyable teaching adults who want some more education, teaching in a community college for example. Or at least teaching adults in a college.

"Kids today in high schools have been there too long and they want to get out and get a job but they know they can't. They know without their parents and their guidance teachers telling them that they won't get good jobs unless they stay in school. Yet most of them have enough formal education to get by on in life and are more than ready for jobs. I call it educational inflation. Used to be that a guy could get into an apprenticeship with grade 10. You still can but a lot of bosses will take the guy with Grade 12 over the guy with Grade 10. In fact, some of the people with college diplomas are trying to get into the apprenticeships so that a guy with Grade 10 hasn't got a chance and he has to stay in school where he hates it.

"I keep reading in the business pages of the *Globe and Mail* that we are short, and going to be even shorter, of so many skilled people, say, in information technology. Why can't we create... with the government in partnership with industry, or with the corporate world... apprenticeships... you know, like in Germany where these guys are respected big time... for kids who have had enough schooling for a while, in areas where we are short of skilled workers, training them on the job."

"Hey, but Colli – hold on there a minute. How would you feel if some teacher told you as a parent that either Nancy or Debbie were not university material, that one of them, or both, should settle for community college, or, worse, for an apprenticeship..."

John burst in. "But that's the whole point, Wally. Look at your choice of words, look at your biases... 'settle for' and 'worse, for an apprenticeship.' You make it sound like as if anything other than university is second class."

"But isn't that how it is, Coli?"

"Only because we have allowed it to be seen as so. Wally, we know now that I.Q. is a crock of shit. It measures very little. But we are coming to know about things like multiple intelligences. That would explain why I have talked to a hell of a lot of guys in the trades who seem a lot smarter than I am. Guys who can fix anything. Guys who have enough confidence to tackle any project. They may have to learn on the way, but that's just it, they are the real lifelong learners."

"Whereas many people with university educations do seem a little dense, Coli."

"Exactly my point. There really are different kinds of learning, not all of them in books, but more hands on. Less into abstract ideas, more into practical solutions. And in Germany apprenticeships are quite prestigious whereas in North America we seem to view these careers as less than…"

"Ironically, Coli, I heard of a guy with a commercial electrician's certificate whose T-4 showed he had made $139,000 last year working at a GM plant in Oshawa."

"Yeah. Yeah. There are quite a few university grads not making that kind of money. All of the teaching profession, for example. There may be a lot of guys who say we don't work that hard but screw them, Wally; we bloody well work, too."

"Coli, something which has always intrigued me is how should a guy be paid? I mean, should someone be paid for the education he needs to do the job, or for how hard, physically speaking, his job is. It's physically harder to shovel gravel all day than it is to sit at a desk. Or should the pay depend upon how much responsibility a guy has to shoulder? Take airline pilots, for example, or the president of a company like Nortel. Or maybe how productive he is? Or on how much money the guy makes for his company, say if he's in sales. Or what about danger? A soldier, a fireman, a cop for that matter, have to take more risks. And as for risk taking… what about the guy who opens up a business and takes a hell of a financial risk. Say he's successful and then employs all kinds of others. That's worth considering, too… As are things like charm, say the ability to relate to people.

So, Coli… what should drive earning power? Education, physical demands, responsibility, productivity, financial contribution, danger, risk taking, social skills? I have often wondered about this."

"Actually, that would be worth a huge debate by a large segment of society, say during an election campaign. But I can't see there being any votes in it, so it will never surface. It's a non-starter, kind of like the environment as an election issue. Though we will likely see that change in our lifetime.

"But, Wally, you're getting me off track. I want to talk about apprenticeships again… Because I see them as satisfying some of what John J. Mason calls the special needs of adolescents, the need for autonomy, for self determination, for money."

"But cool the rhetoric, John. I'm a believer."

"Just listen asshole. Mason says in a book I think I remember as *The Adolescent Predicament* that kids in Grade 11 have needs different from those kids have in Grade Two. But if you walk down the hall in an elementary classroom and similarly down the hall of a high school, and look in on a Grade Two and on a Grade 11, you will see that the 11s are not treated very much differently from the little ones in Grade Two. The 11s don't have a lot more control over the decisions which affect them than do the kids in Grade Two."

"Coli, you ought to go into fuckin' politics... become the minister of education or something like that..."

"No, but listen, you dumb prick... This guy Mason says that no wonder so many kids in high school are rebellious. And I agree with him, Wally. I figure this is part of the reason why public education cannot really deal with gifted kids. Kids who think for themselves will never do well in situations where only conformity counts and succeeds.

"And Illich is right too...

"Who the fuck is Illich? It sounds like a body problem. You're off on your hobby horse, Coli!"

"Why can't kids get out when they are bored with formal education, get some work which satisfies them, contributes to society, cuts the cost of education, and then come back to school when they feel they need for more formal education? They could learn a lot more in the work place than I can teach them about literature they don't care about. They haven't even got enough life's experience to even appreciate serious art. You cannot make youngsters appreciate art and ideas whey they are simply too young to experience any shock of recognition. Let them live a little more. We ought to stop forcing Shakespeare down the throat of a kid who really wants a job so that he can buy that car and take that girl out. Get out from under his parents' thumbs. And there's nothing so wrong with that either. In almost every animal species that I know of, the adults cut the youngsters loose a lot sooner than humans do, and the young have to

make their own way in the world. Hell, we force th(
school so long, without increasing their independence, a... ...
why they haven't gown up at 18 years of age???"

"John, never mind real estate. Again I say it... maybe you oughta go into politics." Wally laughed.

"Sorry, Wally. But I do care about these things. Every time I have trouble with a kid whose pent up energy spills out as rebellion and we have a ruckus, and I have to send the kid down to the VP, and get this, Wally, the vice-principals and the principals today don't want the kids to learn anything about reality, about the consequences of their behaviour, because that might mean standing up to the kid's parents .. These gutless wonders are afraid of the superintendents who want to know why the school has so many suspensions. Fucking principals are afraid of the trustees, and I guess it will soon be the school councils... so these administrators hide behind trying to be social workers, special education masks, fucking counselors, anything but being administrators with authority, without which the teacher has no authority as well..."

"Watch your blood pressure, Coli..."

"No, I mean it, Wally, I take it as a personal failure as a teacher, because I fear that I just haven't reached the kid. But sending him to the office is an exercise in futility. There's no support there for sure, not for me nor for the kid, ultimately. But then I realize, maybe there's no reaching this kid. He just doesn't want to be here right now... he's trapped by his own knowledge that he hasn't got a chance of getting a decent job without more education but he's too bored to endure very much of it."

"John, you can't save them all."

"True, yet it's those kids who make the profession a challenge, Wally. Any idiot can reach the kids who want to be there, who do their homework all of the time. Who come from the families where formal education is really important. Where it's just a continual expectation that there's homework every night. Whose parents love books. Where the fucking television is not on 18 hours a day in the kitchen and the family room. Where conversation still happens. Shit, some families eat supper watching TV. But it's the kid who is about to drop out who is the real challenge. And lately, I'm losing more and more of them and I wonder if the generation gap is just getting wider and I have less and less credibility. Am I simply tiring of the challenge? This is what I ask myself lately. Sometimes I wonder if I could be cut a little slack and allowed to teach adults in a college.

"Coli, from what I can see of kids working one place or another around town, I wonder how many of them are taking their part-time jobs more seriously than their school work."

"Yeah, you've got a point there, Wally. Some of my students are making two and three hundred bucks a week working. Doesn't leave much time for homework. One of my students told me the other day she doesn't even live at home. Needs to make that kind of money to support herself. Maybe that's not so bad. I don't know. I kind of respect her. She's a pretty good student. But what can I ask of such a student in the way of standards?

"And to get back to what I was saying about teaching at a college…Ironically enough, teachers at that level probably have their own challenges of which I am ignorant. And maybe if they heard me ranting like this they'd just laugh and say something like, so you think we have it soft, huh? You might find it even more difficult to teach when the cutbacks at the college level are such that you don't even know whether you're going to have a job shortly. Still, however, I can't help think, Wally, that at least their clients are wanting to be there and that's got to make it a little easier, especially if the clients are adults who have gone back to school because they want to."

"John, I do have to get the hell out of here. And I am leaving now. And you should tape all of this and give it to me later. Just keep talking. You might not even notice that I've left. Sorry. Just kidding. I know that you care a lot about this stuff. And I shouldn't tease you about it."

"No, it's okay, Wally. Louise always said that I ought to write down what I feel so passionately about but I never felt the need or the urge. I never thought it was worth that much, that is, to actually try to write a book about it. Besides, I figure other people always have more interesting and original points of view than I do, so I have no desire to write. No, that's not true. I do want to write but I have no real confidence in the quality of my writing nor in my own ideas as being of any value to anyone but myself except maybe those who love me and are willing to let me rave on at times."

"Well, John, maybe that's a real good reason to begin some writing. What you said about your ideas being of value to yourself first of all. Aren't good writers supposed to write first of all to please themselves?"

"So I'm told. But that's a whole other subject we don't want to get into right now, Wally, because you keep saying you have to leave now, remember?"

"I'm outa here again. You're right." Wally got up and started heading for the door. "John, watch yourself, will you? Just in case that was no fluke last night. You never know in this crazy world what crazies are around doing gratuitous violence. You will be lucky if it was a random act of stupidity."

"Wally, I will walk tall and carry a big stick. I will hold my head up in the corners."

"Stop trying to pretend you were ever an athlete. You only looked and smelled like a jock strap. Still do." Wally laughed as he opened the door and walked toward his vehicle. John watched him as he walked across Lakeshore Drive. John thought he saw Wally looking up and down the road as if he were looking for some clue as to what had happened last night, as if Wally might get a glimpse of the vehicle that almost ran a man down.

When Wally was gone down the road John went to the counter and poured another cup of coffee and then sank into his most comfortable chair with the remnants of Saturday's paper, especially Focus, his favourite part of the Saturday *Globe and Mail*. He read for about 20 minutes and then fell fast asleep again. It was 1.00 p.m. when he awoke.

He showered and dressed and thought of calling his mother to see whether he was expected for Sunday dinner. But then he went to his kitchen table and began marking papers, an activity that he did not very much enjoy. It seemed to go on forever and he never seemed to get done what he had hoped every time he sat down to mark. Moreover, the pile of marking never seemed to go down very much after two, three and even after four-hour sessions. Marking was always discouraging.

Furthermore, it was such a humbling experience. Especially tests and exams. Kids didn't seem to take these assessments very seriously. He swore that the majority of kids didn't even prepare for the tests and exams. No matter how many hints he gave–in fact, some times he downright gave them the essay questions before the exam so that they could prepare answers at home and edit them for quality–many students came in and wrote first draft answers which were largely garbage. It was as if their marks didn't matter to them. He would talk to them, lecture them, cajole them, show them how to prepare, give them mock tests, but it didn't matter. And so he ended up marking the worst drivel. He wondered at many times if perhaps he just wasn't a very good teacher. Yet the kids gave him feedback frequently that they loved his teaching.

Today he was marking a test on a short story he had assigned to a Grade 10 class, Shirley Jackson's "The Lottery". He enjoyed the story's theme, that people can get blindly caught up in customs which are violent, self-destructive and nonsensical. Ignorantly going along no matter the damage. People not being able to recognize the idiocy of it all. The annual draw to see which member of the community would be stoned to death. The story certainly always made him wonder which customs his own society blindly followed, customs which would look ridiculous 100 years from now but which, right now, seemed absolutely necessary.

There was the ritual of divorce, for example. Going to a lawyer and paying all of that money to get a separation agreement when money was already a divisive force in the breakup in the first place. Why would two perfectly sane people, fighting over money so much that they feel they have to leave each other, decide to go to a lawyer and pay this lawyer a hell of a lot of money neither of them have, to get a divorce? Now here was a ritual that people really seemed to believe was necessary. Some brave souls had tried do-it-yourself divorces but when assets were involved they seemed to believe, and lawyers certainly encouraged them to believe, that they would be forever sorry if there was a screw up and they did not get their fair share at the time the separation agreement was drawn up. Lawyers had convinced society to be very, very frightened about not getting it right in the separation agreement, not getting all they could from the other spouse. As if the money both parties paid lawyers would not far surpass any small amount they might not get in the separation agreement.

And John also wondered what other customs might be at work in his society that were stupid. He thought that one day it would come out that medicine as practiced in the 20th Century would be seen to be crazy. Kind of like blood letting. The patient funds the medical system through his tax dollar. Yet he goes to doctors who treat him as if he is someone stupid who must be tolerated. The general practitioner sends the patient to the specialist for a test. The patient asks the technician or the specialist what he saw during whatever technology is being used and gets the answer that the results cannot be discussed with the patient; they are to be forwarded to the general practitioner. The patient who funds the system cannot have the information he is paying for, and the damned information pertains to his body. The implication is that he is too stupid to understand and may do himself harm with this knowledge. Just not too stupid to fund this system.

What a fucking paradigm, John thought. John laughed as he thought how strange it was that when he went to buy a used car he was generally treated with so much more respect by the salesman than he was ever accorded by most of the doctors he had met. Oh, there were some good guys but they were exceptions. In fact, the doctors with the best bedside manners seemed to be female. Too many male doctors just seemed to be on power trips and people seemed to accept this as the natural order of things, especially older people with so little education that they were genuinely intimidated by doctors and the medical profession.

And then there were the antidepressants, like Valium and Prozac, that seemed to depress people, that lead some of them to suicide for shit sakes, and John wondered why there weren't more people blowing the whistle on these fucking drug companies. "Modern" medicine...

It was when John's ruminations carried him to the topic of nurses... their fixation on the imperative mode, issuing shoulds to patients and visitors like there was no tomorrow, that John realized he was getting no marking done, was sitting at a kitchen table as his coffee grew cold, and had better stop with the day dreaming and start with the marking. Besides so what if nurses were obsessed with the shoulds of life; didn't they get it from the doctors? And worst of all, didn't John himself have enough shoulds in own vocabulary. Didn't Wally just tell him to stop with the preaching? Once a teacher always a teacher, he smiled to himself.

After suffering through till 3.30 p.m. and ten tests later, he was delighted by the ringing of the phone, and yes, Mom, he was coming for supper. And, yes, he would be there by five and yes everything was fine and no he hadn't been too busy this past week to call her; he just hadn't and he'd see her shortly. John knew that she had not heard about last night nor did he intend to tell her. That's all he needed right now, to see her worrying about something like this. He could worry enough for the two of them. It was bad enough that Louise had made that morning call and was obviously upset. These thoughts and others continued to preoccupy him while he put everything back into his briefcase, cleaned off the kitchen table, did the breakfast dishes and generally cleaned the kitchen, while also feeling some hunger pangs and anticipated eagerly his mother's cooking. Comfort food. Now here was a ritual he did not want to do away with; here was a custom, a tradition that had to stay just the way it was. Central to the psyche, he thought to himself. Part of the meaning of home.

As John drove over to his mother's he thought of the whole business of family. There were so many articles in the media these days about family. How so many kids have different sets of parents today. How so many marriages are no longer permanent arrangements. The rise of the common law relationship.

Shit, thought John. Who would want this kind of arrangement? It was bad enough making oneself vulnerable with someone who promises to love you forever no matter what. Why would anyone share his deepest self with someone who, by not committing forever, has already made an implicit statement that she's outa here the first sign of hard times?

Common law relationships puzzled John. He was still a supporter of old fashioned marriage of the kind his parents had. But as for himself, he had no desire ever to marry again. He was finished with intimacy. As lonely as he was... still... never again he told himself. And yet, he knew that the single life, like the married life, was incomplete. No one has it all. The married person has to account to someone all of the time, is not in charge of his own time anymore, nor of his own money. Cannot really make decisions even about social life without consulting a partner who may not agree to whatever the other wants.

Yet the single person, for all of his freedom to go drinking with the guys whenever he wants, to go golfing for the whole weekend, even to go south on golf holidays, to spend his money in whatever ways he wants to, to go fishing without having to ask anyone, to socialize with whomever whenever he wishes, still has a downside every time he comes home late at night to an empty apartment. With whom does the single person share plans and goals? To whom does he go when he's upset about whatever? Who listens and comforts and affirms him then?

No, John was of the opinion that the single life was likely not what some unhappily married people might think it is. Far from perfect. And John knew that he was happiest when he was married and he wondered how many other people, refugees from former relationships, also had come to this conclusion. How many singles wouldn't try harder if they had known then, before they split, what it's really like living a split? How many could be really honest enough to admit that you bring your old personality to every new relationship.

Things don't really change because you change partners. Or was he just full of shit? "Didn't know what he was talking about," he could hear someone, whose second marriage was much better, saying to him. But then, John also knew that he hadn't been unhappy married, hadn't wanted to be single again, would have been quite content to die as Louise's husband. In fact, that's how he thought it would happen, although he never gave much thought to his own mortality. Becker may well say in *The Denial of Death* that it was a sickness of our culture not to acknowledge and live as if we were aware of our mortality. Still, John could not agree with Becker, no matter how large Becker's following, which had become something almost of a small cult by now, or so John had heard. For John, to think often on death seemed morbid. In fact, it terrified him, having watched his own father die.

Bone cancer. On the spine. Tumor too big to radiate. Might cause swelling such that John's Dad would lose the use of his legs. In fact, the doctors at Mount Sinai could not understand how Albert was still walking, so big was this tumor on the spine. He ought to have lost the use of his legs by now. They kept asking him to move his legs, as if they did not believe he could still use them. Albert had told John and Emma this himself, about the frequent request to move his legs now.

They were now in Albert's hospital room. Emma. John. Albert lying there. Dr. Mason and his assistants. John did not know their roles. Dr. Mason was speaking.

"The tests we've done show that this tumor is very large and we are afraid to try radiation on it. We don't want the spine traumatized any more than it has been by this tumor, not now by any swelling that is, because we don't know which functions you might lose if the swelling impacts on certain parts of the spine. So our decision as a team is that I should go in and remove the tumor. I've done these before and so you can rest assured that this is not a first for me. But I want to get it out cleanly and then I am going to have to rebuild one of the vertebrae and put a steel plate on part of the spine to stabilize it after this tumor has come out. Some of the bone has been destroyed

BEARE PARTS

by the tumor.
"Maybe I should stop now and let you ask me some questions."
"The tumor is big, Doctor?" from Albert.
"Yes, about the size, I think, of a grapefruit."
Silence. Albert and Emma were very quiet. Either they were in shock or they did not want to ask anything else. Maybe they did not want to know anything else at this point. Couldn't handle it. John had questions but he did not want to ask them in front of his Dad. Not even in front of his Mom. He would see the doctor later. Maybe call him. He was surprised even to be in the room at this time but his Dad wanted him there and told the doctor as such. The Doctor had no problem with John being there. But John had a problem with it. After all, he was only a son. His Dad was the boss in the family. John could not imagine his father ever needing him. But suddenly, there it was. The invitation to attend the interview with Mom and Doctor Mason. Dad had said he actually wanted John to be there. And John was there for the news. Cancer, yes. Surgery, yes. A chance to survive, yes. Not just the surgery, said doctor Mason, but for some more years if this tumor could be excised cleanly.

There was again very little talking after the Doctor and his staff left the room. It was a Monday now and the surgery was to be Thursday. As soon as possible. Get the tumour. Put in a brace. Dad was going to live. Mom was relieved. Dad was white. Not talking. John left them sitting there. Went home. How had Dad handled it?

Lying there. Crying. Trying to convince himself that others have recovered. No pain for once. His side not hurting for a change. What was it they had given him? Why couldn't they give it to him for the rest of his life and forget the surgery? Terrified of the surgery. Remembering his experience with open heart 15 years ago. The doctors had assured him then that they were doing so many of the these bypasses that appendectomies were now statistically more dangerous. Bullshit. Doctors ought to experience the operations they perform. Ought to live with the nausea after all that anesthesia. Try to eat anything for a week after when all you can take is apple juice and you have never even liked apple juice but now it is at least refreshing. Worrying. I am not healing very fast. I find it hard to walk. I am going to die and they don't want to tell me. But they know. They just don't want to tell me the truth. They think I can't handle it so they're not saying. Everybody is in on to it but me. Even Emma and John. That's why they are all being so nice to me. They know how bad things really are.

No place to be if you are an independent sort like me. Nurses always giving me sermons. I should do this. I should do that. I shouldn't feel this way. I should be more patient. I should not worry. Do these people know any word but should? And the residents. The interns. Arrogance. No time for my questions. Just in and out of the room with these chart boards on which they scribble whatever seems important to them. Patient seems hostile? Angry? You're goddamned right I am. A simple operation, huh? I hope the hell you have it soon, you son of a bitch. Try walking after it like me. You won't be taking things for granted any more like I used to, like digesting something without nausea, like breathing without self consciousness, like walking. Like freedom, and getting the hell out of this prison. I want to be home. I want to work in my garden. Yes, he remembered this anger, these fears. And now he lay here again in a hospital bed.

Trapped. This life is a trap. We are trapped in these bodies. Or are we only these bodies? Is there something about me that is alive without this body. I guess I may know this finally, sooner rather than later. Or will I know it? Will I know anything if I die under that knife? Will it matter then? Yes, damn it, yes. I don't want to say goodbye forever to Emma. Fuck off with these tears.

Life. Don't get too comfortable–that's the lesson he had learned.

And someone was holding his hand. He looked up at an older woman. Short. Smiling down at him. Letting him convulse, the sobs wracking his body now. Her smile seeming to say, it's okay, cry, get it out. Who was she? Had he died? An angel? These drugs were doing it. But the pain was gone. Yes, his side did not hurt for the first time in a long time. And the doctor had said the pain was not really in his side. The tumor was on his spine, not in his side. Fuck him. The pain had been in his side. Shouldn't talk like that. Might have to explain to God soon so many things, so much anger, so many sins. A lifetime's sins. But he had been forgiven. Confession.

What was he thinking about? Recovery. Would he recover? Hope. Yes faith and charity were important but so was hope. Where was this coming from? The lady? No, look at her; she isn't saying anything. Just standing there. Holding my hand. Smiling. Hope. Where can I find out about hope? How do I hope? Why should I hope? What can I hope for? Putting this business of leaving off for a few more years with Emma?

Hope. Some kind of a mushroom like I saw one time coming up through the asphalt in my driveway. Couldn't believe it. A mushroom, then another one, then another one. Appearing in my driveway. Right through the asphalt. Strange, very strange, that they have this kind of energy. Yet you try to tear them out, they fall apart. So how do they bust asphalt? Mystery. Like hope maybe? Springing up through the soil of suffering. Against all odds. Against all the evidence. We are going to die, every one of us. Sooner or later. Sooner for me. No proof there's going to be a me after I die. Why hope? Jesus, where are you now? Violent sobbing again.

Hope. It promises. It reassures. I… we… need promises reassurance. When I was young, my mother reassured me. Promised me. I believed her. I believed my priest. I believed my teachers. I got older, I believed Emma. And she's the only one left. She still loves me. She's still with me. Her promise still counts. And I don't want to leave her now. I'm not ready. She's not ready …….

Stop with this crying. Think about promises. I think about promises and I think about politicians. I can even laugh thinking about politicians and their promises. Laughable. That's what I need, a laugh. Stop me from crying. Open even to the promises of politicians, suckered time and again… every election. No one wants to admit it. But we vote on the basis of whose promises we like the best. Even if we don't really believe the bastards. We need good news. We need to believe in better times.

There's so much horseshit to deal with. Look at John. My son believed in marriage. In his Louise. For better or for worse. Till death do them part. And she believed I'm sure in his love. Like my Emma's love. Forever. A promise. And now they're part of the divorce statistics. Hurting each other. Fighting over bullshit. So many people. Love each other. Would die for each other. Then they want each other to die. Promises. Life is dirty, a prick.

Like bone cancer. A painful way to go I remember someone saying. Was it in a funeral home I heard that? Maybe I said it myself. Now I got it. Prick. Life. Go to hell. Life. So quick. It's over. And it's not anything like I expected. Maybe my Mother knew this and didn't tell me. That it always turns out as a surprise. I don't know. I miss my mother. She's been dead for so many years now. Will I see her?

Each generation sees it too late… that it is about to be replaced, buried, forgotten. And then we start looking for reasons to hope. But there are none. Who cares now whether the mortgage will be paid off soon? Who gives a shit about whether I can manage on this pension? Will I be dead forever? I care about that but only because the pain has stopped. When the pain is there I don't even care about that.

It was a Wednesday evening at the hospital when John met Father Bill Graham, who was already at his father's bedside when John strolled into the room. Not short, not exactly tall but heavy set, and with a smile immediately welcoming and somehow affirming. Affirmation from a priest was important to John because of his guilt at being a lapsed Catholic. He always expected that priests would shun his lapsed Catholicism. It always came as a surprise to him when priests and nuns would be nice to him these days.

"Hi, I'm Bill Graham." Not even Father, just Bill. That impressed John, as here was a man who did not have to rely on his title for his identity.

"I'm John Coliani. Albert's son. Nice to meet you Father. Do you know my Dad?"

"We met earlier this week. I have recently been assigned as a chaplain to this hospital, as of July 1. I am just getting to know some of the folks in here. Thought I'd drop up to see how your Father was doing today."

"And you're welcome any time, Father. I was very happy to meet you myself." This from Albert.

"And how are you, John?"

"I'm fine, Dad. How is the pain today?"

"It's not so bad. And after tomorrow, who knows?"

"Dad, did you want to speak with Father alone for a while?"

"No, I have already gone to confession and prepared for tomorrow, with Father's help."

"John, you live here in the big city or up north in Beach Bay?"

"Here. Did I hear recently that you're also at St. Rose of Lima's parish, Father? If you're wondering whether I go to St. Rose of Lima's, or why you haven't ever seen me there, Father, no, I don't live in that neighbourhood. But then I don't really go to any church any more, except maybe once in a while to my wife's, and she's Anglican. I have gone to the odd Midnight Mass and once to a Good Friday service in the Catholic church closest to us. For our kids."

"Oh, I didn't mean to pry or that kind of thing, John. How many children do you have?"

"Two girls, father. A sixteen-year-old and a twelve-year-old. My wife and I have just recently separated. She's a lawyer in town." John put his head down involuntarily as he said these words in case anything came into his eyes.

But the priest knew at once that John's father's illness was not the only suffering in John Coliani's life these days. He was quick to respond. "Hey, John, excuse me for being so forward. You're not going to believe this, but just before supper at the rectory, the Pastor gave me two Leaf tickets tonight. They were given to him by a parishioner and he was counting on going tonight. But he has an emergency to deal with, a very distraught family with the sudden death of a mother in a car accident. So, anyway, I inherited these Leaf tickets and I haven't a clue who to give them to. Could you use them John, or is it too late to find a friend?"

"Father, don't you want to go yourself?"

"Oh, that's not important. It's more important to me that these tickets get used by someone who enjoys them."

"You don't like the Leafs, Father?"

"Oh yes, it's just that I cannot think of anyone to go with at this late time. I thought maybe you might. Your Dad had just been telling me that you enjoy athletics. You play a lot of golf apparently?"

And then John thought, oh oh, what has Dad been telling him about me, about my marriage break-up? John was on his way into anger when Father said, "I play golf every chance I can get, John, which is not as often as I wish but your Dad was perhaps speaking out of turn and telling me that you might take me for a game one day. I am, of course, a greens fee player. I don't have a membership and your Dad said that you do."

This relaxed John and prevented the dive into anger. "Father, I am a member at a very pretty club. Weston. Would you like to play there some time?"

"Would I? Just try me. But what about these hockey tickets? Can you use them tonight? You have 40 minutes before the puck is dropped."

"Tell you what, Father. I could never get anyone to meet me at the Gardens at this time. Too late. But what about you coming with me?"

John could not believe he had just said that. He just met the guy. A priest. And now he was talking about going to a hockey game with a priest. All he knew was that it had all happened so quickly and so naturally.

"You're on. But first I have to cancel one appointment. I'll go down to the nurse's station and use the phone there."

As he left the room, John could see that his Dad was looking off into some far off place. Suddenly John thought he'd made a mistake into saying yes to a hockey game the night before his Dad's surgery. "Dad, do you want me to stay with you instead of going to a hockey game tonight?"

"No, my son. Go with Father. It's good. I want to sleep early tonight and I think they are going to give me a pill to make me sleep tonight. Besides your mother…"

"Is someone talking about me? Should my ears be burning?" as Emma strode into the room all smiles. She was carrying a shopping bag out of which she now took a housecoat. "I brought this for you, honey. You will need it after the operation. She exuded confidence, John noted, and this was a Godsend to everyone in the room. Confidence was essential. Hope was crucial.

Just then the priest walked in and Emma's eyes turned into brown question marks. "Mom, this is Father Bill. He has been visiting with Dad; he's new to St Rose of Lima's. And, because of his generosity, he and I leaving you immediately to go to a Leafs' game, tickets compliments of Father Bill." He let those words just hang there till she came back with,

"I know who Father Bill is, Father Bill Graham, the new Chaplain here at the hospital. I will take your word on the hockey game thing. Tonight?" As if she couldn't believe it.

"Mom, it all happened very quickly. I'll explain it later."

Now it was Father Bill's turn. "It is good to meet you, Mrs. Coliani. I did not want to interrupt you and your son."

"Why? In this family, we interrupt each other all the time. We listen with our motors running. We are Italian. And my name is Emma. And if you ever come to Beach Bay, make sure you come over for spaghetti–the other priests do. And now, both of you go to this hockey game or you will be late."

John said something about his Mom being a Mafia Don. And how he and Bill had better listen to her, while Father bill said he'd be sure to hold her to that spaghetti offer. With that and some laughter they were both gone and Emma looked down at her husband with tears in her eyes. These she suddenly wiped away and tried not to let Albert notice them. But he did.

"You are as surprised as me to see John going to a hockey game with a priest?"

"Oh, if only John would be influenced by this man. Go back to church. Get his Faith back. Maybe losing Louise would be something he could bear." And then she started to cry hard. "I'm so sorry, Albert. This is not the time for me to carry on like this."

And no sooner were these words out, when into the room came Louise, Nancy and Debbie.

The hockey game was no hell; the Leafs lost badly and both Father Bill and John wondered why the fans paid money to such a team to go on in this way. Only in Hog town, could management such as that of the Leafs get away with giving so little to the fans and getting so much back in the way of revenue. No matter what kind of a team the fans got, they attended; they paid to see the nonsense on the ice. And people wondered about the lack of accountability for the educational tax dollar said John to Father Bill.

"Yes, it is true, John, that accountability is often absent in the private as well as the public realm. It reminds one of the big banks always telling the federal government to get the hell out of the market place, to deregulate, and they'll create the jobs. And what do they do? At a time when they are enjoying huge profits, they are downsizing like mad, eliminating jobs as fast as they can. The Prime Minister has every reason not to trust the large corporations when they claim that they will create the jobs if only they are left alone, given bigger and better tax breaks."

John liked this guy. He liked his opinions. He liked the way Father bill was relaxed, not at all the way John thought that a priest would talk. Bill had a way of helping John to relax, too.

"On another note, John, I hear through the grape vine that you have been going through some difficulties lately. You mentioned earlier that your marriage is undergoing some of the pressures of the modern world."

"It's true, Father. Louise and I have separated. It's not my choice but then, maybe I was partly responsible. I'm pretty upset about it. And now there's Dad to worry about."

"John, I brought it up to let you know that I know about it, not to pry, and to let you know that I'm available to do anything I can, even if that is just to listen, without judgments, John. Just to listen if you need a friend to run things by now and then. I'm trained to do that and it's partly why I became a priest, to help people. So if you will allow me, I'll be glad to practise my vocation."

"Thanks Father. I believe you. And who knows, I might just take you up on it some time. But I have to confess, I haven't been a very good Catholic of late."

"John, before you go on in that line. Anyone who hasn't been a lapsed Catholic at some time in his life hasn't been doing much thinking either. There comes a time, and it's different for different people, where I suspect every one of us has to make the choice that theoretically we make at Confirmation. At Baptism, our parents pass on to us the Faith. At confirmation, we are supposed to choose the Faith ourselves. But let's face it. We are way too young to make that choice at 14 years of age.

"So, we go to high school, we go to university, and caboom, our Faith is rocked by doubts. Or we just stop going to Sunday Mass when we are away from home for the first time. Or it happens when we move out of the house for the first time after we are married, and we stop going to church on Sunday. Or some kind of crisis precipitates our descent into the darkness of doubt. A fiancee dies, whatever. For any number of reasons, people come to a point where they have to make the choice for themselves. To believe or not to believe. And to practice that belief or to lose it. Believing by itself is not enough. A guy can say he believes in God, but if he doesn't do something with that belief, it atrophies just like an unused muscle. And without the support of a Faith Community, it does not take very long till he's an atheist.

"I know, too, John the temptation of agnosticism for people of intellect like yourself. And by the way, I know more about you and your teaching than you might think. I already knew who you were before we met. I have met some of your students by the way. And I hear from the kids that you are one of the best high school teachers. Authentic and intelligent. Stimulating classes. Teaching kids to think. And that's great. But getting back to agnosticism. It's the siren song for intellectuals. We cannot prove God. We cannot disprove God. So, let's just sit on the fence and say we don't know if there's a God; that's the most respectable position isn't it? Except that we cannot live on a fence, can we John? Either we teach our kids about God, or we don't, and we can't teach them about religion without letting them experience some of it, can we?

"No, we may adopt agnosticism intellectually, but we will live either theistically or atheistically. Sermon's over, John. Sorry I got carried away, there."

"No, it's okay Father. And I agree with you now. But it's taken a few years for me to come to much the same point as you're describing. But it's a little late now. My marriage is over. My kids are being brought up without much of my help these days."

"John, you're an athlete. You know it's never over till it's over." Who was that Casey Stengel or Yogi Berra said that?

"I'm not sure, Father."

"But I got way off track, John, with what I was trying to say. Adult Catholics have to make adult decisions, so being lapsed just means you are going through your own period of relationship with God when you can no longer live on the Faith of your parents, your teachers, your priests. You have to relate directly to God yourself and come to your own relationship with Him. Your own accommodation with Him. He's already in your life, John, talking to you through the seemingly ordinary events of every day, and especially in the not so ordinary events as well. Has it occurred to you yet, John, that He may well be talking to you right now in this biggest of events, your breakup with Louise? Could it be, John, that our God, your God, has something He wants to say to you, and the only way He can get your attention is through something of this magnitude?

"I'm not saying that God contributed to your break-up just so He could talk to you. I am saying that I have really come to believe that in these kinds of events we will find God. That He doesn't come to us in lightning flashes, on the tops of mountains, but that the burning bushes are right in front of us, if we would but open our eyes. Let

Him into our consciousness and address Him directly right there."

John was quiet now. This priest was hitting him right between the eyes. Maybe he just needed to hear these things. To believe that no matter how he had abandoned God, God had not abandoned him. It was like a drink of water to a very thirsty desert traveler that John received these words. He had a new friend for sure.

"More coffee guys?" It was the waitress in the restaurant after the game.

"No thank you. I'll never sleep tonight." Father Bill smiled at the lady. John noticed something about this smile. It was so affirming. John had been noticing the smile all evening but he hadn't given it much thought. Now, as Father Bill smiled at this perfect stranger, the waitress, John did think about it. Bill had a way of looking at you that said, "I like you!"

And John remembered those tapes he had once been lent, audio tapes by a Father John Powell: My Vision and My Values, they were called. Where father Powell had said that his role was to look at people, to deal with them, in such a way that you showed them not how good you were, but how good they were.

And Powell had also gone on to say that he believed that this was something of the effect Jesus had on perfect strangers when He saw them for the first time. Jesus simply looked so deeply into their eyes with his smile that said, "I like you just the way you are." Powell had said on the tapes that the person was left wondering after Jesus had walked by, who was that guy anyway?

It was this same Powell who had said that there are three of me, the me I see, the me you see, and the me that God sees. John had been attracted to the notion of heaven that Father Powell had elucidated as one in which we see ourselves for the first time as God sees us, without all of the junk we put into out self images. He had really taken to that as somehow being much more attractive as an idea of heaven than sitting around all day playing harps.

And here was this smile on Father Bill's face that made John know that he liked this guy, wanted to see him again. But he never did. For Father Bill was dead the following Monday of a heart attack, at 43 years of age, having been in his latest assignment for a very short time. Another statistic of a young priest dead of a heart attack. John wondered why some bright young sociology candidate did not do a PhD thesis on the average age of priestly deaths.

In his journal the week following Father Bill's death he wrote that one day the church was going to have to answer for the harm done to people because of mandatory celibacy. The damage done to abused kids. To married women. Even to, and especially to, the priests themselves. For sex was a biological thing, naturally, but incapable of permanent repression.

In the week following the news of Father Bill's death, John went back to one of his books where he had highlighted the following passage:

> The more the sex drive is forced down into the subconscious, the stronger it gets, till it erupts volcano-like into some kind of aberrant behavior. For those in whom it does not erupt, they feel it as the kind of tension which wreaks havoc with blood pressure and causes coronary problems, cancer even, till it kills them at too early an age. Yes, the Church will indeed be called to answer for its inflexibility with this mandatory celibacy thing, no matter how many stupid arguments the Magisterium advances as to the necessity of a celibate priesthood.

Now John even wondered whether those Catholics who had left in anger, because of things like this dogma, and other bullshit like the Church's stand on the inferiority of women to men – and that's what it was no matter what they said about there not being any women priests – whether the loss of their Faith would be left on the doorstep of the Magisterium to answer for.

The teaching authority of the Church... the promise of Pentecost, that the Holy spirit would guide the Church, keep it from error in its teachings... but where was this Magisterium to be found these days? In the Curia? In the Congregation for the Protection of the Faith or whatever they called it these days? With the Pope? With the regional and national conferences of bishops?

The Church was not a democracy John had heard. Still, he wondered why contemporary theologians weren't going crazy today over the heresy of clericalism which John saw as the prevailing modus operandi in so many parishes that he'd heard about. Oh, it was fine for Vatican Two to speak about the Church being the whole people of God, but, in practice, from what John had seen when He had helped out with the Share Life Campaign, it was the priest who was the Church and the parish council were rubber stamps to allow strong Pastors, Builders all, to do their thing.

John was angry again. He had lost a friend before he had spent a second evening with him; that's why he was angry. Angry at this very church to whom Father Bill had given the better part of his life. John knew that he would indeed have gone to see this guy again. That he might have helped John. Irony. What was God saying to John in this event?

Well, maybe something, because the very day that Father Bill had died, a Monday that John would not soon forget, John received a brown envelope in the mail. It had a return address on it from Father Bill Graham. Inside was a typed note which read:

March 23rd

Dear John,
Forgive me for taking this liberty but I wanted to share something with you that you might find interesting. Some years ago, at another parish, I went through a crisis which almost saw me give up my priesthood. I went to the Bishop for help and he was kind enough to send me away for a few months. During those months away I went on a 30-day retreat in a monastery and I was placed under the spiritual direction of a Monk who was also a therapist. One of the things this guy did for me was start me in the habit of writing in a journal each day. At first, he even gave me questions that I ought to

try to answer. Eventually, I did not need his questions and even now, I begin each morning with three pages of writing on whatever I choose to write about. It's almost like a kind of meditation except that I don't fall asleep like I do when I try meditating without putting pen to paper.

I have found this morning writing very helpful. I guess the Greek was right, the unexamined life is not worth living. I have found that my own liberation proceeds only to the extent that I find out what is controlling me, what I need to be liberated from. And usually, that happens to be emotions I am feeling but not facing into. These emotions usually control my behaviour to the extent that I do not bring them into the light of analysis.

I don't know whether this will be true for you, too, but the Monk told me that it was generally true for everyone. Strange. My education taught me to respect reason, not emotion, which I was supposed to be suspicious of, since feelings are not a proper way to ground anything. Yet there's not much new about any of my ideas. What makes me who I am is my only particular configuration of emotions.

One of the questions the Monk started me off with was, what are the most important statements I have learned about life so far? It was instructive to me to try answering this question. Would you be interested in trying to answer such a question only for yourself in some kind of journal? One day, we might even share answers to that question. If you wish, I could even provide you with some of the other questions the Monk gave me to try.

Give me a dingle if you should be interested. Again, please don't think I am forcing myself on you as some kind of spiritual director you did not ask for. I offer this information strictly as a friend who has had his own struggles, and I must say I am somewhat scared of taking the risk that you might just tell me to go to hell. Like any other human being, I am not much good at handling rejection, but it would probably serve me right if you did not want to pursue our friendship. At any rate, life is a series of judgment calls, and if I've made the wrong one here by going out on this limb, I will survive as I have my other mistakes, for God loves us, and is there to pick us up when we are down.

Bill

John was flabbergasted. Not at all angry. In fact very pleased that father Bill had thought enough of their evening together to take the time to care this much. It was a risk on his part. Some guys might well reject such an overture of friendship. But not John. He was surprised and impressed with Father Bill. Strange. Who would have thought that Father Bill had any kind of a crisis in his priesthood? He seemed so together. Without any doubts about God, about his vocation. His very smile announced the presence of God.

You just never know, thought John. People may seem to have it altogether and then whammo, some news surfaces that suggests their lives aren't any more problem-free than our own. The Warren Pryor syndrome: despite the milk-white shirts and his escape from the red dirt, he still managed to put a bullet through his own head. Or Auden's character looking down, seeing the shadow of the Average Man attempting the exceptional and running away. We discover so often that heroes have feet of clay.

Is this why heroes are so exceptional? Ordinary guys doing extraordinary things? But sometimes the pressure to do the exceptional when you haven't got exceptional resources must be tough, John was thinking.

What was that question, I should try to answer? What have I learned that's most important about life, or is it my own life I am supposed to write about?

Anyway, John had no time for journal writing every morning. And while he thought it might be a good idea to try some of it some time, maybe in the summer when he did not have to teach every day, or when he did not have an early starting time, he might be willing to give it a try.

After Father Bill's funeral, John gave the writing a try. One morning at a time. Soon he was into it big time. Writing in a journal gradually became a very important part of his life. It was his main contact with a friend who left too soon. It was a way of dealing with the shock people often experience at times of such loss.

Life is precious, and fragile. It is often unbelievably cruel, but still, life is precious. By life, I include good health, good food, good wine, friends, golf, and yes, male bonding around a table covered with draft beer. My wife and children were treasures I have lost but they made life richer. Good weather, especially sunshine, is also important to my life. But so is snow on Christmas Eve, rain on the roof of a waterproof tent, the smell of coffee in the morning coming from a campfire, autumn leaves, the first tulips of spring, and the first robin song before I even see his red breast. In fact, I like all of the seasons and they are an important part of my life.

I am not big on pain and suffering. I have the typical pain threshold of an Italian Canadian. I cry easily. I don't like to see my Dad going through the pain right now in the hospital, recovering from the worst operation I have ever seen anyone have. I still can't bear the thought of seeing him after the surgery, his eyes and gestures with his hands almost pleading with me to get rid of that tube in his mouth, and nothing I can do about it to relieve his discomfort. I'm told he's getting out by the end of this week. Thank God! But is he going to be okay?

Watching Dad, I have seen something of the preciousness of life, something of its fragility. Mortality. Dad has an opportunity to deal with it now. Everybody has to at some time or other. A passage I guess. I wonder if dad afraid of the act of dying? I know I would be. I am! The possibility of choking to death scares me badly. I hear there's choking, gasping for breath. I'm not afraid of being dead, but I'm terrified of dying. Dad might well die from this damn cancer on his spine, how is that healthy? Screw you Becker. Maybe I forget what his thesis really was. So long ago since I read that book. But it didn't effect me like it did my ex-Jesuit friend who put me on to it and told me it was a must read.

I still wonder if I will ever be one of the cognoscenti. Thinking about death seems morbid. But maybe what Becker was saying was that our problem is that we do not live life as if we were aware of our own immortality. That would make more sense. But that could be confused with carpe diem. And we have been told by the Church all of our lives that hedonism is wrong. That living for now is wrong. That this life is only a preparation for the next. That we are not supposed to be happy here in this prison of a body. Was the Kingdom Jesus talked about a futuristic Kingdom or was He really saying that the Kingdom is a now thing? I know that St. Augustine apparently said that our souls were made by God and will only be happy when they return to God. So which is it? Throw our apples into the barrel of our earthly existence or opt for a delayed gratification and mortify our flesh till we meet our Maker? Each one is a leap. Isn't that what Pascal said? Or was it Kierkegaard? I forget.

But it's easier to leap when you can see the other side.

My Roman Catholicism no longer buoys me up. I can relate to Shaw. Dammit I wish I could believe. And take comfort in that belief. Then I could say I am going through this stuff with Louise for a reason. A reason for everything. Something good comes of all suffering, and so on.

Strangely enough, I haven't lost my admiration for who the Christ was supposed to have been. What a guy. If I had the freedom to remake my personality, I'd like to be more like Him. But without the pain, without the Cross. Was there a real Christ on this planet? Did this guy really live?

Why did the Evangelists portray Him without a sense of

humour? I gotta laugh. I need jokes. He'd have been more relatable for me had He a sense of humour. Did they just leave this out? When He was at Cana doing the water into wine caper, was He laughing that day, carousing with the guys, drinking wine? I mean, how do you go to a wedding and be serious all day?

And this Pope today. What does he have to say to me? To my life right now? My Dad sick. My Mom shattered. My wife gone. What does this guy have to tell me about my life? That priests can't marry. That women can't be priests. That Father Bill is dead at 43 years of age because he tried to live an impossible life of celibacy. You'll never convince me that this is healthy for normal guys. How many heterosexuals are entering seminaries these days?

Still, Jung, was it Jung? Who said that we cannot achieve any measure of peace until we make peace with whatever is our conception of God? I never read any Jung. I've only read about Jung. Read other people talking about what Jung said. Should read him myself I guess. But I gather that Jung said something about most psychological problems stemming from an individual's failure to deal with the place of God in his life.

But it's not really God I'm struggling with, or is it? It's the people with the collars who see themselves as the Church, and only themselves. They make all the decisions. Not for me, boys. But maybe it comes to one and the same thing. Maybe my problems with some priests, with some of the hierarchy are indeed my problems with God. For maybe we relate to God only through our relationship with those people in our lives. And He did chose some apostles. But are these guys today really the successors to the apostles He chose? What do they know of service, of washing feet? Why isn't washing feet a sacrament today? Prelates today strike me as power mongers, decision makers, but not as suffering servants. There are exceptions I guess but the media doesn't write about them so I don't hear about them, and I don't see such exceptions locally either.

It occurs to me as I write in the pages of this journal, could my marital problems, and the concomitant financial worries this break-up has engendered – even my Dad's illness – could these circumstances be God's attempt to speak with me? Or is this an ancient Catholic superstitious belief that god is to be found talking to us in the ordinary and extraordinary circumstances of our lives? Would I recognize God's voice in my life if He did speak to me? How would God speak to me? Is the age of miracles not long gone? Or is it visible only to those who have Faith?

I find myself believing more in this life than in any afterlife. And yet having said that, I realize what corner I have trapped myself in. This life is so not so pleasant without Louise, Nancy and Debbie. I can see why people turn to their religions for consolation, turn to hope for a better life after this one. Pain and suffering are great preachers I suspect.

Is this life a mere dress rehearsal? Or is this all there is? Am I going to be dead a long time and therefore foolish not to carpe diem? But where are these flowers to pluck right now?

John was surprised by how much he could write in the mornings. How easily the words would come to him. Maybe it might prove useful to continue with writing in this journal. Perhaps he would eventually discover something of himself not yet known. Maybe a modicum of peace would be his through this self exploration. If nothing else he was doing what his friend Father Bill had suggested and somehow this kept Father Bill around. And John needed him to be around. On another morning:

I am depressed – really depressed. I am pissed at Louise, and I cannot right now imagine calling her for any reason. I know that I ought to forget about her. It is Saturday morning.

I have been out drinking with the guys again last night. That too pissed me off, that I give in and get drunk, and then end up feeling this way the next morning. Same old. Same old. I never learn.

And this fucking weather. The temperature has dropped again. The rain seems now to have been falling for ever. I need some sunshine, damn it.

I care nothing about my life. Nothing about my future interests me. I would prefer to be dead right now. That's how I feel. I am a little bit afraid to acknowledge these feelings. In fact, I am frightened. I might decide to do something which cannot be undone. Suicide is immature. Right. And my mother needs me. It would kill her. Right.

But I do want to be done with this loneliness. I am completely depressed by my relationship with Louise. I wish I had never married her. Why didn't I stay single? Is this really what I wish? I don't know. I cannot believe I wrote that. I was happy when I was married to her, most of the time. Still, now I feel so very vulnerable. We have not talked for what feels like weeks now. Except these stupid fucking letters from her idiot lawyer. Why is she doing this to me, to us? She knows better.

And what really is the sense of writing all this down? Does it really help? Where are you now, Father Bill, when I so badly need to talk with you. Love to see you. Help me, please, to get through this shit. This journal writing seems just to keep me upset. I ought to do some marking, do some reading, just get my mind off all of this shit, but I don't feel like doing anything. Just crying maybe. And I am doing that right now while I write this stuff.

I don't know what I want. Nothing. Other than to be dead. Totally out of this stupid fucking life of John Coliani, teacher. Dad – can you hear me, wherever you are? Every once in a while the idea occurs to me to pick up the phone and call you, and then it is brought home suddenly to me that I can't do this. And it hurts. I suppose that this is part of the grieving process, a process that does not just stop simply because the funeral is over. One of the reasons I wanted to go up to the cemetery after the funeral was to help me bring closure to your death. I thought that if I saw your coffin lowered into the grave, it might help. In fact, it only seemed at the time to upset me more. But perhaps it did help in ways I do not yet understand.

I ought to write down for myself, what I remember as significant during your illness.

Once you smiled and said, "Look who's here!" to me, when I got to your bedside, but nonetheless, I could not believe your condition. In fact, I said to myself, something like the following: "I think My Dad is dying. I cannot believe that he has gone downhill like this when the telephone reports have been so good as to his progress." But you had evidently made the decision to pull out.

Mom told me a great deal after the funeral. What she went through. One night when she got to your ward, she heard two of the gentlemen across from you make some kind of a negative comment, to themselves and to their visitors, about it having been so noisy and their not getting a moment's rest with you moaning in pain all the time. She felt so badly for you, Dad. You WERE moaning quite a bit and seemed very disturbed. When Mom asked you what you wanted, you said that you wanted to die. Tiresias? She also heard that the night before, these guys could not sleep and you had to be moved out into the hall so that they could get some sleep in the ward. Later, she heard that the Resident had told the nurse that maybe he was going to send you back home. So Mom asked to speak with the Resident when he came onto the floor.

When she met this doctor, she asked him whether this was the beginning of the end for you, as she suspected. And he said, "Yes, there's not much more we can do for him."

She asked whether it was true that he had been thinking of sending you home and he said yes. Mom then said that Dad had told her, too, that he wanted to go home. And she wondered whether he might be more comfortable there, rather than in this ward. The Resident, said, "most definitely," and that it was the best thing in the circumstances.

I think that this doctor told Mom something like this, that there was more of a chance of a palliative strategy at home when someone was dying. The emphasis would be placed on making the person as comfortable as possible. Since you seemed most uncomfortable in this ward, in the hospital, Mom agreed that maybe it was the best idea, especially since the Doctor assured her that everything they were now doing for you in the hospital could be arranged for you in the privacy of your own home, providing Mom got lots of help. They would continue with the oxygen, give you the morphine, and generally see more to your comfort. And you had lately told Mom and me so often that you now wanted to die, so that this time, Mom finally tried to see it from your point of view.

Everyone – doctor, nurses – was of the same opinion: that we ought to respect your wishes. So Mom told you, she was going to respect your wishes, Dad; you were going home. And the next evening, back home, you were so much more peaceful. Or so Mom thought. So much so that you did not die. Not then. But eventually you had to go back into the hospital after all, where you did die.

Mom called me at the time and told me most of this even then. She also said that a lady whose husband was right beside you, came over to Mom and told her that she could not help overhear Dad telling a nurse how you had prayed so often to be allowed to die. I told Mom that I wanted to accept Dad's wishes. We agreed completely. So we tried to do that. Ultimately, it was your own decision to go home. It was also your decision to die, and be done with a life you no longer enjoyed. Like I feel right now.

It was tough to accept, Dad, but I tried my best to be a good and loving son to a father who had been so good to me. It was tougher still, for Mom, when at home your poor brother could not understand why you had returned when you were still so sick. He kept saying, "Why isn't he is in the hospital?" Mom likely could not explain much at that point. She never told me, maybe she did not remember, whether she did, or did not say to him, "Leave me alone. My husband wants to die." Your family would not have understood that. I suppose your family thought that Mom was giving up too easily when she was really struggling to accept and respect your wishes. And one or two of our aunts were calling everyone to tell them to come right away, even after Mom had hinted that she wanted to be left alone with you. She knew then that the funeral was going to be very soon.

When I got that final call to come home immediately, I was glad that I had said my goodbye to you, told you how much I loved you, told you what a great father you had been, how we were going to miss you, but also that I had accepted your wishes and that you had my blessing to go if that's what you really wanted. I was crying when I said this to you, and you squeezed my hand, and Mom heard you say, "I love you, too," but I did not hear that as I was just too upset. I was determined that I was going to say something like this to you, before you died. I wanted badly for you to know how much I loved you, how much Louise and our kids loved you. I am crying even now as I write this, as I remember these last moments I had with you while you were still conscious.

Mom told me later that after you were readmitted to the hospital because they couldn't get the morphine to work any more, that it was just after that, that you began to show all of the signs that the pamphlet told her to anticipate during the process of dying. Your digestion shut down first and I guess that's why you could not hold down the antibiotics, the milkshake, the grapes.

Perhaps your death was especially threatening to our uncles and aunts. I don't know; I cannot speak for them. I can only speak for myself, that Mom and I wanted to do whatever made it easier for you because there was no question in Mom's mind, and in the minds of all of the professionals, that this was your ending. The sooner we accepted that, the sooner we could try to make your passing as comfortable as possible. And I am very glad we made the decision we did, because it was absolutely easier for you at home than it was, than it would have been in that hospital ward. You weren't very conscious when you did have to go back to the hospital. You didn't notice very much, Mom said. I will always be grateful to all of the professionals who helped us to deal with what you wanted. I gather they, too, were relieved that they did not have to pretend to Mom any longer that more could be done for you, which I suspect they sometimes have to do with some folks.

I know that Mom and I did everything possible to encourage you not to throw in the towel, to try to get you to keep fighting. But I suspect that you wanted us even sooner to see the inevitable, because you loved us so much. Finally, all that was important was to get you as comfortable as possible in those last hours.

I don't know whether this writing will help my grieving for you, Dad. I sure hope so. Father Bill thought that it would help me, and maybe it will. But I also know that a wake, a funeral mass, writing a journal entry such as this, are still only steps on a journey that may well take quite a few more months. Christmas will not be the same this year. I wish you peace, Dad. You would want me to have peace, too. I truly hope that we made your exit easier. But if there is any kind of life beyond this one, maybe, just maybe, you could speak to me somehow sometime?

BEARE PARTS

My life made so much more sense when you were here. Are you watching over us both now?

Because I feel so much like joining you, Dad. Somehow, I did not follow the model you and Mom gave me for having a great marriage. Mine is toast as you know. But our kids are past their infancy. Do they really need me anymore? I don't even live with them. What's the sense of living for me any more? I know, you once told me that you never stop being a parent, even when the kids are grown up. But I guess I'm thinking more like your kid right now, and not like a parent. Fuck it. I don't have the energy to feel guilty now.

The kids would survive if I opted out. And Louise. It sure wouldn't bother her all that much. In fact, it would make things a lot easier for her and her lawyer if I were gone. She would certainly find another guy pretty damn quickly. So what's keeping me here? That suicide is a major sin? That I'd be damned forever? Who knows? Am I just having a Hamlet moment? Feeling sorry for myself? Perhaps some self-mockery would be just the thing to provide me with some ironic detachment from all of this emotion, this tidal wave of shit which suffocates me.

It isn't just Louise who's getting to me. It's my whole fucking life. Take my fucking career for example. Teaching. Read the papers. Everyone hates us. We're parasites with three months holidays. Doing nothing of value. The government heaps insult after insult and the public eats it up and the government's popularity soars. We are overeducated assholes.

I feel so damned alone. I have no faith, Father Bill, to buoy me up. Agnosticism at times like this doesn't help much. No faith in Jesus. No faith in me. No faith in my marriage. No faith in life, in its value. We are ants on the log over the fire. The gods are watching us, deciding when we will fall into the flames for their enjoyment. Is that what Hemingway wrote? Our Nada. Who art in Nada. Or mere blades of grass which, when we perish in the Fall, will be remembered not at all by the earth which birthed us? And these are the words of the Bible? Some comfort there!

I want to be dead. Is it sinful, Jesus, to acknowledge this death wish? My life has been full of sin. Why stop now? Of anger. Of gluttony. Of drunkenness. Of weakness. Of general malaise. Self-indulgence. Name it. I confess. And of anger – great anger. Perhaps suicide is a natural conclusion to such a life. Dad – help me. Jesus – help me. Don't let me do what I shouldn't do. Am I mentally ill? Or just emotionally distraught? Or a little of both? In fact, are the two really different?

I must remind myself what I know about depression. That when depressed, we tend to think that our lives have always been this bleak, are shit right now, and will ever be this way. That's the power of depression, the way it works. It wipes out memories of happier times and tends to convince us that life is nothing but this shit, past, present and future. I have to tell myself, force myself to remember, that this, too, will pass. But right now, consciousness is not what it's cracked up to be.

Can I give this up now? Has it helped, Father Bill? Am I past the crying, the whining, the drowning in self-pity? Can I go on now with this wonderful fucking life, such as it as, this truly wonderful Saturday morning?

As the weeks of separation went on, and the teaching year came to a close, followed by another summer of golf accompanied, however, by a lot of rain, John continued with daily journal writing. He missed some days but was mostly faithful to this practice. When the Fall brought another year of high school teaching, John thought of introducing the habit to his English classes. As a way on getting kids into writing every day and as a means of self discovery. He did recommend the habit to various classes but he did not formally mandate the habit. Somehow he was cynical of getting most kids to see that anything mandated might have some practical application in life. Anything forced upon kids always seemed to them to be school things. Of little value in their busy lives. It was difficult for so many of them to make the connections between school learning and their lives. John often felt like a failure as a teacher for not being able to get them to see the value in what he was trying to teach them, trying to get them to inculcate something so valuable into their daily lives.

He kept trying to make the themes of literature strike home to them. Kept trying to have them experience the shock of recognition yet at first he judged that so many of them had so little experience of life at this point, that serious literature could not possibly speak to their cares and concerns. Lately he had begun to conclude that they had so much experience of life but the problem was that it was so different from John's growing up, from the experience that older authors wrote about, that he felt they needed their own literature. But it hadn't been written yet.

The pervasiveness of the drug culture. The huge increase in influence of contemporary music's lyrics. Indeed the variety of musical genres, most of which John was not even familiar with, not to mention the personalities speaking to these kids today. The unbelievable increase in single parent homes, and the number of kids with multiple sets of parents and grandparents owing to frequently changing co-habitation arrangements. This was not the world in which John grew up. It was not the world as described by the novelists and poets he had been trying to teach these kids.

Perhaps it was for this reason that he knew that the teaching of writing was as important as the teaching of reading. Yeah, some things never changed. When Lawrence wrote about power balances in heterosexual relationships, or Joyce struggled with coming to terms with the Faith of one's youth, they had hit upon themes still worth discussing today. But on the other hand, many of today's youth were most obsessed with homosexual coming out, with the admission of lesbian tendencies, with the failure of marriage in their parents' lives. For many of these kids, there was no Faith to come to terms with. They had been brought up in atheism and agnosticism. Their parents had ridiculed main stream religion.

John despaired about getting them to appreciate Western Literature for many of them had very little knowledge of the Bible. Frye, of course, was correct in stressing that Western Literature was a series of footnotes on the King James Bible. But John and so many of his students did not share a common understanding of the place of the Bible in their lives. They could not, therefore, easily be brought to a love of Western Literature. One couldn't presume that they knew very much about either Old or New Testaments.

He figured he was getting old when he began to become too aware of the differences between his and his students' generations. It was always the oldest and most out of it older teachers who ranted about this young generation's differences. John did not want that to happen to himself. He wanted to leave teaching when he thought he would reach the point when he was out of touch with kids. And yet for all of his attempts to stay tuned to what was on the minds of these kids, he felt himself slipping beyond their kens. Beyond their preoccupations and into his own. He wondered sometimes if his students would be making fun of him behind his back the way he had often heard them laughing at the oldest teachers on staff, the way these guys "were out of it," with their ties, their suits, their attitudes so laughable to the kids in the hall, in the lunchroom, in his classes.

It was a bit frightening for John because he had not groomed himself to think in terms of escape from the classroom via the administration route. He wanted to stay in the classroom, kibitzing with teenagers, getting their eyes to light up. But he worried how long he'd be able to do that. And then what? When burn-out came, what option was left for him? None that he knew about.

Teaching did not open any doors. You chose it, you did it, and then you got promoted out of the classroom. Or you burned out in the classroom. Bored. Not much effort or energy left. No new courses to teach. Not much effort in terms of new lesson planning. Use the old stuff. Thank God for file folders. Counting the days till the 90 factor. Hoping like hell you could hang on till then.

John did not feel this way yet but it was a pretty accurate summary of the kinds of feed back he got from the older teachers on his staff. The ones who got into pyramid schemes of one kind or another. There was one guy who had suckered John into attending an Amway presentation in the guy's living room. John had never forgiven the guy and was wary of every invitation since then.

It was in June of his last year in his Toronto high school that John accepted that his father was not going to make it. Over the past year Albert had been to Toronto for a second set of radiation treatments. The first set had been in conjunction with some chemotherapy at Princess Margaret, and John's mother had stayed with him in his new apartment, while spending most of her days at the hospital with Albert. That had been in September. But in May of the following year a cat scan showed more tumors and Albert had gotten 10 radiation treatments, some kind of maximum dosage attempt to save his life. But without admitting it to each other, both Emma and John somehow knew that it was futile. The surgery had given Albert perhaps a year more of life, and the ability to keep on walking. The initial tumor likely would have crippled him eventually. Other than that, the surgery seemed to have been something to endure which produced far less in the way of results than were to be hoped for after such suffering. Albert had gone through a hell of a lot and for what?

It was in early August that Emma called John in Toronto. Crying as she spoke:

"John, I know you were here last weekend..." And her voice went silent. She could no longer speak. (Indeed John had been up most weekends, signing a contract to teach back home, getting a place to stay, spending time with his dying father, trying to deal with his own grief over the split.)

"Mom. What's wrong?" Trying to help her because he knew why she couldn't speak. It always happened to him, too, when he became so overwrought that all he could do was either cry or be silent till he got himself back together. "Is it Dad?"

"Yes, your Uncles and Aunts are here with me... And..." Quiet sobbing.

"Mom, if there's a nurse in the room with you now, put her on."

After a few seconds which seemed like a very long time to John. "Hello John? This is Brenda Jordan. I'm on duty in your Dad's room today."

"Hi Brenda. I remember meeting you this summer. Is Dad in trouble?"

"Yes, John, your Dad is slipping away now, and it will not be much longer. His breathing has that sound to it which usually signals the end is near, although sometimes patients do come out of it. But I think not this time, John."

"If I left right now, it would take me four hours to get there. Do I have time?"

"I don't think so, John. I suspect it will be within the hour. But one never knows how long the process will take."

"Thanks, Brenda. I'll try any way. Please tell Mom I'm on my way."

It was 9.30 a.m. on a Saturday morning in August. John was in Beach Bay by 1.45 p.m. and instinctively he went by the house on his way to the hospital. There was no need to go any further. All of the cars were in his parents' driveway or in front of his parents' home. His aunt came out to the driveway and told him that his Dad had passed away at 11.45. His Mother was inside the house with other relatives.

John went inside and merely nodded at the uncles and aunts he saw gathered throughout the house. When he got to his mother, he saw an older woman than the one he had left last weekend. She was kind of bent over even in a sitting position and looked up at him, tried to smile but started to cry as he went to her and enfolded her shoulders in his arms. She stopped crying shortly and said nothing then but just stared silently ahead of her at nothing. After about five minutes of total silence in the room she said to John, "Have you had anything to eat?"

"Mom, don't worry about me right now? All of my uncles are going to think I'm spoiled." There was finally some laughter in the room and an easing of the grief. Even Emma looked more like herself and though she didn't smile, she seemed to be staring less intently at nothing. It was as if she was establishing eye contact again with the people in the room. She was momentarily back from wherever her memories, her grief had taken her.

John got up and went into the kitchen where one of his aunts was doing dishes but there were Italian cold cuts laid out on platters on the table, bread in wicker baskets too. And cheese and pickles and roasted peppers and someone's homemade melanzane. And two or three kinds of olives. Family was important John thought. And he was hungry, too.

He was well into his sandwich when his Mom came into the kitchen and said, "I hope you don't mind son. But I already went to the funeral home with Uncle Andy and picked out the casket. There wasn't much to decide as your Dad had made most of the arrangements himself. The plot for him and me were purchased years ago and the package at the funeral home your Dad had already discussed with Mr. McKee. He would even have chosen his own casket, apparently, but when he went to see McKee there was some uncertainty as to which models would or would not be available. Any way, that's about all I had to decide and it was a little cheaper to take one McKee had in stock today. And to decide the times of the visiting hours. We start tomorrow afternoon at 2 p.m. then Sunday night, Monday afternoon and evening, and the funeral is Tuesday morning at 10 o'clock at St. Lucy's. Is that all okay with you, John? As I say, I didn't really have to decide very much, or I would have waited for you. I also figured that you'd be just as happy to have this done with."

"Yeah, Mom, it's all just fine. I just hope that you can get through these next few days okay. You look exhausted, Mom."

"I'll be okay, honey. I just need to cry and to rest a little. Of course, we all knew it was coming, including your Dad. We were helpless to stop it. We tried to accept it. We prayed about it and then we cried together. He cried like a baby so many times, John, right in my arms." And then his mother started to howl and almost collapsed into John's arms. They hugged each other a long time and he let her cry.

Eventually, some of his aunts and uncles left to leave them alone to rest. But around supper time, some came back and more came over. And one of them became a bartender, and drinks and food were served in abundance till at least 11 o'clock that night, and there were tears but there was also a hell of a lot of laughter, although not in the living room so much, where Emma sat quietly on the chesterfield and received her relatives. In the kitchen, however, jokes were being told. And memories of Albert were cherished. The time Uncle Eddie had fallen in the creek trout fishing and Albert had tried to help him up and he fell in, too. And they were drinking wine and drying their socks and pants by a fire when a man and his daughter went walking by, fishing too, and here were these two guys warming themselves by a fire in their underwear swatting mosquitoes. It seemed so funny the way Uncle Joe told it and he hadn't even been there.

Other memories came forth and other tellers of tales helped to lighten the pain of the evening, their first evening without Albert. One of his cousins had his own father tell the story of his being lost in the bush with another guy for two nights. John remembered that time when his own Dad had gone out to help look for his brother, John's uncle. The funniest part of the story involved his Uncle and his friend coming upon another guy in the bush who, upon seeing the two of them, said, "Thank God you found me. I've been lost for two days. And my Uncle exclaimed, "Found you? We're lost, too." They were all of them found very shortly thereafter without suffering much more than some damage to their self-esteem as hunters, and some pretty powerful appetites.

There was also the memory of John's Dad bouncing on the bed upstairs in the home he grew up in until he put the legs of the bed through the kitchen ceiling while his own parents were entertaining some neighbours downstairs at the kitchen table. And the memory of one of John's uncles lying on his back in the bed in that same upstairs bedroom and using his legs to bounce one of the smaller brothers into the air, just as they had seen in a western movie. One unfortunate kick of his legs sent the lighter youngster way too high

BEARE PARTS

into the air so that he was sailing right toward the window and would have gone right on through had not had his arms extended, which abruptly brought his debut as Icarus to a rapid halt against the window frame. Grandpa downstairs was evidently none too pleased with this caper either.

There would be many more such evenings without Albert, but without these memories, without this laughter, without the family support.

And it was in the aftermath of this funeral that John moved to Beach Bay in late August of that summer. He moved not only his material possessions but also his own recent memories. One of these was of Louise's being there at the funeral with the kids to help him and his Mom. He was grateful for her presence and yet hurt, too, that there wasn't much intimacy between them. Louise, too, looked very hurt by the loss of her father-in-law and in her pain, did not seem capable of reaching out to John except on a certain level which somehow was not enough for what he needed. Oh, he didn't know what he needed then; he was so upset, so confused, torn between an urge to cry out in rage, in sheer grief at not being able to hug his Dad again, to share a glass of red with him, and stupid, unbelievable goddamned giddy laughter.

He hugged his daughters after taking them up to the coffin to see their Grandpa. And when Debbie began to cry he broke down, too, and sobbed convulsively out loud. He was dimly aware then of being hugged by more than one person. He remembered Louise's perfume, and Nancy's, "Dad, I love you so much," and Debbie crying just as hard as he was. Then his Mother's look and he knew he could not cry like this because she needed him to be stronger and he just stopped suddenly, or so it seemed, and went over to her, and stood beside her where she sat in the wing chair on the side of the room. He was still holding two little hands; Debbie on one side of him and Nancy on the other. Louise was hugging one of his aunts by the casket when he finally managed to lift his eyes from the floor.

And so it had come and gone, the time in the funeral home, the meals at the house surrounded by relatives, the funeral morning, the church service, some little Italian priest he hardly knew, and the reception downstairs after the cemetery in the church hall. The cemetery had not been as bad as he'd feared. Not like when his one Italian Grandma had tried to jump into the grave with her own "Johna" as she cried and cried when John was so much younger. It had left an indelible impression on John to see his Grandma so heartbroken at the cemetery when his Grandpa John had died at 67 of a heart attack. Now his Grandma was dead, too. And he saw their common grave stone sentinel-like, as if guarding the memories of these two people, not far from where his own Dad was now being interred.

Spooky. These bodies all lying down under this earth. And now his Dad's, too. He couldn't remember now any other thoughts he'd had standing there that day of his father's funeral, except looking into the face of one his uncles and wondering whether this uncle had traded his car again. Every time he saw this uncle, all he wanted to talk about was his car. He drove more new cars than a car salesman and John wondered whether trading his cars all the time was an effective way of coping with old age and the pain it brings, like this: seeing his brother now in the grave.

And now, a year and a half later, in June when his first school year in Beach Bay was coming to a close, John enjoyed the mornings immensely. He liked to get up just a little bit earlier and sit outside writing in his journal at the picnic table to the sound of bird-song, coffee nearby on the table, knowing that sleep-ins would be just around the corner whenever he wanted them. July was a great month despite the mosquitoes and shad flies. It was golf unlimited. Bike rides. Walks. Barbecues. If only Louise and the girls were up here to enjoy this sandy beach, these morning robins singing away. It was during one of these morning sessions when John thought he heard someone calling him by name.

He got up from the rickety old picnic table, varnish peeling from every exposed surface, four-inch nails going the wrong way because of winter frost's extractions, and walked around the cottage to see

Detective Desfresnes knocking on his front door. "Hello, Detective. This isn't Tim Horton's but I did buy some doughnuts yesterday and I'll bet you can smell the damn things."

Laughter. "No wonder you hang out with that crooked real estate asshole. The two of you are both smart asses." More laughter.

"Now don't be comparing me to the company I sometimes keep, or I'll tar you with the same brush. Seems to me from what I hear that you and Wally have killed the odd bottle of scotch yourselves while pretending you were fishing."

"True enough, John. True enough."

There was some silence then as if the Detective began to remember the good times he had shared with their mutual friend Wally. But the silence only looked that way. In fact, there was another reason for the Detective's awkwardness. And it came out as, "Uhh, John, I realize it's a hell of a time to come calling, even if you do have the goods to attract any cop any time, namely doughnuts, and probably fresh coffee on the stove as well, but the truth is, I really need to talk to you and now." This "now" was said with a kind of urgency that John could not miss.

"Sure, Detective Desfresnes. Come on in, or do you want to sit outside at the picnic table where I was sitting before you drove up?"

"John, in this briefcase there's something I want to show you. And I'd just as soon we talked inside if it's okay with you this morning. An' you can call me Gary even if I am here on business, since I'm calling you John anyway."

"Thank you, Gary. Here sit down. What's up?"

"When was the last time you saw this Barry McDevitt, John? Anywhere, at school or just anywhere?"

"I... lemme see. I don't know. Maybe a week or two ago, come to think of it. Sometimes I see the guy in the parking lot, sometimes in the hall, never in the staff room. But mostly I see the guy if I request the use of an overhead projector or a VCR in my classroom. It's his job to provide teachers with A-V equipment in their classrooms when they put in written requests, and they follow his rules and protocols. If you don't request the stuff the way he says, you don't get the equipment."

"But, it's June now, Gary, so I'm actually reviewing with my classes and trying to show them how to prepare for exams and going over possible exam questions and tentative answers for these questions. In other words, Gary, I'm no longer teaching any new material and so I have nothing to do with McDevitt. Other than chance meetings, and now that you mention it, I haven't had any of those. I'll bet I haven't seen the guy for two whole weeks, since I passed him coming out of the main office one day back in May. We had a staff meeting about exams and end of year stuff last week and he wasn't there that I can remember, but then I think he misses a lot of those staff meetings and the boss can't seem to do a damn thing about it. And the boss wants everybody at those meetings all of the time.

"But so what? As I said before, McDevitt's weird and no one pays much attention to him anyway. Has he done something wrong?"

"John, I got a call from your Principal 10 days ago. It seems McDevitt had missed a Monday, Tuesday an' a Wednesday last week, the last one in May and he'd not called in sick. Your Principal and your Vice-Principal had both attempted to reach McDevitt at his home but got no answer. There was no answering machine so the Vice-Principal drove over to McDevitt's house on Thursday morning of last week.

"What he saw there was junk mail piled up on the front stoop because the mail box is tiny and couldn't hold very much and it was full of flyers and advertisements. You know how it is on a Monday, John; my damned mailbox is full every Monday too. Any rate, there was also a large dog tied up in the front yard and he was barking like hell. Almost insane with eagerness to see the Vice-Principal. And looking as if he needed something badly by the way he was jumping around, barking, and actually howling, not in anger but as if in pain. The Vice-Principal noticed that the dog, a German Shepherd, had no water or food in his bowls and had worn some kind of a path on the front of the lot, where this chain thing would allow him to walk, up and down, up and down.

"The dog's behaviour was apparently so strange to the Vice-Principal, and what with the junk mail on the stoop, that he went back to your school and told the Principal. I guess your boss also took into account that McDevitt's been away for three days and hadn't called in, so he called us.

"Well, we didn't do much about it last week other than find out that McDevitt doesn't have anyone in the way of family to call. And his house is located at the end o' that street so that his neighbours don't have anything to do with him anyway. And there was a suggestion from one neighbour that McDevitt has always wanted to keep it that way.

"I went over myself on the Friday and got into the house to see if the guy was sick or something and couldn't get help, and there was no one in the house. Dirty dishes in the sink and the place looked like a bachelor's if you know what I mean. Not that yours is like that, John."

Here Gary smiled. But the smile left quickly.

"Each room had functions you normally associate with it. Like a canoe stored in the living room, tools all over the kitchen, and the bathroom had the look of a greenhouse. What might have passed for a second bedroom had dismantled computers and other such equipment all over the place, including the floor. The bathroom was so dirty it would be hard to imagine anyone using it without barfing. And the main bedroom was like a tornado had hit it; clothes, newspapers, magazines, dirty cups an' bowls an' silverware spread in a such way that I was hard put to walk into the room.

"But no sign of McDevitt anywhere. So I just left an' went to the station and filed a report of what I had found, and called your Principal to ask him to notify us if he heard from the guy soon.

"I spoke to my Chief about the affair and then I decided to let the matter rest till Monday. On Monday, I called your Principal and still there was no word from McDevitt, so I put the missing persons word out to all the various agencies and went and had a nice visit with your Principal and Vice-Principal. You sure were telling the truth when you said this guy was weird and a persona non grata on your staff. And how they couldn't get rid of him. Well, maybe now, the problem is outta their hands.

"John, everything I have told you so far I would not normally share with other than a police officer. But I have told you what I've told you, because as you're going to see, this is only the beginning. We've put a few men on this case and done a great deal a work since Monday of this week and we've found out a hell of a lot more than we ever expected. Not that we understand much yet... how things go together I mean... but certainly some strange things.

"You will recall the weekend that thing happened to you in the wee hours in front of your house here. And we checked out McDevitt and found he'd been in Toronto that night and so couldn't have been the one trying to run you over." Here he paused, obviously wanting a response from John.

"Yes, I remember being impressed that you had already checked out McDevitt before coming down here to interview me that Sunday morning."

"Thanks, John, but it's just routine. Anyway, it has now been discovered by our folks that McDevitt is in Toronto most weekends. Spends a lot of time with a guy name of Alfred Harris... guy goes by the name of Alf. By a pure fluke, and I mean fluke, one of us... well, shit it was myself... noticed something strange about the photograph of Harris. I am not sure yet how it happened because this guy is now 86 years old and there is no way I ought to have seen it. But I did and if I die now, or if they fire me immediately, it'll be okay. My work life makes sense now. Something's been bugging me for too many years.

"John, you were a young man in this town at one time. You have to remember the case of the missing Falwell couple. June 1957 they went missing at their cottage on Clear Lake. And the news coverage was such that everyone in these parts knows the story of their disappearance and all. You gotta remember this story. And of course, your buddy Wally's involvement with the case."

"Yes, of course I know the Falwell tale and I often think of it as one more of life's little mysteries to go with all of the other stuff I don't understand like cancer and divorce and heartache." And then John stopped suddenly, embarrassed that he'd said this to someone he hardly knew, a police officer at that.

"John, the photograph of Alf Harris reminded me of someone I couldn't place for a whole day. And then when I was shaving the next morning, I almost dropped my razor and I guessed I yelled something out so loud my wife jumped out of bed and came running into the bathroom to see if I was okay. I babbled something to myself, then I yelled out something, then I talked to myself, then I yelled something to her, and she thought I was having some kind of seizure I guess because she started to cry right there in the bathroom.

"Then I came to myself enough to tell her excitedly that Edward Falwell was alive. That he was Alf Harris an' started to get my clothes on as fast as I could and, while trying to explain to my wife that I couldn't tell her much right then, and trying to assure her that I was indeed still sane, I picked up the phone and called my Chief and asked him if I could meet with him immediately. He doesn't normally come in till around 9.15 and I wanted to see him right away, I told him. He knew enough about me to agree immediately. I did not want to have to handle this alone.

"I got to the station, pulled the file, and I knew then I was right. Alf Harris was Edward Falwell. Only it was Edward Falwell at 86 years of age. He'd gone missing in 1957 at 47 years old but still, there was no doubt in my mind. I had stared at those photographs so many times in the 50s and the 60s that I knew that face about as well as any face can be recognized. The Chief came in and I told him everything I could but he didn't see the discovery in the photograph as quickly as I did but he wasn't the Chief in those days back in the late 50s. He didn't know the case like I did. But when I pointed out the distinguishing features and how I knew it was Falwell in Harris' photograph, he agreed and could see that I was right."

All of this time John was very quiet. Stunned by this information. Wondering what it had to do with him. Why was Gary here this morning?

As if sensing John's puzzlement, Gary looked at him and said,

"John, I have another photograph to show you this morning. It's not of Harris. And by the way, McDevitt is still missing, and now, so is the old guy, Falwell-now-Harris. They're both gone. No trace of either of them. Haven't been seen for at least a week. And we think their disappearance has something to do with this third guy."

And here the Detective reached into his briefcase and pulled out a photograph, and laid it on the kitchen table in front of John, who saw a guy somewhat Oriental looking. That was just before John's jaw dropped in shock, his eyes went very wide, and he breathed inwards somewhat noisily as he recognized the face belonging to the driver of that car that night back in June.

Chapter Four
Family Life in the 90s

"How long did you say that we have been coming on this weekend, Horney?" This was from Buns.

"None of your fucking business and don't start with the bullshit, Buns, you prick." It had come around again. The annual fishing weekend when no one fished, just drank. They had already been at it for half an hour now and the usual was beginning – cutting up the food, the accommodations, each other. Strangest shows of affection known to anthropologists, and to ex-wives, like Horney's. Barb was her name and John remembered her well. For she had grown up with them and indeed many a party had been held at Barb's parents' home down on the lakeshore close to where John's rented cottage was now. Barb had always teased the guys about the male bonding thing.

"This shit on the table would never pass for food at any other establishment. We're definitely not paying for any of it, Horney. Beside you probably bought your year's supply of peanut butter and hid it before billing the rest of us poor sluts. We'll no doubt be asked to pay for this on the tab.

"What do you think, Jimmy Jones? Horney's ripping us off again, right."

"Yeah, and we're all sick on Monday from this shit he serves us all weekend, most of which he gets behind the Salvation Army kitchen when they throw it out as inedible," yelled Jimmy Jones though he was standing right beside Buns. Jimmy was drunk already as he had attended Friday night service at the watering hole before joining the guys here at Horney's cottage on the shores of Lake Timachi. How he drove after drinking all the time and never got caught was a mystery to John.

"You're sick on the Monday because you drink too goddamned much, Jimmy. In fact most mornings are Mondays for you, Jimmy, and there's a u in the morning."

"Well, ain't you the witty fellow today, Knockers." Jimmy threw a beer cap at Knockers who ducked and threatened to throw some of the beer in his bottle at Jimmy Jones by putting his thumb over the bottle's end and shaking it.

"Grow up you bastards, and don't make another mess of my cottage, you assholes. Knockers, if you spill beer on the floor, you're cleaning it up. Last year you pricks didn't lift a finger to clean up before you all left on the Monday morning. And Coli, you prick, you can't say you have to beat the traffic this year and get out of here early Monday morning without paying and without cleaning up. We've got your number this year." Everyone laughed.

"Yeah, make the prick pay double this year, Horney. And make him clean the place up for all of us. All those years he came up here, and left early, the prick."

Just then the ghetto blaster from the next room exploded into Leader of the Pack by the Shangri-Las.

"Turn that fuckin' music down, you asshole, before you bust my speakers," Horney yelled.

"Fuck you," came the answer.

And when someone stepped out onto the verandah for a leak, it was invariably, "Shut that fucking door."

And when Horney's dog, Puke, so much as barked at an insolent chipmunk who thought he owned the shoreline, it was, "Shut ta fuck up." In fact, so often was this screamed at Puke that someone quipped that the dog always needed therapy for his identity crisis when he got home not knowing whether his name was Puke or Fuck Up.

And so this annual weekend went, especially the happy hours. Golf on the Saturday, weather permitting, golf on television, different guys taking turns with the cooking and the clean-up, although each one bitched that they had already done enough work and that it was somebody else's turn. And on and on. A video or even an audio taped version of the weekend would have been an educational experience for most of them when they were sober at home. They might have asked if they had really participated in such a weekend. Yes, every year for 25 years. And none of them would miss it.

And as they got older, they appreciated even more what they had in this group of guys who had grown up together, married around the same time, some of whom divorced and were supported by the same crew over the years. Most of their lives were not planned in the ways they came out, but so their lives had evolved until this weekend was one of the few constants they could count on. Most everything else was a matter of change and still more change.

Horney, in fact, Larry Bastien, was French Canadian by birth. He had gone to the same Catholic high school where John went and was now teaching. Horney had married Barb when each of them was only 21 years old. They were the first to marry and John was an usher at the wedding. Larry's brother Mike was the MC; it was the last time Mike had partied for he was dead one week later in a car accident. Horney himself had already had open heart bypass surgery and had given up his job as a school superintendent and was now selling cars and enjoying his reduced teacher's pension. Horney had gone into teaching right after one year of teacher's college, because he had taken Grade 13 and was able to get his teaching certificate in those days with only one year of teacher's college. He had taught elementary school for years and taken university courses at night in the summers till he got his degree and then switched over to teaching math in the public high school.

He and Barb had three children, for one of whom John and Louise were godparents. Paul was his name; the other two were Angela and Patricia. Horney was not satisfied with one degree, so he then got his B.ED., got his Principal's Certificate, his M.Ed., his Supervisory Officer's Certificate, and climbed the usual ladders of department head, vice-principal, principal and assistant superintendent. Because he had gotten into teaching so young, at 20 years of age, he had reached an 80 factor at 50 years of age and had opted for a reduced pension after his bypass surgery. He had gone to sell cars at a car dealership rather than stay with the pressure of a school superintendency. To all appearances, he had done the right thing. He seemed happier now than John had remembered seeing him in a long time. But John remembered, too, what had often been said about appearances.

Of course, there had been pretty big changes in Horney's life, for he and Barb had split up way back when Horney had only been about 43 years of age. She got the house and the kids stayed with her. Horney was a Principal by this time, and one year after their break-up Horney had been promoted to Assistant Superintendent. He lasted at this position for about five years when he found out that he had to have open heart and upon recovering from that experience resigned within the year. People were shocked, even John. For Horney would have had a much better pension had he lasted another five years, which would have given him his 90 factor and an unreduced pension.

But Horney had other ideas. Something to do with wanting to live another five years, he now said to John, the two of them alone on the verandah, sipping a beer, watching the night sky do its thing. Listening to Horney, John felt his old friend was making eminent sense:

"John, I came to a point in my life when I knew that what I did for a living was not what I seemed cut out to do. I had suspected that this had been true for a long time. I figure I'm not alone, too. Education's like that. You get in and you can't get out. There's nothing else to do for teachers. Or so they think. So we work our asses off to get promoted out of the classroom and then one day we find out we have to have our arteries fixed because they're plugged and no one, including the entire medical community can tell you why for sure. They talk about booze, smoking, hyper tension, over weight, lack of exercise, and stress. And so on and so on.

"But nobody could say for sure what it was in my case. I'm not overweight and it's never been a problem for me. I have never smoked. Yeah, I drink on the weekends but only when I'm with the guys. Barb never liked booze very much after we had kids so we didn't drink much in the home and I kind of lost interest because of the impaired driving possibility that I saw some of my friends get nailed for. I have always been a runner so exercise was not a problem either. I did have high blood pressure and I still have to watch it but I figure that stress is the main culprit and there's nothing more stressful than a job you hate. And I hated many of the Trustees I worked with. Really ignorant people on power trips who don't give a damn about kids. And there's no pleasing the bastards. Always talking about standards and yet many of them never finished school themselves. They did not have the self-discipline they preach at students and teachers alike these days. The fucking hypocrites have no credibility. They generally fuck up education and make life miserable for kids and teachers, under the guise of bringing accountability to the system. I actually witnessed some of these fuckers 'borrow' school computers "to try them out at home" which left kids short computers in the process. Their preoccupation with their honoraria, with mileage reimbursements and with their trustee salaries fooled no one but themselves–they didn't care much about kids from what I could see, yet they prefaced much of their long winded bullshit with apparent concern over the kids' welfare. Reminded me of the lyrics to, 'I'm only thinking of you,' in *Oliver*.

"Being a Principal wasn't as bad as being a superintendent but when decision time came, I didn't want to go back to that either. Been there, done that kind of thing. Wanted something entirely different. Figured it'd be my second and maybe my last career change. Didn't want to go back to school either. Had enough of the submissive posture all students have to assume to last me the rest of my life. I can't stand the 'yes sir, no Mam' one has to practice in order to be a student and that's true whether you're in Grade 3, Grade 11, a Master's program, or a course leading to a Supervisory Officer's Certificate. No more submission for this guy. That, too, was stressful.

"I have always enjoyed cars, John. And people. Always thought I could sell if I believed in the product. Guy came to me years ago. A damn good friend at the time and tried to tempt me to leave education and go into insurance. The guy's worth a lot of money now. But I told him, no, I couldn't sell insurance because, other than term, I didn't really believe in insurance and didn't think I could sell it convincingly. Couldn't convince myself I guess. But cars? That's a different story. I love 'em.

"Burt Simmons came to see me in the hospital after the surgery and we got talking about me doing something different for a living. It was me that broached the subject of my selling cars for him at the dealership. First, he thought I was kidding and I had to insist that I wasn't. Then he got really interested and said, 'Larry, I'd love to have you at the dealership and I do think you'd have a lot of credibility selling cars in this town. Long as it wasn't to some kid now turned adult whom you'd thrown out of school.'"

"And, John it turns out to have been the best move I've made. Unlike my marital moves."

Just then Buns joined the two of them on the verandah. They got to talking about marriage, about the huge costs of separation, emotional and financial. John made the statement that the real cost was not financial for him. Whereas Louise had asked for $700 a month, John had insisted on $1,000, with $300 to go each month into a trust fund for the girls' education down the road. When he told Horney and Buns this, they scoffed. "You are like no other guy – this is like no other break-up, that's for fucking sure," said Buns.

"John," Buns said, "the way you and Louise get on today has me really wondering why you two couldn't patch things up."

John was sorely tempted to suggest that Buns ask his wife Bonnie that very question but he held his tongue. "Most of the time," Buns said, "the financial negotiations are what turns an ordinary agreement to separate into one of acrimony. Two people can go their separate ways, agreeing beforehand to who's taking what, and yet a few months down the road they aren't even talking to each other. Lawyers get blamed I know for fanning the flames of this bitterness, but in truth, it isn't just the lawyers who are part of the problem. It seems that many couples who agree to a peaceful separation have second and third thoughts down the line about what they think ought to be coming to them from their years together.

"My own law partner right now is paying $3,500 a month to his ex and both of their children are grown up, educated and working for a living but Ron still has to pay Genevieve $3,500 every month. Now here's a woman who's got a B.A., a nursing certificate, and is only in her late 40s. But her lawyer convinced the interim judge that since she had never worked outside the home, at Ron's insistence (and Ron denies this like crazy; he says he asked her to get a job many times), she could not now use her nursing certificate because it would mean a year's upgrading. Moreover, this lawyer convinced the judge that she is not feeling all that well since she has fibromyalgia, that she needs this amount, this unbelievable $3,500 a month to live according to the way she had when she was with Ron.

"Ron, of course, is having a rough time with this monthly payment as $3,500 a month is a hell of a lot of money. Too bad his ex-wife can't get a fucking job like the rest of us. And get this, she left him!"

"Am I ever glad to be out of that shit every month myself," said Horney. "When Barb and I split up, she was working and so I didn't have to pay her the big bucks I might have. I think I did okay. She got the house, the cottage, and I got to keep my pension. Plus, I had to pay nine hundred a month for the kids. But that stopped when the last one of them graduated high school. Two of them went to work and only Patty went on to university. I helped Patty out at university for four years running to the tune of $500 per month but that's finished last year as well. Barb is married again, and I have nothing to pay per month now and it's great."

"Consider yourself a lucky guy, Horney. And all of that tail you are getting now as well. Fucking car salesmen are all ladies' men, right, John?"

"Oh, I wouldn't know, Buns. Is it true, Horney, that you have all of this tail these days?"

"I know nothing. I see nothing. I tell nothing."

"Yeah, but we know, Horney, you randy old prick."

"Actually, Buns, if this is the single life, you can have it."

"Aren't you having fun, John?"

"Truth is, he's pining for the Ex, aren't you, John. Know what Buns, I tried to line him up with this gorgeous creature two months ago. She came to me and asked me if I thought John was a free agent and the dummie here wouldn't even call her... said it was because she had kids in his school."

"Actually, she called me one night and we chewed the fat on the phone for about an hour. We mostly talked about what was happening at the school, that kind of thing, but I could tell that she was calling me to see if I were interested in getting together for coffee. I let her know as gently as I could that I was not the right person for her. She hung up eventually and I haven't spoken to her since. It was awkward though, having to pretend that she called me out of the blue to discuss what was happening at the school. I don't even teach her two sons."

"You are one crazy bastard, John."

"Maybe you're right, Horney, but with having to deal with the split, missing my kids like crazy, and trying to help Mom and myself handle Dad's death, I just don't seem to have the emotional energy for any new intimate relationships. And as for sex, there must be something wrong with me, because I don't even miss it. When I am running every day, I feel some of the old libido returning, but most of the time, I just don't give a shit. I sure didn't feel that way at 20 years of age!"

"Yeah, you know it is funny how I have noticed the same damn thing. Ripping one off just ain't what it used to be. I mean, shit, a woman wouldn't even have to take her panty hose off for me them. I'd just drill her right through. Now I'm lucky if the little guy wants to come out and play once a month."

"Buns, I always said you were a fucking queer anyway."

"Eat shit, you moron." Laughter and more of the same repartee till John said that he was turning in, and he was just going to do that, when Buns said to Horney, "Would you split up again, Horney, if you had it to do all over again? I mean seriously, Horney, would you? I often wondered if you guys who packed your marriages in, got all of this freedom back, were actually happier than when you were married. You sure make it look good, what with all of those ladies I see you with.

"Not that I want to try out the single state again. Bonnie and I have our difficulties, but basically, no matter how often we fight, in calm moments I know that I would marry her again."

There was some silence among them now as the moon danced on

the ripples in front of Horney's cottage and a loon crooned his loneliness somewhere out past the moonlight. Finally Horney spoke, with John still leaning on the verandah pillar, which was as far as he had gotten when Buns had popped this question to Horney.

"I figure it this way," Horney finally answered Buns, "that no one has it all. The married guys have someone to answer to, have less freedom, and can't do anything about the single unattached women running all over the place these days. Oh yes, a few of the married guys do screw around now and then, and perhaps there's more than a few of them, but that doesn't interest me any more like it used to. Those guys are just asking for heartbreak themselves, theirs and their wives'. As I know all too well. But for the truly single guy, even like myself right now, there's more action out there right now than I ever saw as a teenager.

"Still, to answer your question, Buns, the married guy has some of the goodies, too. He has someone to come home to and I will tell you, night after night of coming home to an empty condo gets to me. It's fucking lonely and maybe other divorced guys will admit that and maybe they won't. Maybe they don't get lonely, but I know I damned well do. And my final answer, Buns, no I would not split up again. I'd try harder to save our marriage. I still miss the whole idea of family living together. In fact, I even appreciate being friendly with Barb these days. We even meet now and then for coffee when some item or other has to be discussed. When anything important comes up.

"When I had that heart bypass, it was really bad for me. I wondered if this was it, and I wanted more than anything for Barb and I to be still married so she could help me to face this shit, this violent surgery.

"But I knew Barb was gone forever from my life and lying there in that hospital room I thought a lot about that and I cried, too. Ten years after we split I'm lying in a hospital room finally admitting the truth to myself. No, I would not break up again and I'd fight like hell to stay together. I'm tired of not having anyone to really talk to, especially when I'm upset. I think the married guys have it better. Planning a future is just not as exciting when you have no one in mind to share this future with. That's how I feel, anyway. Sorry, John, if I don't seem more positive about being single and maybe you don't need to hear this shit these days. I know you're hurting."

John didn't know what to say. He knew that deep down inside he wanted to do a couple of things, hug Horney for his honesty and cry like a son of a bitch. But he merely came back with, "Horney, you're not telling me anything I didn't know."

With that John left Horney and Buns alone on the verandah and went into the cottage to climb into his sleeping bag, thankful that he hadn't done much drinking this evening, and would be able to get up in the morning without feeling as tough as he had yesterday morning when he and the guys had partied so hard on the Friday night of their arrival at Horney's cottage.

Eventually, the weekend came to a close and there was the usual laughter when it came time on the Sunday to settle all of the accounts. Horney totaled the food up and said that each guy's share was $25 and the usual remarks were screamed out. Buns demanded that the cost of his six bottles of red wine be deducted from his $25 bill because "all of these sluts" had drunk his wine all weekend.

Jimmy Jones wanted to be paid for his having given up an otherwise good weekend to come and endure the "rest of you assholes" all weekend. Knockers wanted to pay his $25 but only on the condition that the fishing weekend never be held in this "rat's nest" ever again, and on condition that they be allowed "to torch this piece of shit for a cottage" as a last entertainment laid on by Horney. Sam wanted to "get the hell out of here to go to an eye/ear/nose/throat specialist to see if serious damage had been done to his ears because of the snoring he'd had to put up with all weekend."

"Fuck off, Sam, you just want your throat cleared for your next blowjob, you cocksucker." This was Horney's final shot as the guys left him and John alone in the driveway. John agreed to stay behind and help Horney clean the place up a bit more than the whole crew had done this Sunday morning.

"Well, Horney, another good reunion you've just hosted."

"Yeah, the guys seemed to have a good time. John, if you're not in too much of a hurry, why don't we stay the day? Put the boat in and do some trolling for lake trout. Cook one up for supper and go back to town tonight? The clean up is bugger all, just to get the beer cases organized, the garbage thrown at the dump, and some floor sweeping. That won't take 30 minutes with both of us, then we can go fishing. What do you think?"

"Well, sounds all right to me, Horney. I told my Mother already that I probably would not have dinner with her tonight anyway. I think she's going out to the Italian club for dinner with my Aunt. She said that I could join them if I got back in time but the thought of some quiet fishing sounds great but I don't want much booze today. Want to give my stomach a rest."

"Yeah me, too, Coli."

The fish eluded the two of them that day and about 4.00 p.m. they had cleaned the cottage and were on their way back to Beach Bay, neither of them saying much to each other on the way down the highway. They were talked out but contented. They stopped for a burger at 5 o'clock and then Horney drove John home and the annual fishing weekend was finished. John reflected at home on how it was different coming off this fishing weekend because for the first time he did not have to drive all the way back to Toronto in heavy weekend traffic. For the first time he had the Beach Bay guys' advantage of merely having to drive as far as Beach Bay and not 220 miles back to the big city.

"Some blessing," he lamented. What preoccupied him was the bitter sweetness of it all, for he would much rather be driving home to his family, to someone who had missed him, than to an empty cottage. Not even the location on the lakeshore could cheer him up, because he was oblivious of the charms of the waves, having lived with them all weekend. Like any other blessing become routine, he was no longer noticing it. The lakeshore existence always looked so much better when one lived away from the lake, as in a Toronto suburb. And so with a marriage partner – same phenomenon. John thought to himself: the song is right – "you don't know what you got until you lose it."

He laid down on the couch about 6 p.m. and fell fast asleep. In his dreams he remembered a particular morning awaking beside Louise from a nightmare. He was glad to awake and to discover that it was only a nightmare but still the nightmare had haunted him. For in the nightmare he dreamed that he and Louise had been to a party, where later in the evening John had found Louise lying on a family room couch when he knelt down and suggested that she come home with him now. She suddenly and without warning had insulted him with, "I am not going home with you right now. And your breath really stinks."

Worse, a lady was sitting just around the corner from where this couch was located, and the woman had her head around the corner and was taking in this whole ugly scene between John and Louise. After standing around waiting for Louise to get up off the couch and come with him, John finally went outside and got into his vehicle. It was idling when Louise eventually came out, walked up to the passenger window, and said into the silence that she wasn't getting into his vehicle and then went and got into some other person's car.

John remembered that in that nightmare he was driving down the street by himself – totally destroyed. And then he awoke, got dressed, and sat at the kitchen table with a cup of coffee trying to make whatever sense he could make of the nightmare. When Louise got up, he told her of the nightmare, and she had hugged him. He had thought the woman represented the social humiliation, the shame he had felt whenever there had been a scene between them caused by his having drunk too much. And there had indeed been such times, some too painful to remember. Like the night driving home from some golf course party and he was totally pissed and suddenly took it upon himself to want to drive. Louise had sat there in the driver's seat, saying no way even after John had removed the keys from the ignition and the car had come to a stop on the side of the road.

What had happened then was simply something John did not want to think about. A police car had driven up at this time of night on a country road, out of no where. And out of it had stepped a female OPP Officer who had listened to Louise's story, and she told the truth. The OPP Officer had ordered John out of his own car and told him to walk the rest of the way home, as it was not that far. John did walk and was even offered a ride by one of his neighbours who stopped on his way home from a late shift at the airport where this guy worked. John got home and then raised hell in the bedroom but not for long as his parents were guests in the house that night as his Dad was down for some radiation treatments in Toronto. And then he got in his car and drove around in defiance of the OPP and when he got home late next morning, having fallen asleep in his car on a side road somewhere, he was too ashamed to be grateful that nothing worse had happened. He never could look this neighbour in the face again, although John had heard that this guy had marital troubles of his own.

But John didn't see this so much as a marital trouble as he did a drinking problem. And his life had been full of the same kind of thing. Every once in a while he would stop drinking, or at least try to quit, and then he would experience another social event like a dance or something, and realize how quiet, how subdued, how unsociable he was, without a drink. He didn't like to dance for he was very shy without a drink and Louise, who loved to dance, certainly didn't have as much fun. So he would begin to drink all over again.

That morning that he told Louise about his nightmare, she was very comforting, and told him that she loved him, and that she, too, had mornings when she felt worthless, that she did not want to go on, as she had nothing to offer anyone. She had told John how she prayed some mornings that God would teach her how to forgive herself, how to see that without God she was nothing. That if anything was important it was that only by being in tune with God could she do anything of value.

John remembered that morning how impressed he had been once again with Louise's spiritual depth, how grateful he was for having married her, for having landed this wonderful woman. And yet, he had said to Louise that morning, but if we see ourselves as worthless, as junk, how can we achieve anything? How can we bring love into other people's lives, like my students, like our two little girls, like each other, if we don't love ourselves first?

Louise had answered that first we must be honest with ourselves in order to forgive ourselves, to have some necessary humility, some truth about our good points and our limitations, then and only then, could we live with ourselves in peaceful acceptance of our identities, and then we could reach out to others, but not before achieving at least partial peace with who we were as individuals. "No acceptance of myself, no love for anybody else either," she had said to John while hugging him and wiping away his tears.

John's memory of that morning he had told Louise of the nightmare was all too vivid as he woke up now in a dark living room in his cottage, as lonely as he had ever felt. He got up and went to the kitchen and turned the light on. The electric kettle was filled and turned on so that he could make a cup of tea. He got his current novel from the night table and sat at the kitchen table to read but he could not stop thinking about that morning when Louise had been so comforting. Finally he got into the novel and read until 11 p.m. and went off to bed after flossing and brushing his teeth.

The next week had only one event of significance that he could now remember. Shirley Spattafora was the event. She had been very nice to him all year in the staff room, in the office, in the halls, and John could not help notice the charm she was expending upon him but he was not at all that interested. Indeed he was not even sure that the effort on her part was anything more than sympathy, or maybe empathy. Shirley was separated herself. One ordinary day she had come home to discover that the man she had been married to for ten years had packed up and left her. He also left her everything, the house, the sport utility vehicle, the dog, but not the bills, for there were none.

Apparently they had been married for ten years, had no children, and were one of those couples who just seemed to have everything going for them, a brand new house with every amenity and bright new appliances. Their outdoor patio was discussed as a work of art, complete with pool, and many a party was held at this home. But Shirley's Garth had discovered that he enjoyed the male penis more than any part of the female anatomy. And that was it. He left his marriage and came out of the closet both at the same time.

Evidently there was not much bitterness between them and even now they were supposedly good friends. Garth had decided to get out of his marriage and had also decided that since, he was pulling the plug, Shirley should not have to endure, as well, any financial hardship. So he simply left her everything, moved to Toronto, and was apparently now living with his third significant other since Shirley had been his wife. Shirley, of course, had continued to teach at the Catholic high school where no one had any problems with the break-up of her marriage. Indeed she was looked upon as something of a martyr whose only mistake was to have married the wrong person.

It was said that Shirley married him knowing Garth could swing both ways but that was never verified for who would ever ask her this. It was generally accepted, however, that she knew long before he finally left that Garth was at least bisexual because there had been incidents at some of the drunken bashes around their pool apparently.

During the past year, Shirley had been especially friendly with John. She was another English teacher like John and she had copies of some old movies that John had heard about but never viewed. One day she was teasing him about this beautiful cottage he was renting and asking when she going to be invited for a swim in the lake. Or was he hoarding the whole lake to himself? John had countered with something to the effect that anyone with a pool such as she had was in no need of a sometimes polluted lake in which to swim.

She then offered a challenge. "How about coming to dinner and trying out the pool for yourself provided I get a chance to try your lake out?" It was all done in fun but John was nervous, too.

He saw no way to be anything but a gentleman so he reluctantly agreed to the challenge, as long as she would show him Casa Blanca. "And do I also have to cook what you suggest," she teased.

"No, I eat anything. Can't you tell by my waistline?" He was inwardly proud of that waistline as he had taken off 20 pounds this past year.

He had gone to dinner at Shirley's and had a thoroughly delightful time. He had helped her in the kitchen, making the salad like a good Italian ought to, while she was so busy with her preparations that there was little time for any intimacy and flirtation which might have scared John away immediately. They had dinner and a bottle of wine but John was careful to have one and one half glasses and that was it. During dinner they discussed their marriages and John thought he had made it very clear to Shirley that he was far from over Louise, far from being open to any new relationship with anyone. He was happy that she seemed quite content with that, yet it didn't seem to cool her warmth with him.

After dinner they did watch Casa Blanca and the Maltese Falcon. John had enjoyed then both very much, especially the line in Casa Blanca where Bogart predicts that the problems of three people wouldn't amount to a hill of beans in a short time or something like that. The line had taken him to a point of personal reflection and he was still thinking about it when he had driven home that night.

And he was glad to be able to get out and drive home for Shirley had gotten quite cuddly after the movies, moving closer to him on the couch, and John had to be quick to get up and say how tired he was. Shirley was attractive; she was free; she was seemingly interested in something more than dinner and movies. But John was not, and he wanted to be up front about that right away.

When he almost jumped up she got the hint and did not try again to suggest anything more intimate between them. He thanked her graciously for a wonderful Saturday evening and left for his place.

It was at least two weeks later that she teased him at school about the return engagement, even though he had not really tried out her pool; it had been too cold and there was not even a thought about going swimming that night at her house. He began to think that he had been wrong about her; that she was not really interested in anything more than company for he had been pretty overt in his attempt to get away from her that night and she had to have noticed his unwillingness for anything more than an evening together. That she still wanted to get together again for an evening suggested to John that perhaps she knew he wasn't interested, had accepted that, perhaps never even wanted anything more than that, and yet still wanted to get together again on terms similar to his. "So, hey, why not. Company is better than loneliness every damn night," he told himself.

He invited her over for a Friday, June 14, and she accepted. John had gone for a couple of beers right after school but he did not tell Wally or Horney about his plans for the rest of the evening. When he tried to leave the pub about 5.30, he got a lot of flak. He wanted to stop by the grocery store, pick up some steaks, some garlic bread, and the salads he needed to entertain Shirley that night. But the guys kept the pressure on him and he didn't get out of there till 6 and even then they refused to understand that he had something else to do that night. He finally lied that he had to do something with his mother later and wanted to get home for a rest first.

Fortunately, Shirley had been invited for 7.15 and that gave John just enough time to get the groceries, and have a shower before she arrived. He had already thought of the wine the week before and had stocked up. He also had a plan that it might be a good idea to go out for dessert later and leave the cottage.

Things went pretty much as he had planned. The steaks were barbecued at about 9 o'clock, just as the sun was doing its slow dive across the western sky out over the lake and it was as if John had laid on this perfect sunset. Shirley loved it, as she sat on the steps, and he barbecued, and they sipped their Lindeman's. He also had pre-boiled potatoes and these were now wrapped in foil with some creamy cucumber and mayonnaise and were now roasting on the barbecue. Plus mushrooms sauteeing in butter in a foil pan on the side grill. Shirley had cleaned and prepared the mushrooms for him while he had prepared the potatoes and the steaks. He had bought a pre-mixed salad package and a loaf of garlic bread.

They were about to make the coffee after their meal when Shirley spilt the remains of her glass of red wine all over her white slacks and, knowing that wine could stain a white fabric, John suggested she get into something of his while he soaked her slacks in the sink to prevent the stain. They were looking very domestic indeed when a knock came to the door. At first they hadn't heard it because John had just told Shirley

"… about this old priest hearing confessions the first Saturday in Lent in another priest's parish. And this guy says into the darkness of the confessional, 'Excuse me Fadder, but I stole some plywood.'

"So the priest tells the guy to say five Hail Mary's, make a good Act of Contrition; the priest said that he would give him absolution and he knew that God would forgive him.

"The next Saturday, it's the same priest again helping out with Saturday confessions in his friend's parish, and it's the same voice in the darkness saying, 'Scuse me Fadder, but I stole some plywood.'"

"Again the priest gave a penance. This time it was a decade of the beads. And again he asked for an Act of Contrition, gave the guy absolution and assured him that his sins were now forgiven.

"This went on for five consecutive Saturdays in a row until the light went on in the old priest's head: Holy Hannah. This is the same guy every Saturday who steals the plywood.

"'My son', began the old priest, 'Are you the same guy who confesses to stealing the plywood every Saturday?'

"'Dat's me, Fadder!'

"'Well, we were taught in moral theology, that when sin becomes habitual, you need extra Grace from God to help you break the sinful habit. And obviously, I have not been giving you a penance each week to generate a quantity and a quality of God's Grace sufficient to the task of helping you to break this sinful habit. Now for your penance this week, I am going to have to give you a much more serious penance, my son. Do you know how to make a novena?'

"The answer came back quickly and enthusiastically: 'No, Fadder, but if you get the fucking plans, I get the fucking plywood.'"

Shirley was laughing so hard, and John was so enjoying her response, that not only did they not hear the soft knocking that had been going on, but also it took their eyes a few seconds to focus on the figure standing in the foyer of the cottage who was staring dumbfounded at the two of them.

What particularly caught Louise's eye was the housecoat Shirley was wearing. It had John's and her initials sewn in gold thread onto the front, very conspicuous against the red background of the velour material. The housecoat had been a Valentine's gift from her to John from Halpern's some years ago. It was as if this housecoat had now taken away her ability to speak until finally,

"John, I... I... I'm sorry. I didn't know you had her... I mean... I mean company here tonight. I knocked and no one came and yet I heard laughter so I thought maybe you were on telephone. I mean... I'll talk to you later."

And she was gone as suddenly as she had appeared. For a moment, there was no talking. John quickly processed, "how much have I had to drink?" No. That was fine. Not much. It was really Louise. What the hell was she doing here? And then suddenly, panic. He ran to the door but her car was just driving away, down Lakeshore Drive.

Finally, "Uh, John, was that someone you have been seeing lately? Or should I ask? I don't know whether to keep quiet and pretend I didn't just see that, leave quietly, or stay and help you clean up. You look white, by the way."

"Uhhh, that was my wife, my... my ex-wife... no, my wife... it was Louise, Shirley, and I don't know what the hell she was doing here." And then tears came into his eyes and he was really angry at this development and stormed into the kitchen and began cleaning scraping plates of debris into the garbage, even perfectly good pieces of steak that were left over.

"John, why don't you let me do that, and you sit outside or relax somewhere?"

John couldn't talk. All he could do was to keep cleaning the kitchen and so Shirley merely helped, without talking any more. John kept wondering in his mind: "Louise, what are you doing here? Where did you come from? Why are you here?" Over and over again, these questions went through his mind like water running somewhere and he finally focused on it and caught himself listening somewhere in his head.

When the kitchen was cleaned up, the table cleared and wiped, Shirley excused herself and told John that, really it had been fun, and she was sorry that the night had ended in such a way that John seemed so upset, but that she understood, and thanked him again profusely for the steak dinner, the great culinary skill, the perfect sunset and the great jokes. She hoped that they could share another evening together. She left and while John was sure he had said goodbye, it didn't seem to matter at all. He just wanted to be alone. He was sitting outside at the picnic table, looking at the smallish waves glisten their way onto the beach and listening to their soft repeating swoosh, when their soothing sound was interrupted by a phone ringing in his house. It was 11 o'clock.

"Hi Daddy!" Debbie.

"Debbie, is that really you? Is everything okay?"

"Yes, Daddy. Everything's fine. We surprised you for Father's Day, huh?"

"What do you mean, honey?"

"Well, Mom told us that she didn't tell you about us coming up this weekend. Not even Nanna knew."

Quickly John realized that this could get even more embarrassing. He had to stall somehow. And he got a break.

"Were you surprised to see Mummy, Daddy? Are you having a good visit together? Oh, just a minute, Daddy, someone's coming into Nanna's now. It's Mummy. I thought she was still with you, Daddy."

John could hear voices in the background. And then suddenly Louise was on the phone but only after he had heard Debbie getting heck for calling Daddy so late and why was she still up?

"John, this is Louise. Look, I know you have company and I'm really sorry and embarrassed that I disturbed you and that Debbie seems to be falling into her mother's footsteps by interrupting you tonight but neither of us knew you... were seeing... had company. I'm really sorry. But I'll hang up now and we can maybe talk some other time."

"No, listen. Louise. Please. First of all, I'm alone. Secondly, it's not like it looked."

"John, you don't have to explain anything. Oh, I'm so damn ashamed." She began to cry and told John that she would have to hang up now. Which she did.

John was about to dial his mother's when he got a another idea. He grabbed his jacket, his keys and ran across Lakeshore Drive to his car. Within minutes he was speeding right through a radar trap and, sure enough, the cherry began to flash on the parked police car, which now pulled out to catch up with him. John pulled over and realized he had no wallet with him.

The policeman got out of his car, strolled up to John's window, made some comment that John seemed to be in an awful hurry, and asked for his driver's licence. John replied,

"Officer, I just got a call from my wife whom I did not know was in town with both of our daughters.

"Sorry for speeding, but this is really important to me."

"But where's your licence?"

"In my wallet, back at my cottage. My name is Coliani. I can go back and get it if you wish."

"Are you a teacher at the Catholic High school?"

"Yes, I am, and I'm sorry I was speeding. But this is important."

"Listen, my name is Constable Redford and my son Gerry is in your class. I wanted to meet you anyway, but not this way. Slow down and carry your wallet with you next time. And by the way, I hope that booze I'm smelling wouldn't put you over the limit. There are other guys out patrolling tonight whose sons aren't playing football for you. Good night."

"Thank you." John had to be careful that he did not spin the tires on the shoulder of the road as he left, thanking God for Gerry Redford, one of his students and a star player on the football team. He thought himself an asshole for speeding while he had been drinking. But right now, all that mattered was getting to his mother's house.

Without further incident he made it to the familiar driveway. And saw an unfamiliar vehicle. As he got out of his car in the driveway, noticed the Budget Rental car sticker, he put together that Louise must have rented a car to drive up. It occurred to him that it was bit late to be dropping in but he figured that his mother, his daughters and his wife would still be up celebrating their being together again. He caught himself knocking at the door of his own family home, said to himself, "What the hell am I knocking for," and was about to open it, when he realized that after all, maybe it was a good idea to knock, given who was inside.

He was saved from having to think any further about whether or not to barge right in when he heard, "Daddy!" shouted from somewhere inside. The door was suddenly open, he was standing in the foyer hugging Debbie, when Nancy threw herself at the both of them and almost pushed the three of them back out the door. This was what John needed more than anything else in the world right now.

"Hello, John," from the top of the stairs.

"Hello, Lou." A sheepish smile that could have been one of shame or of joy was on his face.

"Surprised to see you tonight, John. I'm so sorry to have barged in on you earlier."

"Lou, I hoped you were not gone to bed and wanted to come right over."

It was difficult to say the so much more he wanted to say, as his mother joined them for her hug, and the girls were chattering all at once. John wanted badly to be alone with Louise to explain some things. He just couldn't talk there to her. He realized he had to go with the flow and that meant having hot chocolate in the kitchen, telling the girls all about his cottage for the seventieth time, only this time with a difference. They were coming to visit him tomorrow they said and they wanted him to tell them again all about it, and the beach, and the neighbours, and the kitchen, and the bedrooms, and on it went. They asked him what he did with his time on the weekends, whether he was with his old buddies every weekend, whether he still liked teaching at his old high school, would he be getting a puppy, could they visit the school, would he barbecue for them all the next day like he used to do on Saturdays, whether he and Mom would have a date on Saturday night… at which a full silence ensued for some seconds, until Louise piped in with, "Now girls, leave Dad alone with all of these questions. Let him catch his breath, and don't be planning Dad's Saturday night for him. We may see his cottage tomorrow but only if that's convenient for Dad. He may, after all, have other plans. Don't forget, he did not know we were coming up."

"No," John, countered. "I don't have any plans. Well, I mean I do… but I can get out of those. I mean I will get out of those. I mean, you have to come over all weekend, I mean if you want to, if you don't have other plans. And Mom, you come, too. And, yes, I will barbecue, just like the old days. And maybe we can all go to the show tomorrow night, or something…" And then he realized he shouldn't have said that, because he really would like a date with Louise, just the two of them.

But John knew somewhere deep inside himself that this was not going to happen this weekend. Whether it was premonition or simple fear, he knew that he would have no date with Louise this weekend. He had to spend the time with his daughters. His mother tried to help out:

"John, if you would like it, these gals can stay with me tomorrow night, that is, if you and… I mean… and Louise… wanted to…" And she caught herself in the act of being Cupid and stopped talking and it was painful for her. Louise rescued her.

"Why don't we all get a good night's sleep and play it by ear tomorrow? But, John, you mentioned having other plans with… I mean, you…that is, if you have something else on, we are fine with Mom here. We could visit you in the daytime and your evening would be yours, as planned, if that's okay?"

John's mind was suddenly of little value. How he wanted to say that all he wanted to do was be with her but he couldn't say it. Was it fear of rejection, pride, embarrassment? Words of any kind seemed beyond him. As too often happens, there are moments of suspended animation when words of reassurance are necessary. Louise wanted very badly to hear that she and the girls were welcome, that John wanted to see them, and her, too. But silence would choose now to assert its dominance. Nancy broke it with,

"Dad, did we make a mistake not telling you we were coming?"

"No, honey. I am so glad to see you all. Really, I want us to be together all weekend. Honest, I have no plans that are important, or anywhere near as important as your being here." As he said these words he glanced at Louise, who looked away as if she did not want him to see her eyes at this point. It appeared that John was not the only one struggling with feelings. Lou seemed to have some of her own that she wasn't sure she wanted.

"Daddy, could we stay up all night with you?" Debbie asked.

"No way," said her Mom. In fact, I was just going to ask Nanna about your going to bed. It's almost midnight.

"Why are we sleeping here at Nanna's, and not at Daddy's cottage?"

Again the awkwardness. But Louise was quick off the mark this time. "You know why we are. I already told you that Daddy would not be prepared with enough beds and sheeting for the two of you. Besides it's so late now, I want you in bed within the next 15 minutes."

John knew that he would not win this one. First of all, he didn't have the beds for all of them. Not even enough blankets or even sleeping bags. Besides he knew his mother would be hurt if he did not let everyone stay with her for at least tonight. So he said nothing while his mother and Louise called all of the shots as to who would be sleeping where. He listened and supported Louise when she finally insisted that Debbie go brush her teeth, floss and get ready for bed. Nancy might have been allowed to stay up later but in sympathy with Debbie, or maybe because she was just tired, she accompanied her younger sister to the washroom. Maybe she wanted her Mom and Dad to have some time together.

Emma said nothing but followed the girls down the hall, getting towels and face cloths, and just generally wanting to be with her granddaughters–like the old days.

"Oh, John, it seems so sad to be in this house and not have your Dad falling all over us." And she started to cry all of a sudden. She looked away. Before John could short circuit emotionally, not knowing whether to hug her, or just respect the space between them, she recovered almost completely, except for the tears on her cheeks. "I am so sorry we didn't call you first. I felt like such a fool earlier tonight." And the tears seemed to come back again, but she did not acknowledge these. "I did not mean to embarrass you, nor your friend."

"Louise, one of the main reasons I came over was to tell you that the lady you saw, despite the appearances, is a friend, a colleague, and nothing more. And I realize how stupid that sounds but it is the truth. She had come for dinner and spilled red wine on her slacks after dinner, while I was making coffee or something.

"Honest, that's... she's... not important. What's important is that you're here, that you brought our daughters up for Father's Day. Debbie told me on the phone... And I am so sorry I was not alone to greet you when you came to the cottage..."

For the first time Louise stopped concentrating on her own embarrassment and noticed John's pain, his sadness, the look in his eyes which somehow suggested that he was pleading to be believed. And at once she felt somehow relieved. She did believe him. He was telling the truth and it did matter to her that the woman wearing the housecoat she had bought him all those years ago did not mean what Louise had feared the woman meant to John. There was still hope.

This was really the reason she had come with the girls to Beach Bay. Father's Day's merely gave her the excuse. She knew the last time she had left her therapist's office that it was time to face up to a few things: number one, she still loved John Coliani; number two, she wanted to be his wife again; number three, she wanted him to be the father of their two daughters; number three, she wanted them to be a family again; number four, she feared that John might no longer be interested in fighting for the survival of their marriage since after all, he had been dating women she had heard; number five, she had no idea how all of this could come to pass since he was not about to move back to Toronto and her career still demanded that she work for her Toronto firm, and she could not even consider giving up that career. But, "what the hell?" she had told herself just before proposing the Father's day venture, "I have to try, and leave the results to God." And here she was looking into the face of the man she knew she still loved.

"John, if you want us to come tomorrow, we will come, and we will have dinner there, too, if you like, if you are being honest that your other plans are not that important... In fact, I had kind of promised the girls that we would stay with Nanna tonight but that somehow we would all stay with you tomorrow night... unless you don't have the room, and if you'd rather, I could always stay here with your mother." Testing, testing, testing.

John's face beamed. "Fantastic," he said. "You just made my day, I mean, night, weekend, whatever." He was tempted to say, life, but held back, although he really wanted to hug her with gratitude, and with... love. But again, he held back. frightened that he was making too much of what he was hearing.

"Louise, I know how much you detest driving long distances. In fact, I seem to remember a certain someone sleeping all the time right beside me in the car and always pretending that she was just resting her eyes..." They both laughed then, which relieved the pitch of the emotion they were both feeling. And she poked him in the ribs.

"You were always claiming that I was sleeping but I always answered you when you spoke to me."

"If you call a snore or two an answer." More laughter.

"John, that's not true. I don't snore."

"No, and chain saws make no noise either." He looked at her and she at him. They wanted to say more things, to keep the joy alive but suddenly it dried up as quickly as it had come. What were they both thinking about? How could this be happening? Too much had happened between them in the last two years. They were not a couple anymore. There had been all of these lawyer meetings between them. This carrying on was definitely too story bookish. And weren't they both afraid of rejection? For whatever reasons, John tried to do the loving thing:

BEARE PARTS

"At any rate, knowing how tired you must be from having driven up here, maybe I should go home now and let you and the girls get some needed rest?'" Testing, testing, testing. But she didn't notice it. She was once again locked into her own timidity. It was not what she wanted to hear from him. She wanted him to stay. She wanted him to propose a ride, a coffee shop, anything but this gentlemanly departure; she was, however, scared that he himself might be really tired, that he'd had company for dinner, that he might have to go home to clean up, whatever, that she'd sprung this visit on him without notice and that it might not be quite fair to him, so she simply acquiesced.

John found his Mom, kissed her good night, Nancy and Debbie as well, and after tickling both of them in their bed, just like in the old days, he left them giggling, and went home, floated home in fact, and did not seem to need the car. His happiness lasted right until the knife to his back which forced him down so quickly.

Louise, too, was a stronger, more upbeat, more hopeful person than she had been in years when John left her that night at his mother's place. It was not until the call from Wally Misener that her short-lived euphoria changed instantly to fear, anxiety, bowel-moving paralysis. Her scream brought Emma, John's mother, running to the kitchen telephone, where Louise had a complexion worse than even the fatigue from a car trip could induce. Louise was also sobbing uncontrollably.

"What is it, Lou?" Emma asked in terror.

"It's John. He's been stabbed."

Right at that moment, she could not process having said that. Nor did Emma believe she'd heard those words. "What did you say?"

Louise could not talk. She was crying too hard and by now the girls had come into the kitchen, direct from their bed. Louise saw this, got a measure of control, and said to them. "Daddy's been hurt. Mr. Misener–Wally– just called. He's on the way to the hospital. I am going, too. Oh, God!"

"Louise, what is going on?" The girls were now crying, wailing in fact. "What is this all about?"

"Mom, I don't know much. Wally just called to say he had been in touch with a Detective who called him at his house. A Detective Du-something or other, and John's has been attacked in his cottage and has been taken to hospital, and… and… and…it's very… bad!" She could not say another word; she could only yell, cry, shake, sob, and hold on to the counter. Emma grabbed her and held on, and cried too.

"I must go now. Mom, Nancy can stay with Debbie. You will want to come, too." Questions from the girls were handled with, "Try to be brave. We'll call you from the hospital." There was no sense trying to get them to stop crying; it was not possible; there was no time. If only they had not heard this yet. If only Emma could stay with them. That, too, was not possible. But Louise was adamant: they were not coming to the hospital. In case… in case… in case, what? Louise was sobbing again. The girls were still crying when Louise and Emma ran out the door.

They were at the hospital in another 10 minutes.

"Louise, I did not expect to get you on the phone. I'm sorry to have been so blunt. I was too stunned to be more gentle. I'm really sorry. But I had just been called by Gary Desfresnes." And he saw how devastated Louise and her mother-in-law looked standing there. He knew it was only going to get worse.

"How is he, Wally?"

"Ahhh, the doctor was just here asking for next of kin, I mean, for someone to talk with, and he's going to want to chat with you. I'll go find him." It was all Wally could do not to bolt from there at once. He did not want to have to tell them what he had just heard. He almost ran from them to go find the doctor. Mostly so he could get away from the inevitable.

A man came into the emergency waiting room, not the large public one, but something smaller and more private where somehow Emma and Louise had been led by someone of whom they took no notice… they had been both unable to sit down, but had stood standing with vacant stares on both of their faces. Wally had gone to get the doctor, or so he said, when this man in white came in and asked them both to

BEARE PARTS

sit down.

"I am Doctor Gilbere, the resident in charge of the emergency room tonight. Are you Mrs. Coliani?"

"We both are. I am John's wife, and this is his mother. Is he okay?"

"I am afraid that John is not doing very well right now. He has suffered severe trauma to his neck and back, inflicted by a sharp instrument, likely a knife. He is not conscious as we speak. He is also receiving blood. His heart rate is very slow. We have a patient whose life is in very grave danger. I'm sorry. But we are doing everything we can to save his life, and we may yet be successful. The next couple of hours are critical."

Both women cried softly. Louise began to tremble and shake. Emma looked as if she suffered the entire news in her face; she was white, and seemed to be mumbling to herself.

"I can only try to imagine the impact of such news on you both. My experience has taught me never to believe I can feel what you are feeling right now. But what I can do is to help you is to provide some medication to help you both get through the next few hours or so, or even days... if need be. Will you allow me to prescribe something for both of you? I also have to get back into the emergency room. I gather from the police that neither of you would be able to offer information as to what happened. But I would like to know right now if John has allergies to any medications we might need to give him. Or any medical condition we ought to know about right now as we proceed with our work."

Here he stopped and looked intently at the both of them. No one said anything. Until both tried to speak at once.

"He has no allergies..."

"Sorry. Yes, he does, Mom, to penicillin. He never had that when he was younger but after we married, he reacted one time to penicillin and was told he could not take it ever again."

Emma did not reply. She just sat there, without visible sign that she understood anything right now.

"Anything else we should know? How is his heart generally?"

"Fine. No problems that I knew of." Louise also said: "Other than recurring indigestion, John has had pretty good health most of our married life. Emotionally... he..." and she broke down again. "We haven't been living together..."

"I see...well, if there's nothing else right now I must excuse myself. The nurse will be right in for you both, and some other members of out hospital emergency response team. Excuse me for now." He jumped up and was gone as fast as he had appeared. Emma and Louise were now in each other's arms. Wally Misener came back into the room. He, too, hugged them both.

After some time, they all sat down and Wally said. "There is someone here for whom I have a lot of respect. He is an old colleague of mine and a good friend. John has met him more than once, as well. If you are up to it now, he'd very much like to chat with both of you. He is, of course, a police officer."

"Wally, I think I can talk now; it's the breathing I'm having trouble with. It feels like I have just had the breath knocked out of me," Emma said. "Louise, are you ready to meet Wally's friend?"

"I want to call our daughters. Where's a phone?"

"Down the hall, Louise. I will take you to it this very moment. Of course, call them." This from Wally.

"But do you think it might be better if you waited a moment to calm down a little? Maybe help them deal with it better, Lou?" asked Emma. Or... maybe I could call them... no, I guess that's stupid. How silly of me. You'd want to call them yourself. But if you want...

"Oh, I don't know what I'm trying to say. There's no way to tell them... this... this news. God help us now."

"Detective Desfresnes is out in the hall. He's a good guy, an understanding guy. But I know he's going to have to get on with his work immediately. I thought maybe you might want to hear him before he leaves, but I have to tell him now..."

"Wally, we'll talk with him quickly then... I'll call the girls right after. Maybe with more information... no, I won't tell them what he says. Oh God, does he know things about all of this?"

"I'll go get him." Wally left the room.

Seconds later Detective Desfresnes was warmly shaking Louise's hand, and then he did the same with Emma. "You son's... your husband's... a fine man. I know him. We've had coffee together. This should not have happened. I am truly very sorry to meet you both like this. Please sit down. I want tell you what we know, what we do not know. And to see if you can help us in any way.

"Obviously, this is not a good time to bother you with questions. Please understand. The nature of our work does not allow us to pick our times. We want to act as quickly as we can. Speed sometimes helps get results. It can, of course, also cause problems. In the case of information, however, we need all we can get, as fast as we can get it.

Detective Desfresnes then began the narrative with the near miss with the car that night on Lakeshore Drive, the interviews after. He did not tell what else he knew. Certainly not the most recent information he had. What he told them was just enough for them ask no more right now, to have them trust him, to open them up to tell him what he might not yet know. He did not even tell them as much as he had shared with John recently; and certainly he had shared even more with Wally, but then Wally had been a trusted colleague. Desfresnes also did not want to upset these two women any more than they were already disturbed by the events of this evening.

Left alone, Louise said to Emma. "I feel weak by all of this. I want to go to our daughters. I want to stay here. I don't know what to do. I ought to pray, but the energy seems not here."

"Louise, why don't I go home for a bit. Get the girls a little more settled, if they have not fallen asleep, and then come back? I won't sleep tonight. But maybe I can stay there awake if you will call me at the first sign of news. That way the girls won't be alone anyway."

"If you do that, it will be such a relief. Then I can stay here and use what little energy I have to pray, to worry about John. Right now I haven't the strength to worry also about our girls and I feel so guilty admitting that."

"Louise, you have enough here at the hospital. I'll leave immediately. But please, even if it's small news... anything... I beg you, call me."

"Emma, I will, of course."

Emma left then, and Louise noticed then that Wally was walking up and down in the hall. She knew she couldn't sit down, so she walked out to him and he smiled at her. "Want to walk with me? Not much of a stroll but I am so scared I can't sit down in the waiting room. I don't want to read, either. I just want to see Doctor Gilbere with good news all over his face."

"Wally, do you hate me just a little for what happened with John and me? I mean I know you love your friend a lot."

"No, Louise. I don't hate you. What happened has often been a matter for me to think about, but I try even in my thoughts not to give in to judgments. We are all of human, and none that I know are perfect. I am so aware of my own faults that it would be sheer hypocrisy on my part to hate you for whatever yours might be.

"I guess I believe that you and John have struggled hard like the rest of us but people change, sometimes in different ways, and that likely causes them to rethink their living arrangements.

"I also figure there are so damn many pressure working against long-lived marriages today that it's amazing people stay together as long as they do. Careers generate so much pressure. So do financial obligations. I won't even speak of our own individual addictions."

Louise looked at Wally. Recognizing different dimensions in someone she thought she knew, but obviously didn't. Someone who previously didn't seem capable of this kind of attitude. It crossed her mind that maybe she had never really known Wally Misener.

"Do you and Brenda ever have doubts about your marriage?"

"Louise, if you are asking whether all is harmonious between us. No. Hell no! We sometimes fight so hard it embarrasses me after to think I behaved like that, yelling and screaming, over what very often looks in retrospect to be such trivial bullshit. But at the time, these things look to be so important. Probably because of buried insecurities, angers, rage hidden inside me that I don't understand. Could be that I direct this rage at Brenda. I don't know. I just know that sometimes we fight big time.

"But, as to wondering about whether we should have married?

Whenever this has crossed my mind, I realize pretty quickly that if Brenda never changed one thing about herself... if I had known when I proposed to her, what I know about her now, I would still be eager to marry her. I guess that means, now that I think about it, that I am still very much in love with her. With the person she was and still is.

"Does this mean I have never been attracted to another woman? No. There have been many other attractive women. But even when I have been attracted to another woman, it did not mean I was no longer attracted to Brenda. But my libido seems to be able to handle more than one attraction at the same time. But attractions are simply that... attractions.

"I cannot conceive of starting a long-term relationship with another woman again. Brenda and I are just too bonded now. She is too much of my life now. I wouldn't want to be out even playing the field like some of the guys these days. What about you?"

"I have had the chance to date this last year, Wally, but I've been too busy so far. I only have so much energy and it goes to my girls and to my work. The house needs this and that. The gardens... well, I'm embarrassed by them. I feel guilty as hell when there's no energy left over for things like my church which is important to me. At least my religion is. I rely on my belief in a God who loves me, is looking after us. Yet I don't seem able to give Him any of my time. Even my prayers are very quick little things said between other priorities.

"No. There's no time to date. and besides... I... oh shit, I'm going to be honest about this... and not because..." She started to cry. They continued walking. Wally wisely let her cry; he said nothing. He did not try to comfort her in any other way but by letting her cry privately, respectfully, as if he were not there, but he wanted to seem to be there if she needed him to listen.

"Not because I want you to go tell him... if ever he can... hear one of us again... like a high school nit who tells a boy she likes his friend so he'll tell the friend... not because I want to manipulate you, or John... but truthfully, Wally... I still love John. I want no other man. I want our family back."

Having blurted this out, she sobbed more uncontrollably now.

Again they walked. An orderly noticed them and looked away. The hall smelled of hospital smells. What were these, antiseptic cleaners? What were the component smells of hospitals halls? Wally thought of iodine but knew that iodine was not used these days. Nor was ether. So what were these smells? Why did hospital halls always have this smell? Flowers? The smell of flowers always reminded him of funerals from when he was an altar boy. To this day flowers in large amounts smelled of funerals. Wally shuddered inside. He did not want to think about funerals. He was close to tears himself now.

"Wally, when John and I separated, it was his idea. But I said little to stop him. I couldn't seem to say anything. I didn't know why then. I think I know why now. I had made a hell of a mistake with a guy from our office. John found out about this one-night stand. I was so guilty I had no right to ask his forgiveness. I did not ask. He left.

"I was so broken up I went, am still going... to therapy. Trying to adjust to not having him anymore. And cannot seem to accept it. Oh we fought, too. There are things about John I would still like to change. And I know those kinds of wishes do not make for a good relationship. But... his drinking... his golfing all of the time... his overly carefree attitude to the spending of money... his refusal to accept the demands of my career... we did grow apart over the years... let less important things come between us... took each other for granted... both of us, I guess... didn't work at our relationship... me just as guilty, maybe more guilty than him of this... anyway, that affair I had was the natural culmination in some way of the death of our trying to love each other.

"And I see now, I did some time ago... that my not saying much about his leaving wasn't just from my guilt over that affair. I guess a part of me I'm not now very proud of, was wondering whether I still loved John. Whether we shouldn't try separating for awhile. I wasn't smart enough to see that this could be a dangerous experiment when I'd been taking John's love for granted for far too long. That I could lose it completely, forever. That he might find someone. But part of me couldn't/wouldn't accept that he was serious about this split. I kept thinking he'd be coming back, that he'd want to reconcile, that he loved me too much to make this split permanent. And then I began to realize that maybe I was wrong. With increasing terror I saw little by little that maybe he did mean it to be a permanent split. That he was really through with us…And I have never been the one to find it easy to start the healing between us after one of our fights… it was usually John who made the first move…

"I got more and more terrified that our marriage was indeed over and that I had allowed it all to happen. That's when I started therapy. Like so many things in life, I had to lose John to know what I had let die, our love, our marriage. And I am so angry now at myself for having to learn it this way. My stupidity has hurt the girls, too, big time, because they need their Daddy. How I have wished we could try again."

Wally said, "I sometimes wonder how many separated people, divorced folks, in some part of themselves, feel the same way. Or is this just a kind of wishful thinking on the part of those of us who have stayed together."

"I can't speak for anyone else, Wally. I just know what I believe now. You can stick trial separations in your ear as far I am concerned. Trial separation was a mistake, a cop-out, at least for me. Maybe not for John. I allowed my lawyer to make his life miserable. I ought to have fired the guy. In fact, I know why I came up this weekend… to talk to John… to see what he was feeling, thinking, about us…whether… and now he's…" Silence. Walking. For about three minutes.

"Louise, John still loves you. Only you. Surely you know that!"

"I want more than anything to believe that. No. Right now, more than anything, I want him to live."

She was crying so hard now that she walked into the more private waiting room and threw herself sobbing down onto one of the black vinyl chairs. Wally walked in and sat down beside her, saying nothing. They did not speak. She cried.

Wally did not know what to say, could not then think of anything hopeful to say because he was so damn scared himself. He looked about the room, noticing the end tables, two of them, the little lamps with the off white shades, a few magazines on each of them, the black vinyl on all of the chairs, the cream coloured walls, a photograph or two, of sailboats at sunset, of sunrise also on water, and the couch against the far wall where someone had left a bed pillow, a remnant of some other lonely vigil.

Wally wondered whether this other person's vigil had ended with good news, whether this vigil he and Louise were keeping would now end with good news. They were unable to talk much now, both too tired, exhausted from worry. They must have been sitting like this for another hour. The nurse came in. "Mrs. Coliani?"

"Yes?" Would there be news now?

"There's a telephone call for you. You can take it at the desk, the nursing station, if you'd like. I will bring you there." Wally noticed it was now 2.45 a.m. His wife Brenda walked into the room and ran into his arms. Behind her came Horney and Barbara. It did not even seem strange to Louise that Barbara was here with Horney. As if they hadn't broken up all those years ago.

Louise had already followed the nurse to the phone. It was Emma.

"I am sorry for not calling you, Mom, but there's been nothing. No news at all."

"Oh, well, Nancy has finally fallen asleep but Debbie just can't sleep and she has been crying non-stop – me, too, for that matter – and she begged me to call you for news. I couldn't resist because I wanted to call myself but have been trying not to. Forgive us. We cannot stand the waiting, both of us.

"I suppose it's worse for you and I feel stupid for bothering you."

"That's okay, Mom. There's no news, no change. May I speak to my little girl?"

Debbie was crying, asking about her Daddy, why anyone would want to hurt Daddy, was he going to die, and it was all Louise could do to talk calmly, try to answer a couple of the questions, mostly let Debbie get it all out. Eventually, Louise settled her down a little, enough to say that she did not know very much yet, that Daddy was sleeping and being looked after by some really good medical people

BEARE PARTS

who were doing their very best to help him get better. Whether it was the soothing effect of Mommy's voice, or the words Mommy delivered over the phone, or the fact that Debbie was simply exhausted, she began to yawn on the phone. Louise jumped at the opportunity to say,

"Honey, it would really be a help to me and to Nanna right now if you could try again to fall asleep until morning so that we can think only about Daddy, and pray for him, and not be worrying about you. Do you think you can go to sleep now like Nancy did?"

"I'll try, Mommy, honest I will."

"Thank you, Sweetie. Remember that I love you, and Daddy does, too. And we are going to survive even this. Good night, Sweetie. Let me speak to Nanna now."

"Louise, I think she's going to go to sleep now. So don't be worrying about her now. Just call me if anything comes up. I am going to be on the couch here reading a magazine if I can, unless I doze off."

"I will call you with any news and thank you for being there with the girls. Bye for now."

She cradled the phone at the nurse's desk and walked slowly back to the private waiting room to find Wally, Brenda, Horney and Barbara all sitting chatting quietly. Silence happened when she crossed the threshold.

"No one has come in, Louise" said Wally, as first Brenda, then Barbara, and finally Horney gave her a hug. She cried a little while the hugs were given but not too much. She didn't have much energy left to cry. But she would find much more.

"Would it be more helpful if we sat here with you, or if we left you here to try to get a little rest, and just went down for a coffee and checked back on you now and then?" Wally asked.

"Well, I don't really know what to say. I appreciate having you all here, honest... but I don't know whether I will be much company," said Louise.

"Honey, you don't have to say anything, do anything, feel anything, be anything. You just sit there and we'll play it all by ear.

You don't even have to decide anything, like whether we should stay or go, unless you feel strongly one way or the other." We'll sit with you for a while and see what happens." This was Brenda.

Louise smiled gratefully at her and within about three minutes, had closed her eyes, her mouth fell open, and she fell sound asleep. At which point, Wally put his fingers to his lips and gestured to the three of them to follow him. They left her in one of the black vinyl chairs, although her eyes opened ever so slightly to see them sneaking quietly out of the room. She said nothing as the sleep was feeling oh so good.

She did not know how long she had been sleeping when the three of them were seating themselves ever so quietly beside her in the waiting room. They had been downstairs or somewhere she guessed as she rubbed her eyes and tried to smile at each of them. "What time is it?" she asked.

"Four fifty-five," Horney replied.

No sooner were the words out, when all five of them looked up at Dr. Gilbere coming softly into the room. "Hi Wally," he said. Horney, Barbara and Brenda joined Wally on his feet as he shook Dr. Gilbere's hand and quickly introduced Horney and Barb to the doctor, who already knew Brenda. They left the room as soon as these introductions were over.

"I have some good news, Louise," said the doctor. "We are not completely out of the woods yet but it is my belief that your husband's life will go on for a while yet… it may be a changed life…we don't know that yet… but the bleeding has been stopped… the spleen and the caryatid artery have been repaired… and he is sleeping now with the help of the anesthetist, Dr. Jordan. The team has worked very hard and the repairs to the caryatid artery went as about as good as we could have hoped at this point. Same with the spleen. There also appears to have been a blow to the skull and this injury is more serious than we initially figured and we are anxious about complications from the severe concussion he is now experiencing. We had to wake him a little after we finished the surgery and we were worried that it might be both difficult and dangerous after the trauma of the surgery, and given the concussion. But he did wake up and I asked him who he was and he replied and said he felt very sick and we immediately put him back to sleep. We will be watching his vital signs very carefully now in intensive care where he is about to be moved.

"But I want to say that with some luck and some prayers I believe the worst may well be over. If he can get through these next few hours without seizure from the concussion, I think he is going to do just fine.

"He will be, I would guess, in intensive care for 48 to 36 hours, and then be moved into a room in which he will recover slowly. But I see him here for a week to ten days. I am very tired now and I'm going to get some sleep but I will be in the hospital if they need me should complications arise.

"I won't presume to tell you what to do. Nor do I even know if you are the person who should be there when he wakes up, but he's going to need lots of love. Someone should be close by, to come to his side. You mentioned being separated so I am conscious of choosing my words carefully.

"If John has a lady friend to whom he is close, it would be good for her to be here. He needs no added stress now... if your relationship is one of stress for both of you. If on the other hand, you think you should be the one to be there when he wakes, I'll leave that to you. It's your call.

"Please understand that your relationship is none of my business. But his recovery is. And I want to ensure that I leave no stone unturned. The psychosomatic thing is very real; healing is definitely aided by emotionally supportive relationships. I have to be blunt, Louise. If you think it would help with your not being here, make the tough decision. I also have to tell you that our own son is in one of your husband's classes and I have heard that he lives alone.

"On the other hand, if you have still a strong bond between you, you can help him tremendously by being there for him when he wakes up.

"I'm sorry to have seemed to intrude where it is not my place to go. But I know you will understand that right now I have my patient in mind. I'm sure you do, as well, or you wouldn't be here all night." Louise could not help herself. She just sobbed and sobbed and the poor doctor, who had been here before, could not help but feel useless for what he had said. But it was a judgment call; he had made it, had said what he knew he had to say to her. He was silent for some moments and then said,

"Louise, you do not have to say anything to me, and I am so sorry I had to say that to you, but now I have to go. I want to ask you if you would like a sedative or anything of that kind. I can also get you some counseling. It's sometimes great to have someone caring who really knows how to listen. We find that people get a lot of help just by being able to talk out... what it is they think and feel. They make better decisions; they give better support to the patients, when they are themselves helped to be in touch with heir own psyches.

"We've got some damn good people here, and some of the best are volunteers, so you wouldn't be talking to someone who gets paid to listen. They really do care, Louise. Again, it's your call and you don't have to decide anything right now. But if you want anything right now, say the word."

He waited a moment and then, when she smiled a little at him, and threw her arms around him, and thanked him for saving John's life, and between sobs, told him she'd be just fine without any sedative right now, he felt better leaving her to herself in the waiting room he had come to hate so much.

This was a part of medicine he hadn't thought much about when he made the decision to become a surgeon those ten or so years ago. Yet he had come to realize the importance of this room and what went on inside it, not only for the people he talked with in this room, but for the patients who would so need the support of the people suffering so much in these rooms.

Had he his way, these would be very different kinds of rooms. One hell of a lot more comfortable, more... whatever it would take to make them places of serenity... he was no psychologist... no designer... but somebody must know how to makes these places less like morgues. These were his thoughts as he sought out the bed he needed so badly right now in the residents' resting quarters.

Louise sat quietly for a moment and wondered what to do. Should she believe John, that this woman she had met earlier in the evening... when was that... it was only last evening for heaven's sake... it seemed like a week ago now... before all of this stuff... how life can change so damn fast... it is frightening... I must be too damn tired right now... wearing his housecoat... Shirley was her name... would Shirley be more of a help to him when he woke up... or was he telling the truth... maybe he was trying to let her know gently that he had found someone... in which case my being here would be part of his problems and not part of his healing... how the hell can I know the answer now... we didn't have the chance to talk... oh shit, why did I let him leave me at his mother's... why didn't I tell him right then and there that I wanted us to go out immediately and talk and talk and talk... why did I have to keep my mouth shut... what was I afraid of... why didn't I speak... he would not have gone home... I could have prevented this, this fucking stabbing... who the hell did this to him... who the hell is this Shirley to him now... I don't know... anything... it's not fair... I must be guilty... I let him go in the first place... I deserve all of this and more... no, no, I don't know... She sat there and thought and thought and thought and wondered and cried and sobbed and thought and...

Wally came into the room by himself, looking like hell, as if he'd been awakened on a park bench. His hair was sticking up, what was left of it, at the back of his head . . his shirt was a little out of his waistband... his eyes looked a little puffy and rings were visible at their bottoms. The park bench idea was not far off the money. He had been sleeping in his car. Everyone else had gone home. It was now 7.05 a.m. "Want coffee?"

"Where's everyone else? Home, I hope."

"Yes, Louise. They all went home because we found out most of the imminent danger to John had passed. That barring further complications he was going to make it. I drove Brenda home; she left her car here. Didn't want to drive by herself. Too upset. Then I came back and closed my eyes in the parking lot for a moment and I think I slept about an hour, or just under."

Before he knew what was happening he was being squeezed and told that she loved him as John's best friend. She was crying, her tears were warm on his cheeks, and he hugged her back and cried himself.

"The doctor told me I had to make a decision, Wally. And I don't know how to make it." And she cried some more. Wally let her find her voice again.

"He said I should be here for John only if I thought it would help John. Not stress him. But I walked in on him last night to surprise him and there was a woman at his place. We were all very embarrassed and maybe John has a new person in his life. And I deserve it all. And maybe I should leave now and let her… be there…" And she couldn't talk any more.

"Louise, who was the woman?"

"Someone by the name of Shirley. I… she was wearing his housecoat, Wally…"

"I think I know who she is, Louise. She teaches with him. But I did not know he was seeing anyone, Louise. One thing for sure: John Coliani loves his wife. Whether he is having a relationship with any other woman, I don't know. And I am a good friend as you just said yourself. But I know this much: John is not over you. He still loves you. His heart is broken for not living with you. I would bet a year's salary on that. He hasn't said as much to me. I wish I could tell you that he has. But he keeps his pain to himself. I do know this man well enough to bet that year's salary. Say the word and you and John could get back together again. Here. Toronto. I don't know about the details, but John wants to be married to you. Wants his family back. Wants you."

Louise was crying again.

"Stay here, Louise. John is going to need you big time."

All of a sudden. "Oh my God, Wally. I have to call Emma! And the girls."

Chapter Five
More Fishing

The Evinrude chugged along smoothly, not a miss to be heard. Sometimes, after listening to it for hours, it began to sound as if it was saying the name "Ralph". Only the name was drawn out slowly, rhythmically, as in "Raaaaaaalph, Raaaaaalph, Raaaaaaaalph." This observation was going through Wally's head now. He and Gary Desfresnes had been talking for some time and now they had gone silent with each other... thinking about what had just been said.

Trolling used to be more relaxed than this. But then, Wally didn't normally have his closest friend lying in a hospital bed, struggling for his life, while Wally was out for a day's trolling. In fact, Wally didn't even fish much any more. There was no time for fishing these days. There should be, thought Wally. Why the hell wasn't there?

But the fact was, he did not get out fishing much any more. And the truth was, here he was, a sunny Wednesday morning in June, loving it, basking in it, except for thinking about Coli. Which is why he was here in the first place. Having said yes to the coaxing of Gary. It wasn't for the fish Gary was here. But they were fishing nonetheless.

"So let me see if I have this straight. City Police, OPP, RCMP, and MNR all want me to catch a fish. So much so they're paying for this little outing, Gary?"

"That's about right, Wally. You think I'd waste my good booze on the likes of you?"

"Precious little I've seen of any libation, Gary. Remember the old days when we could enjoy a drink on the water without breaking the law? Now, not even a beer, you cheap prick."

"Now, Wally, don't be harsh with your old buddy. After all, it was drunks like you who abused the privilege for the rest of us more moderate types. And that's why drinkin' an' boatin' an' fishin' ain't ko-shure no more. Not in the eyes of the law.

"But the vodka is back at the camp; so is the beer, any time you want to head in, Wally."

"No, we haven't been out very long. And the fact is, it's been too long, Gary. I'm enjoying this. But I'm still trying to process what you just told me. McDevitt, Harris – alias Falwell – mixed up with black bear gall bladders. Chinese aliens trying to buy as many of these organs they can. Unbelievable."

"Yep. I figure we got more police people working on this business than any case I have seen in a long time, Wally."

"And this guy you think did the hit on John, this Jean-Guy Fong... where did you say he lived?"

"We're not sure of that, Wally. But the RCMP guys figure he's mostly on the move. Buying wherever he can and going between this Oriental ring and his Canadian suppliers. He's all over the country quite a bit I'm given to understand."

"And when did you find out the MNR was onto him?"

"When the OPP requested a meeting with me and our Chief. The MNR were there, too. As were the RCMP. I thought it was a law convention when I showed up that morning."

"How long have these guys been on to McDevitt, Falwell and Fong?"

"About two months, I think. I've known for about a month myself. I am so damn upset with myself because I shoulda been watching out for John better."

"But you say you had a man watching out for him?"

"Wally, without telling him, we put a guy onto it as soon as we got the news. But you know the drill, Wally. We don't have the dollars to do 24-hour surveillance unless we are positive it should be done. So we do it intermittently. Watch someone, stop it, watch again, back off. Keeps the guy in the dark. We didn't want John to know he was being watched... protected. Wanted him relaxed... normal. Weren't sure anyone was going to bother him. Chief said we had to balance the risk against the dollar cost.

"Besides, intermittent surveillance is harder to detect by anyone else who might be watching John. And that's the one we want to catch. We were never positive that anyone was after John. That the night he was first bothered was really an attempt to get him. We had only our suspicions. When we got the news from the RCMP, the OPP, well, we were suddenly more interested but still not sure John was a possible target. Without the certitude we needed, we couldn't do the 24-hour thing. And, as I said, we did have a man on that night and it didn't help us…him.

"Son of a bitch was inside that cottage and we didn't know it when our guy came on duty and John came home. Only saw the prick running out and bolting when it was too late to prevent things. Lucky to get the plate I.D. though. Or we still wouldn't know who Jean-Guy Fong is."

"Gary, seriously. Hadn't been for you guys. Could have been a lot worse." Though given what he knew this morning he wasn't sure about this. And he was a little uneasy about whether John had been used as a decoy. And the news was not good.

"Yeah, we didn't stop the knifing but I guess we might've stopped the bleeding. Saved him from dying right there on the floor. Thought of that many a time myself. Tryin' to hang on to that, I suppose, to cover up what happened in my head, I guess. But still, I wish I could have stopped the whole fuckin' thing."

"Not your fault and you damn well know it. But… I appreciate your feelings. He's an awfully good friend. Damn it, I hope he makes it." And Wally went silent.

When Gary could see that Wally was in control again. "Wally, you were too good of a cop… too sharp… not to know I had to get you up here to tap your mind."

"Yeah, I figured you were interested in more than trout fishing today. Shoot with the questions."

"Well, Wally, everybody working on this damn thing wants to know more about how McDevitt got tied up with Falwell-Harris… who would now be about 86 years of age. We also want to know what kind a marriage Edward Falwell had with his wife when she went missing in June of '57. How both Falwell and McDevitt got into it with Fong and his crowd. We know you didn't even know about these things. But we also know you knew the Falwell family as good as anyone after the incident in 1957. What we want to know ain't in the newspaper. And we don't want to interview too many people yet, not at this point.

"Shit, anyone who knew the Falwells in those days – neighbours, friends, whoever – is probably goin' to be stunned when they find out Edward Falwell din't die in June 1957. In fact, they know nothin' of any of this. That's what we believe right now, anyway. We don' want them to know now. Not right now. We may have to go to them down the road. But not now.

"We want to find out as much as we can without tippin' our hand. We're already uptight that so many police officers, law enforcement agencies are into this... we want this hushed. This could have international implications with the smugglin' shit, this bear parts stuff. The RCMP are goin' nuts about keepin' it all tightly lidded.

"They wanted me to talk to you... because you knew so much at one time, Wally. See if you could remember anything that might help us piece some stuff together. Why would Edward Falwell not contact anyone after what happened in 1957...whatever did happen? How does a man leave everyone he might know and move to Toronto? And not only how... why? What the hell happened? Does someone know more'n we know? See why we can't contact them yet?

"Wally, I know you were one of the best. But I gotta say this. I went on record with everyone involved that you could be brought into this even though you aren't a cop any more. Told them all, swore to it, that you could contain what I have to tell you, to get you to try to remember. One asshole Fed even suggested paying for the costs of a hypnotherapist for you, to help you remember... if you agreed. I told him to get real. But it's true, Wally, even the smallest detail could help us. But I told the people I met with... if it weren't in your reports of those days, it wasn't important. Yours were always the most thorough and reliable of police reports. But we surely would love to get those bastards before they scram."

Gary was watching Wally's face intently. It was important to register the expressions on Wally's face now. Did Gary still know this guy? Was Wally the same guy Gary used to work with, fish with? Could he still be relied on? Was Gary right... taking the risks he had taken with Wally, putting everything on the line as he had done with the people now in charge of this investigation? It was now no longer merely his own chief in charge but the RCMP?

Believing he was still right in his assessment, Gary spoke. "There's more, Wally."

"I figured that, too. Don't tell me anything you are shaky about telling me. I don't need to know enough to get you into shit, Gary. You're right, I still remember the drill."

"Got to. Want to. Have authorization for what I'm going to say right now. We got McDevitt." He paused, watched Wally's expression change, become more tense. "Falwell's dead. Both of them hit. McDevitt's in a Toronto hospital. He's our biggest hope... but fuckin' near dead." He scanned Wally's face again, watched the eyes get even bigger.

"Doctors won't let us anywhere near him. But our guys are in the halls. Harris and McDevitt were hit two days ago. Monday some time. Or Sunday. Not long after John Coliani had already been nailed on the Friday night. If we can't get McDevitt to cooperate, you're about all we got, if you got anything we haven't thought about. Obviously, you and I are not having this conversation. I never even came fishing today."

"I hear you, Gary."

Just then, while Gary made the turn with the boat, something hit Wally's line – unmistakable. "Fish on! Or off. No, on! Gary, this is more like it." He had the rod tensely in his hands, was reeling with his left hand, making sure no slack was left, but not setting the hook too hard, for fear of jerking it out of the mouth.

"I will cut the motor as soon as we straighten out your line, Wally. Son of a bitch hit on the turn. Typical. Never fails. If they're going to bite, it's on the turn."

Gary cut the motor when the line was straight out behind the boat. But that didn't last long, for quickly Wally was standing and facing a taut line heading straight away from the midship line, heading due west. Wally had a smile of excited pleasure on his face. "Hey, he might be more than a keeper, Gar, he's got a lot of pulling power." The tension sang while the line spooled out from the reel. The fish was making a run for it. But Wally kept reeling and trying to make sure his efforts at least equalled those of the fish trying to get away with the line.

"The tension on that reel might be set just a little loose, Wally. Give it a click or two."

"No. I'm in no hurry, Gar. Let the bugger have his day. I want to enjoy the contest. It's been a long time."

"Yeah, but there aren't that many around to lose one so I hope he doesn't clean you out of line while you're enjoying yourself, dickhead."

"No, we're under control here, Gar. Call me Santiago! In fact, I think he's coming this way for a change. Like a big marlin." The reeling went on while the boat drifted on the chop. Gary made ready the net, stood up, as if to see if he could get a look at the fish but it was too early yet. He remained standing, net in hand, hoping he would not blow the netting operation soon to be required. Every fisherman's fear–to blow the netting of a buddy's big fish. Gary was already worried about missing other big fish these days.

Wally was winning the battle. And eventually he brought the fish closer to the side of the boat where both of them got a glimpse at the beautiful lake trout struggling in the water. They saw him about four feet under the water on the starboard side before he made yet another dive. Then up again he came, but again the fish dove, this time as if to go under the boat, which worried the hell out of Gary because he did not want the line cut under the keel so the trout could get away. Luckily the trout came right back up again and Gary made his move, getting the net under the fish just in time before it could try again to make another run under the boat.

That the fish could have mustered another effort was readily evident when the net was placed on the floor of the varnished 16-foot cedar strip. Violently the grey-blue water-shiny denizen of Lake Timachi lay waste to anything within close reach of his flopping, struggling, tail snapping contortions on the boat's floor, the lure long since spit from his mouth and caught now in the mesh of the net before either Gary or Wally had made one move, both fascinated by the size of this beauty doing his death dance on the cedar slats, worms spilled all over the floor, and a tackle box in danger of having its contents similarly thrown helter skelter all over the place, till Gary finally seized both the moment and his tackle box out of harm's way.

Wally, too came to his senses, and grabbed the net out of the way, seeing the lure still caught in the mesh. Gary then reached down, and with authority, grabbed the fish from behind, over the top of his head, his thumb and forefinger expertly placed at the opening where the gills are to begin, and held the fish fast. The fish stopped its struggle, while Gary then reached for the cooler lid, took off this lid, dropped the fish in, and replaced the lid, while the fish began another struggle, bashing and thrashing around inside the cooler. But this time the struggle was somewhat muffled and now controlled in time and place. Both men sat down, but only after a hearty handshake, accompanied by the broadest grins this boat had seen today.

"I wondered if we were going to get that one, Gary. I really wondered."

"But you didn't sound that way, you crazy bugger. You didn't want to change the tension."

"Truth was, I was too scared to stop reeling for one second, even to change the tension."

"You didn't say that. Too excited I guess."

"Right on. It's been too long, Gary."

"Well, we got the bugger and I'm goin' to weigh it soon as it quietens down sum-more. Fan-fuckin'-tastic, Wally! The sucker's gotta be six to eight pounds."

"Yeah, I figured it was a keeper, more than a keeper by the way he was fighting."

"This calls for a drink, Wally. And some breakfast, too. How about eggs, some pee-meal, a wack of toast, but only, or course, after a caesar or two? I think I even got mushrooms to fry up. 'Sides, it's ten o'clock and all this work's got me hungry."

"Yeah, you earned it with the netting. Good job, Gary. It's about time you got one in the net considering all the fish you lost on me in the old days."

"You lyin' prick," Gary said. "It was your tendency to damn near winch the damn things into the boat before I could even find the bloody net that used to lose us those fish, that is, if you hadn't already set the hook so hard you damn near yanked the lure back into the boat before the poor fish even knew he'd bitten something."

They were both enjoying the morning, the laughter, the teasing, the triumph of catching a beauty when Gary pulled the cord, started the Evinrude, and pointed the boar toward his dock at the end of the bay. Up and down, up and down went the bow till it planed out and left them both sitting there smiling, as the little cedar strip sliced through the chop toward an old fashioned breakfast, to which Wally was looking forward. That is, until his mind returned to John Coliani, reminding Wally of the fish now lying quietly, lacking the energy to move much. For Wally had heard just this morning before leaving to drive up, that John was now in a coma, and back in intensive care, and on the critical list. Louise had called from the hospital, and Brenda had answered the phone and then upon hearing, had passed the phone to Wally.

"Do you want me to come to the hospital right now, Louise, the police officer, Gary Desfresnes, needs to talk with me today. He's an old friend and we were going to talk at his cottage for the day. But I could change the plans if you want."

It was quiet on the other end. He knew why. Finally, after giving her time, "Wally, you go ahead with your plans. I'll be okay at the hospital but I'll call and leave a message at your house if there's a change. Maybe you can do more good... by helping the policeman today. When are you coming back?"

"Oh, I'll be home this evening for sure, and I'll come right over to the hospital. And you have my cellular number now. Call me right away. Even if the damn thing doesn't work well up there, I will check my messages if I can find a high point of land where the phone works. Okay?"

"Yes, Wally. That's fine. I want to get to the hospital. They just called here. Bye now."

Wally and Brenda had talked. Wally said he felt like calling Gary and canceling. He knew, however, that Gary had really sounded like he wanted to talk to Wally. Brenda said that she would take the day off and go and sit with Louise and her mother at the hospital. Louise had sent the children down to Toronto. Frank, her brother had driven up to Beach Bay to pick them up. Louise wanted to be free to be at the hospital all of the time if she chose. Frank had said he would gladly look after the girls, get them to school, while Louise needed this time in Beach Bay.

It was now 10.05 in the morning. Louise was flipping through McLean's, not reading much of anything. Across from her was Emma, her mother-in-law, looking tired and beaten, as Louise thought she probably looked herself. Louise wondered what Emma was thinking about. Losing Albert, John's father, to cancer a couple of years ago? Worrying about John most likely.

Yes, Emma was worrying about John. And yes she was thinking also about Albert. But she was also thinking about herself, about what she had been living with and telling no one. That her cancer had metasticized into her liver. That the lymphoma everyone said was the easiest of the cancers to treat now appeared to be killing her. That she wondered if she'd made the right decision in saying no to all the radiation and chemo therapies. That she had decided not to undergo any of the suffering Albert had suffered in order to save his life. That Albert's suffering had been in vain anyway... he still died, probably no later than he would have died, had he not taken the treatments, which he himself said were at least as bad as the cancer. Only the morphine and its cousins whose names Emma could not right now even remember had helped a little, although she suspected the last dosages had actually hastened his death, but that was okay because the suffering, the pain toward the end was unbearable for him, and for her watching him die.

All alone in that hospital room, for hours at a time. She would not ever forget those days and weeks. It had been so lonely–his death had come as a relief when it came. No one sat with her. The nurses kept telling her to go home.

John was not even living in Beach Bay then; he was still in Toronto. Ultimately, she thought, we die as we live–alone. Hadn't she read that once somewhere a long time ago? Yes, she had been there with Albert but he was not conscious much of the time toward the end; he just lay there moaning. And she crying, listening to him die in pain.

She believed that younger folks are simply not aware that it always comes to this. She herself hadn't thought much about it before this; of that she was sure. Perhaps it was better than prolonging one's death, than dying ever so slowly, a little bit each day, in one of those places, one of those nursing homes where because you are old, you simply don't matter. She remembered the poster she saw once; in fact, it haunted her to this day, because of the visits she had made over the years to see one person or another in these desolate places. She had deliberately memorized the words out of boredom and because they so impressed her:

> *You are young; you are wise. You live in the houses we did. You have the jobs we had. The path is well worn. And it ends here – in a nursing home.*
>
> *This place is nothing, whatsoever, like home. But I can't do a thing about it. I'm not very well at all. That's why I am here.*
>
> *Do something about these places before your eyes grow dim. The path is well worn; you're on it, and it ends here.*
> Arnold Williams, age 87
> From a CUPE nursing home poster

Emma knew about death; she'd lost her mother and father long ago; and a brother, and a sister. And then Albert. And now, she was going to die. The doctor told her he couldn't say when but that since there was secondary cancer in the liver now, it would not be much longer than a year before she joined Albert. That's how she preferred to see it… going to Albert. But really, though she tried to take solace from this, she wasn't really sure she would ever see Albert again. She didn't really feel the reassurance she would like to feel. Her Christian hope was not as strong as it could have been. She resolved to talk about this to a priest the next time she went to confession. St. Paul may well have said that the greatest of the three was charity, rather than faith or hope, but right now what Emma needed was hope.

When she went to church every Sunday and said out loud that she believed in the resurrection of the body, she felt like a hypocrite for she did not really believe in the resurrection of the body. Wasn't Albert's body right now decomposing in the ground up at St. Mary's Cemetery? Wouldn't hers do the same dance with the worms a couple of years from now?

She hoped that if there were no resurrection for her, no reunion with Albert, there would at least be an end to pain of all kinds. No more suffering for Albert, no more for her, when her time came. She did not think much about purgatory, nor even of hell, thinking these were tales told to frighten uneducated people in the old days. She thought they were stupid tales now, and gave her religion a bad name. And this was sad because her religion was important to her. Not so much for its promises of life after death. No, because it told her how to live while alive. She always figured that those who lived by the teachings of their churches lived better lives, less unstable, less subject to the controls of their whims, their appetites. She preferred disciplined living. She liked having values which guided her in her marriage, in her raising of John, in her dealings with everyone.

So what had gone wrong? Why was John's marriage finished? It couldn't be the mixed marriage, the nonsense she was told about mixed marriages when she was a teenager herself. No. Here was this young woman, Louise, a good person, with a knack for family life, a skill with raising children, a seemingly good mother and wife, whose own religion, albeit not Roman Catholic like Emma's, but Anglican, was very important to Louise. Her own John had abandoned his own religion for some time but a priest had told her not to worry about this because when John came back to church it would be like he had made the decision for himself, not because his parents had made it for him at his Baptism. He had only started going back to church a few years ago.

No, there was nothing intrinsically wrong about theirs being a mixed marriage. They were both good people. Well brought up. Emma knew both of Louise's parents, and approved of both of them. Always had.

Emma thought she knew what had gone wrong. But she could never talk about it to Louise and to John. It was none of her business. They had to work this out for themselves. It was tough as a parent to watch two young people hurt each other and not be able to say anything for fear of being seen as intrusive in their marriage. They had the right to make their own mistakes. They weren't kids. They were adults with all the rights and all of the susceptibility to self-inflicted injuries. But Emma knew anyway, or so she thought, what the problem was.

But what she could not figure out was how this problem had come to be. For she and Albert had not taught John that career was more important than marriage. Than fatherhood, than being a husband. She did not know what Louise had been taught but she suspected that Louise's parents had lived for each other, for their children, in the same way that she and Albert had treasured their own relationship, their own family. So how had this business of career become so damned important that it had destroyed a perfectly good marriage, one made in heaven like all good marriages?

Emma loved Louise like a daughter but Emma was not stupid. She could see that for Louise, her lawyer work was very, very important. And for John, teaching was probably the same, although Emma realized as she thought about it that John did not seem as ambitious as Louise. He didn't seem, for example, to need promotions in education. In fact, his golf seemed more important to him that any vice-principal's position. She had heard that her John was a very well respected teacher and so she wondered why he hadn't chosen to pursue promotion through the educational hierarchy. But she didn't really care, as long as John was happy. She was proud of her son the high school teacher, as Albert had been proud, too.

But she had come to the conclusion that Louise's career was somehow at the heart of this marriage failure. She knew her son wasn't perfect, however. She wondered about his drinking, about all of the time he was with the guys on the damned golf course. She didn't really know what had precipitated the final separation, nor had she asked. She suffered it in silence, her heart breaking when John, and then Louise on another occasion, had told her this news she had never gotten over. She did not believe that either of them loved a third person.

At first she had worried about her granddaughters. But so far they had not seemed to be suffering any negative effects, though she could see how much they wanted their Daddy home again. They talked about it sometimes as if it were a possibility, as if Mommy and Daddy might still one day live together again. This always broke Emma's heart for she knew that lawyers had been involved and that papers had been sent back and forth. John would not have moved back to Beach Bay had there been any chance of reconciliation, or so she had concluded, and tried to accept.

Why couldn't young people see what was important in life? A job is still just a job, no matter how many names we try to hide it with, what was that word she learned just recently, yes, it was the perfect word for this... euphemisms... like the word "career". Fulfilment, happiness, such as they are available in this life, come from people surely. And the most important people are our marriage partners, Emma believed, and our children. One has to risk everything for that belief. "But, I guess, if the marriage fails we are very vulnerable," Emma thought. So people only make half commitments to each other, to their relationships. The world keeps telling us that only in our job successes are we of value. Prestige comes from our jobs, I guess, not from our marriages, not from our life as parents. Emma hated that.

She saw it as ironic that if you don't commit your entire life to your spouse, to your kids, the marriage, the family, both are likely doomed, she thought. And then folks are left trying to find happiness elsewhere. Emma thought that many people were very disillusioned in their jobs... with their bosses, their colleagues, with their clients.

Her thoughts rambled on as they did so often. And always she came to the same conclusions: any fulfillment has to be in raising our families for heaven's sake! God–we failed to show him this? How did we fail? We tried to live like this but they didn't buy into it, this younger generation. Did we make a mistake by encouraging them to get all of this education, by telling them to get more and more of it, so that they could get bigger and better jobs. Did we tell them without realizing it, that jobs are more important than we ourselves believed?

Are we at fault for their value systems more than we realize? Did we think we were teaching them one thing, but were really showing them something else? Was becoming a teacher, a lawyer as wonderful as we really thought it was? Is that how we really came across to them? Look at Louise, such a pretty daughter-in-law. I want to hug her, hold her, tell her I love her. Tell her that I wish she and John could try again. Not for the girls. The girls are okay. For each other. Tell her how hard it is to say goodbye forever to someone. It's too late for Albert and me now. But it's not too late for Louise and John. and damn it, I know they both love each other. I know things. I know they are hurting... living like this. These two deserve to be sat down and to be told what life is about. I don't care how old they both are! They need to be told what's important. What their hearts tell them!

Oh, it's not my place. I know that. I always have. I say nothing. I just cry inside for them. I want them to be happy. They are not happy. Is she happy with this lawyer's job? Does it turn her crank 52 weeks of the year, seven days a week, 24 hours a day. She may work most of those hours but I do not believe she's happy. What the hell is driving her? What the hell drives all of these young people? Why can't they see?

Do they think they need more cars, bigger houses, more cottages, more vacations? Is that what drives them all? Addictions all. But I don't believe that's true for Louise. She has her head screwed on right with this stuff. She believes in family, in marriage, in friendship, in loving and caring, in being a good person, in her God, in being a good Christian. So what the heck is going on? Maybe I don't know my son, not as a husband, not as a father. But he seems okay to me. What do I know? Maybe living with him is too much for Louise. I just don't know what the hell is wrong with these two. Maybe I am too tired now, too worried about John. Where are those damn doctors anyway? Why aren't they telling us something? Another case of, "No news is good news?" I'm not convinced.

And as if to reply to her accusation, into the waiting room strode a tired Dr. Louis Gilbere. "Good morning to you both," he said as both Louise and Emma jumped up involuntarily to hear the news. Dr. Gilbere waited for them both to be seated after he sat down facing them both, pulling a chair in front of them, thereby signaling that he wanted to chat with them.

"To get right to the point, John's carotid artery ruptured in the night. At a place immediately adjacent to where we repaired the artery in the early hours of Saturday morning. I had seen the additional weakness there but thought John had taken about enough surgery and anesthesia at that point and closed up the neck hoping that the weak area I did not repair would last for a while till he got stronger.

"Nature did not cooperate. The weak area let go in the night, or maybe even sooner. We can't be sure. He was hemorrhaging there for a period we cannot determine. But he lost enough blood by last night that the technology monitoring his vital signs rang the alarm.

"We have this morning gone into his neck, repaired the artery once again, and had a long look at its overall length. We decided against a simple repair this time and went for a complete bypass around the whole area damaged last Friday night. This is a brand new technique, this bypassing of the problem in the carotid artery. The hemorrhaging is now stopped. We have one major worry here. How long was he bleeding? That is, how much blood did he lose and for how long? Our worry comes down to this: Did John sustain brain damage from any loss of oxygen to the brain while he was hemorrhaging? That about sums up the crisis we have been dealing with since the early hours of this morning. Can I answer any questions for you?"

He did not get a chance because Emma fell on the floor. Neither Doctor Gilbere nor Louise could prevent her hitting her head on the terrazzo. But he was quick to respond after that, as was the nurse assistant who must have been standing just outside the waiting room door, because in another instant she was in there, too. And then the whole waiting room seemed full of medical personnel, nurses, orderlies, the doctor… and Louise had somehow been asked to step outside for a moment, where she was being held in the arms of Wally's wife Brenda, who somehow also arrived seemingly out of nowhere.

Louise found herself wondering if there were all a dream, no, a nightmare. But it was real, as she saw the stretcher wheeled rapidly down the hall, then Emma's body on it going in the direction from which the stretcher had come. She found herself eventually sitting down in the waiting room, drinking a glass of water given to her by a nurse, having her hand held by Brenda… Emma nowhere to be seen. Had Louise caught it all, or had she passed out? No, she hadn't fainted or anything. It all just happened too quickly.

After some moments – she didn't how many – she was talking quietly with Brenda. "She must have fainted, poor Dear, dealing with all of this stuff… John her only son… losing her own husband not all that long ago. Still, it was amazing how the staff reacted so dramatically to someone fainting. I had no idea that fainting could be such a matter for concern. Probably she'll be embarrassed now, and they'll be bringing her back in a minute or so."

But inside Brenda wondered if she had convinced herself… let alone Louise. Something was going on here that she felt queasy about inside. They weren't long waiting. An hour or so had gone by and then another doctor stood in front of them.

"You must be Mrs. Louise Coliani. I know who you are, Brenda."

"Hello, Gary. Louise this is Gary… I'm sorry… Dr. Gary Benjamin. He's a doctor here."

BEARE PARTS

All Louise could do was to force a smile and extend her hand. She said nothing.
"Mrs. Coliani. Would you be up to coming along with me to see your mother-in-law now? She is recovered and wants to speak with you. I have been speaking with her. I have been treating... uh, working with Emma for a while now. She is my patient."
Brenda's face turned colour. She looked down at the floor so that Louise would not notice her feelings of terror. Gary Benjamin was Beach Bay's one and only oncologist. Seeing him usually meant one thing... the big "C." Before she could worry long about Louise's powers of observation, Louise had walked off with Gary, and was headed in the direction of wherever they had taken Mrs. Coliani.
Brenda sat down in one of the black vinyl chairs, wished she still smoked, decided against going to get a coffee, but jumped up quickly and went running for a phone.
The stupid cellular phone will likely fail now, she thought to herself. Shit. I want to talk to Wally. These bloody phones. She never understood how the CRTC had ever allowed the use of the damn things. The public was being ripped off. The things malfunctioned more than they worked. More calls were lost all over the place. Didn't seem to matter how many towers were erected. Whether it was Bell or Cantel, the service was less than adequate. Yet the CRTC allowed the damn things in the marketplace.
Her own company was making big money on them. People in Toronto were the biggest and first market for them in Canada. Yet she knew that customers were complaining about losing calls even on Yonge Street. Still the damn things had spread, were spreading... no matter the complaints from customers... like a fungus all over the country.
She dialed the number and was soon listening to "the customer you are calling is not available at this time." She cursed to herself. She tried again. It was not what she wanted to hear. The second time she heard Wally's voice asking her to leave a message and he would get back as soon as possible. This was at least a chance of getting hold of him. So she pleaded an urgent message into the mouthpiece,

to the effect that he should call her immediately at the hospital; she was in the waiting room on the fourth floor.

By the time she made it back to the waiting room, she was wondering about the futility of trying to get Wally in this way. But she was wrong. For a nurse came in; it was a friend of Brenda's from the curling league.

"Hi Brenda. You look like you could use a friend. Your hubby's on the phone down at my desk. Come with me."

"Thanks, Janie. I need a friend and a drink, and my husband right now. Men. They're never around when we need them." She tried to use humour to lessen the feelings of anxiety she was experiencing, and the hot flashes. Brenda was going through menopause.

"Hi, what's up?"

"Wally." Brenda began to cry.

"What's happening? Brenda are you there? I can't hear anything. These damn phones..."

"Wally... please come here right away. Emma is sick now. John has been hemorrhaging. Louise is with Emma. I need you here now."

"I'm on my way, Honey. I will be there in two hours, maybe less. Are you okay?"

"No. I am upset right now. Even with myself. Maybe I am overreacting. I don't know. I just found out that Emma is under the care of Dr. Benjamin. And she collapsed in the waiting room in front of Louise. Maybe I am worrying about nothing. But I wish you were here with me. I don't like the feel of everything here today. I need you, Wally."

The phone was breaking up. "Brenda... listen... we can talk when I get there. Hang in there. I am on my way. I have to hang this damn thing up now before I throw it."

The click was followed by Wally's looking into the face of a sympathetic Gary Desfresnes. "Now it's Coli's mother; she's collapsed. I better get home, Gar."

And at the hospital the click was followed by Brenda's stare at a very white-faced Louise who was coming toward her.

"Brenda! Can this be happening?"

"I'm afraid it seems to be, honey." She hugged Louise. And held her tightly.

"I could not see her, Brenda. Some medical people were in there with her and Doctor Benjamin said something like, okay, I could see her in a little while but he thought that he and I had better talk a little bit first.

"He asked me what I knew of Emma's condition and I told him I knew nothing about any condition. He asked me if I thought her son knew the score and I said that I did not think so and told the doctor we had been separated. Benjamin seemed to know that. What he did not know, he said, was whether his patient was handling her own problems entirely by herself. He then left me for about half an hour in some office and came back to tell me he had just had another discussion with Emma and that she was almost ready to see me now but that he wanted another 15 minutes with me first.

"Then he spilled the beans. Emma has cancer in her liver. It began as lymphoma but has spread into her liver now. Evidently she has been seeing him about this lymphoma for years and only her husband Albert knew that. She had sworn him to secrecy when she first heard, had refused any treatment for it, and evidently it had gone into some kind of remission totally on its own. But since Albert's death, it has resurfaced as full blown liver cancer evidently, and this development came only recently.

"She has steadfastly refused any treatment. She did not, does not, want to go through any of the effects that Albert went through from his treatment... all for nothing, or so she believes. She is convinced that Albert was not helped at all, but in fact was made to suffer more by submitting to treatment. She views chemo therapy as a kind of modern blood letting the doctor told me. She just wants nature, as she calls it, to take its course, and to be no burden to anyone. Also, if it is her time to die, she has this powerful hope that she will be with her Albert again. And so she is only a little bit afraid of death. All this Doctor Benjamin told me while I must have turned white because he kept asking me if I was okay. Which I was not, am not!

"Evidently, Emma gave him permission to tell me what she could not tell me herself. What she could not, would not even tell her only son. Now she is scared of losing John, of dying herself, and of not saying goodbyes to anyone. So she allowed Doctor Benjamin to tell me. I am going to see her for myself as soon as the medical people get out of her room. They came back in again just when Benjamin and I finished talking. So I came down here. To walk maybe. To get hold of myself. I don't know why. Maybe to ask you if this was happening. Is it just a nightmare? I don't know where to go and sit, whether to talk, to cry, to yell, to scream. I feel like I'm part of a scene in the book of Job!

"How the hell can I talk to her now? I can't. I will start bawling like a baby." And Louise Coliani did start to cry, with huge wracking sobs, while Brenda held her trembling shaking shoulders yet again. "And what's worse, I can't help thinking that I am partly responsible, because breaking up with John has probably brought this cancer out of remission."

"Mrs. Coliani would like to see you now," said the voice in the white uniform. Brenda released her hug. Louise just stared at the nurse. Finally, "Okay. I'm coming. God help me."

"I will walk down the hall with you but leave you at Emma's room," Brenda said. "I'll pray that you get through your talk with her. That it will be okay, honey."

Louise went into the room to find Emma smiling at her, her head propped up on pillows. "I'm so sorry," was all Louise could say as she took the hand offered her and broke into the very crying she was trying to avoid.

"It's okay, Louise. I mean it's okay to cry. I've done a little of that myself, as well as a hell of a lot of cursing, too. But it's okay. Go ahead and cry. I'm okay with that. In fact, other than this damn soreness in my abdomen, I'm okay with everything right now. I am ready for whatever. Honest, honey, I am. Except for a couple of things. Like saying goodbye to John, your girls, and you, but we will have plenty of time for that if only John…"

And Louise cried harder. But they eventually talked and Louise was told again why Emma had made the decisions she had made about her own illness, about why she had refused treatment, but Louise could not accept Emma's not telling John or her about how sick she really was. It only made Louise feel guilty that Emma had concluded that John and she had enough on their plates without knowing of Emma's illness. Louise asked whether Emma would have shared the news had John and she not separated.

"Honey, all I can do is guess at that. I don't know how else I would have handled the news. I only know I wanted to talk to no one about it. Your circumstances–your relationship with John–I don't know what it would have been like had it been otherwise – I can't say for sure – I only know that I had to deal with it my own way when I found out – aybe I was a little crazy I don't know – I missed Albert – wasn't even close to coming to terms with his going when I found out–and I don't know… it just didn't seem right to tell John either. I knew he was in pain over losing you, his kids… I don't want to talk about that. It is not my business and I do not want to ever appear as the meddling mother-in-law, Louise. I have tried… am trying… very hard to respect whatever decisions you and John made… make… as a married couple. I hope I have enough understanding to know that two adults must make their own decisions without interference from interfering in-laws… parents who can't let go of their children and let them have their own lives. Anyway, that's past.

"I'm sorry if I didn't handle it right but I did what I could do. And now… I only want my John to have the rest of his life… to see his children raised… to have some happiness… you, too, honey, to have some peace and joy… whatever way it works out for you. I want my John to get better, dammit, is that too much to ask?"

And she started to cry now. They were both crying until the energy of it all was spent. Grief sustained its own storm-like intensity for as long as it needed to and then the waves diminished, the ocean slowed down a bit, the wind abated.

"Do you want me to get you anything? A glass of water, or anything like that? A drink… "An exhausted Louise was trying to come back from the storm.

"No. I'm okay now. Just some Kleenex if you will... I am not going to be in here long, I'm told. I will be released probably today or tomorrow. I only collapsed because of the stress of John. I am going to go on with my life for a while, until I must go. But it's not so bad right now. I am going to get a morphine pump they tell me. I guess it'll get worse, but right now there's just discomfort in my abdomen quite a bit and some pain, for which I take Tylenol Three. And evidently I can still take all the Tylenol I want to. Codeine is bothering my bowel, however, so I have to take a stool softener, but really, Louise, I want you not to worry about me too much right now. John is the one we must pray hard for."

Louise stayed beside Emma and held her hand for an hour or so before she felt a little bit of hunger and then the lunch tray was brought into the room by a Filipino lady whose smile, thought Louise, if it could be bottled, would be as effective as any tranquilizer to pick up the most depressed of spirits.

"Why don't you go get yourself a bite now, Louise, and see what you can find out about John?" The truth was, Emma too was exhausted now, and she wanted to close her eyes for a minute or two ... maybe even say a prayer or two for John. Why aren't they saying anything to us now, she wondered. She wanted some news.

"Maybe I will. Besides I want to tell Brenda to go home. Or to work. She has been sitting all morning trying to be there for me." After making sure that Emma's lunch tray was as conveniently placed as it could be within Emma's reach, and after giving both of Emma's hands a gentle squeeze, Louise left the room. Louise was scared now of adding to Emma's pain by hugging her too tightly. She realized that she would have to say something to her girls at home about Nanna now, about not hugging Nanna too tightly. But what would she say to them? How much would she tell them now?

Thinking about such questions, and then entering the hallway, Louise found Brenda still waiting with loving eyes for Louise to resurrect from the tomb which Emma's room had become in Brenda's eyes.

BEARE PARTS

In another hospital, this one in Southern Ontario, a man was taking very seriously one of the corporal works of mercy – he was going to visit the sick. Anyone suffering from such intense anxiety as Barry McDevitt was indeed sick. Or so this Oriental man chuckled inside his head. His role, as he saw it, was to comfort the afflicted. He would play the doctor to the patient. But he would pretend otherwise for he was now dressed in a patient's gown himself.

And he laughed again in his head. As he put on the standard issue hospital robe, he commended himself for bringing the paper bag which held the medicine he intended to prescribe for his patient. All free for the needy patient – isn't the Canadian health care system wonderful, he chuckled almost out loud – even if he doesn't have a drug plan laughed the hospital visitor who pretended to check the numbers on the walls as if to find where an old friend might now be residing in his sickly state, poor fellow.

He smiled at the nurse's aid who glanced at him walking calmly down the hallway, without a care. He pretended to be someone who was just about to be sent home from the prison every hospital becomes for those who have recovered.

Ah, it was grand to help those in need – Mr. McDevitt was in need? No problem. Worried about something? I will help you, chuckled this quiet man with bagfuls of reassurance about the necessity of his mission today.

So McDevitt and Harris were worried about exposure, about the heat from the stupid RCMP, were they? Didn't I already solve the problem for poor old Mr. Harris? 13 stabs did it just nicely! He worries about nothing now. Imagine. Both of them about to wimp out and sing long songs to the RCMP. To protect their own necks.

But "Doctor" Fong had spotted the signs even before they stupidly told him about their plan, and had idiotically tried to include him. They were ever this dense, but having seen such signs before, he had competently handled the problem on instruction from his masters.

Of course, these two idiots knew little of Jean-Guy's real service to the enterprise. Actually, he usually played the part of a frightened go-between who only did this kind of work part-time for the extra money it provided his family. Sometimes he made out that he was a poorly paid silly servant with children to feed. Having them see him in this way gave him a hand to play when he sometimes had to play the hand of surprise.

Thinking he might want to join with them, they spilled their reeking guts to him one weekend not very long ago. In fact, two weekends ago. They had wanted to negotiate a deal with the guardians of justice. That's what they were proposing. Sell out while there was something to sell.

But they had deliberated. They had hesitated. They had pondered the possibilities. And Jean-Guy liked to sing a little bit himself. Not in the shower so much, but sometimes when it pleased others to hear his songs of loyalty, of gratitude. And so he did–to his principals. And he liked his principals. They had introduced Jean-Guy to a lifestyle to which he had grown very "accustomed". The good life. Flying here and there. The best of restaurants. In fact, the best of everything. More than a taste of honey – a veritable daily banquet of honey.

When told about the anxiety attacks of Misters Harris and McDevitt, the Principals had been quick with instructions. Put them out of their misery before it could spread. Both of them, and soon. His salary would be increased for his trouble. Plus a bonus. Ah, why not make it a whole weekend of work, Jean-Guy had thought. A trip to Beach Bay on the Friday night. Get rid of that poor unfortunate meddling teacher guy who might have heard what he should not have heard one night in the basement of a Beach Bay restaurant. Jean-guy was not sure what the fellow had heard. But he was indeed sure that chances could not be taken.

Risks were sometimes good and sometimes stupid. This guy was certainly adept at sidestepping on-coming cars, even those without headlights. The hit and run idea hadn't worked? Well, a more direct approach would be taken. And then back to Toronto the same night to Old Harris' place and… child's play it would be. All in a weekend's

BEARE PARTS

work and then out West on the Monday.
The heat was too high for his Ontario suppliers? Jean-Guy would turn down the thermostat for them. Their body thermostats. He would remove them from the enterprise; he would be enterprising. He would give them the cool dark spaces which have about them that earthy smell, and that refreshing dampness where none do there embrace. Isn't there a poem that goes something like that from somewhere in my high school days, he wondered?

On his own initiative he had taken proper care of Mr. Coliani in Beach Bay. The teacher had fallen heavily to the floor, his neck cut properly, blood going all over the place. No need to linger. Jean-Guy had not dallied. His exit had been swift, just before the teacher was to have an apparent visitor. For the visitor had been spotted strolling toward the cottage and Jean-Guy, not wanting to hang around in the dark and possibly have to treat another patient he had not counted on treating, decided to bolt.

He had run out the door and jumped into his car before getting the guy's card, without getting a good enough look at the guy to see if he could be recognized. The guy had clearly seen Jean-Guy jump into his car. Nothing could be done about that now. But the visitor had seemed more interested at this point at running into the cottage than in making the acquaintance of the ever affable and polite "Doctor" Fong, who was immediately speeding away from the patient's residence. Ah, I must be one of the few doctors who still make house calls, this "doctor" had laughed to himself.

The very next day, compliance with Jean-Guy's orders took the form of 13 knife wounds to poor old Mr. Harris, who did not even moan after the sixth one. Not so easy with McDevitt, who had returned to his regular weekend rendezvous with Old Harris with more than bear parts last weekend. McDevitt had come with some kind of a black jack under his coat which Jean-Guy had not prepared for. And after only three stabs at McDevitt in old Harris' basement work room, McDevitt, the plucky little fellow, had swung hard at Jean-Guy and managed to hit him on the arm, the shoulder and the... damn it... the head, which still smarted quite a bit, fucking little prick, before running up the stairs and into the Saturday night air.

Must have been some great anxiety attack which the youngster had been suffering again. But these attacks would soon trouble him no longer. Especially now that Doctor Fong had established the routine of the police officer on duty–a bathroom break each day at mid-morning and mid-afternoon. And, of course, there were the trips to the payphone when he called in to his superiors, sometimes even strolling down to the cafeteria to buy a coffee.

Jean-Guy had seen the relaxed attitude with which this policeman did his job. 'You deserve a break today' was very much a part of this guy's outlook. And when he took his break this morning, well, Jean-Guy intended to avail himself of the opportunity such a break provided–to give the enterprise a bigger break by eliminating one of its former employees, who had decided he wanted to become a choir boy and sing, sing, sing his way to peace of mind.

Jean-Guy pretended indifference to the policeman calmly walking past him, who did not even seem to notice this patient, dressed in his patient's gown. This time things would be different. Mr. McDevitt had inflicted some damage last time.

So what if this poor patient had needed two treatments… if the always thorough "Doctor" Fong needed two appointments to bring closure to this case… for sure, the treatment would be completed today. Mr. Coliani had also needed two treatments and those he had been granted, chuckled "Doctor" Fong.

And so it was with great excitement that he turned the door knob and entered the room of his younger and former colleague, whose staring eyes now bespoke real terror. These are not words of welcome, chuckled Doctor Fong to himself as he sprang to the bedside, grabbed a pillow and quickly, oh so quickly, had it placed over the top of his patient's head, before the patient could do a hell of a lot of anything. And almost as quickly the medicine was out of the paper bag, his favourite surgical implement for healing the sick.

Attempting to hold the struggling McDevitt still, with the pillow jammed over his head to stop his screams from going anywhere, while stabbing the knife into him, was proving more taxing than

"Doctor" Fong had anticipated. Had McDevitt not been so seriously stabbed from his last encounter with Fong, he might well have successfully wriggled free from the hold Fong now had on him with the pillow. Indeed, given the three stab wounds from the previous weekend the patient proved remarkably strong under the pillow and nearly got the pillow from off his head.

He did manage one scream but Fong had the pillow back in place and was now stabbing randomly at the writhing body fighting so valiantly for its life. Where the knife was entering could not be accurately determined because of the confusion of the victim's desperate movements under the sheets and coverlet. Fong would have preferred to strip the bed covers to see how effectively he was doing his job but there had been no time and even less cooperation from the uncooperative Mr. McDevitt.

Suddenly his hurried musings were interrupted, as was his bloody work.

As it happened, there were other medical practitioners who wanted to see Barry McDevitt at precisely this same time and it was a group of them who saw much more than they expected when they entered into Mr. McDevitt's room: blood all over the patient's bed.

"Doctor" Fong was quicker to respond than they were, pushing the shocked nurse out of the way, her clipboard falling to the floor as she joined it there, losing her balance, Fong slashing with his knife at the intern who tried to prevent his exit, drawing blood from an arm, another very young doctor standing staring... completely immobilized by these proceedings, as if these were merely chimeric, a show laid on for his tired eyes, the sheer craziness of killing in a place dedicated to the protection of the living, Fong out the door, and almost down the hall and around the corner, with words shouted at his back.

"He tried to kill the patient," yelled by someone to the policeman now striding toward them, coffee in hand, from the other direction. The coffee dropped to the floor, and, surprise, surprise, the officer did not pursue immediately but instead, did what ultimately tuned out to be exactly what he should have done... he instructed a nurse to call for back-up. She ran to a nursing station, picked up the phone and reported to the policeman's division what she thought had just happened. And by now the policeman had run off into the direction into which the runner had left. About his having gone for coffee, he could only give so much time to right now. There would be time for guilt and worry later.

Fong was down the exit stairs two and three and four at a time, knife still in hand. A Filipino cleaning fellow had no time to be terrified, so fast did Jean-Guy Fong pass him on his way to the parking lot, and to his waiting Honda Accord EXR. Out of the lot, smashing the barrier arm as it lay in a horizontal position, and onto the street, and go man go he thought to himself. That was close. But what's this?

Sirens. Cruisers. Three of them behind him as he sped down University Avenue. Shit. Two more across the road in front of him ahead. One of them an RCMP car. Gotta run for it. No chance to drive away this time. I can run. Watch me gentlemen. And you will never keep up with me. And as he ran, the car left idling on the sidewalk on University, he marveled at how fast he was, until the crack, and the burning in his back and the concrete taking the skin off his forehead, cheeks, hands, and his teeth smashed by something he didn't know what, and the pain in his shins hitting the parking meter and it was pain like pins in the backs of his eyes all over for what seemed so quick and then… nothing.

It was all so fast. Terrifyingly fast. Simple. Final. Jean-Guy Fong lay dead on the sidewalk concrete with his neck on the curb, his face on the asphalt. Blood trickled out of his mouth, and out of his chest. The two red pools forming were strangely conspicuous on the beige-grey of the concrete. The fine thread between a life and a death had been broken again. This time at the corner of Adelaide Street and University Avenue in downtown Toronto.

The commotion forming now of running police officers, curious pedestrians, the sausage on a bun guy with his little cart, gawking motorists, all seeming to wait for the same take-charge authority being witnessed at a hospital not far from this scene, as Barry

McDevitt was being rushed into a surgical amphitheater. As ambulances pulled up to the curb on Adelaide, soon to discover that here there was no longer any real urgency, another medical team was hoping that haste and skill would save the life of a man stabbed repeatedly... while recovering from a stabbing he had experienced only six days previously.

And in yet another hospital, in fact in Beach Bay, Ontario, another victim of a stabbing was waking up with an appetite.
Louise was summoned by a nurse, told that Mr. Coliani was asking for her and for something to eat. Emotions work like a yo-yo at times, or like a teeter totter. Tears of joy came down her face when she heard these words. The nurse asked her if she needed anything, and she said, "No, you've just now given me more than I was hoping for. Can I see him right now?"
"Yes, that's why I came to get you. Come along."
Louise had been sitting with Brenda in the same old waiting room, which was now getting very familiar to her. She had seen a great deal of it lately. They had some lunch in the cafeteria, looked in on Emma afterwards and found her sleeping, and so came back to the waiting room, where they waited for news, and for Wally's return from Lake Timachi. Brenda had not wanted to leave Louise who said she'd be okay if Brenda wanted to go to work now.
This was fantastic news. Before Louise saw Wally, who was now in the hospital elevator, she was off down the hall to see John, asking the nurse all kinds of questions.
"What can I expect?"
"Well, the doctor sent me to get you. He has been sitting with Mr. Coliani since the wee hours of this morning. He knows better what you can expect. But I have been in the room myself and John... Mr. Coliani... seems aware... no apparent – and I stress apparent, because it may still show itself – brain damage from the hemorrhaging and the oxygen deprivation... he may have been very lucky... in fact, miraculously lucky... but I don't want to say too much for fear of getting your hopes too high. You had better speak with the doctor.

"Certainly you can expect the apparatus of modern medical technology to be all around your... er, husband... ex-husband? He is getting blood to replace what he hemorrhaged. He was getting oxygen, too, although I think they have stopped that now that he has awakened. Anyway, you will soon see for yourself. But things do seem better and I suspect that some of this crisis is over. Again, however, wait for the doctor to really fill you in."

And they were now outside a room in critical care. The nurse knocked on the door and then opened it, asking Louise to wait for a moment in the hallway until she came back to get her.

It wasn't long before Doctor Gilbere stepped out into the hall and said, "Hi." He looked tired, but he smiled nonetheless. "The worst is over," I hope. "The operation on his carotid artery that we did early this morning seems to have been successful. There would not appear to be any hemorrhaging at present. Most importantly, he was conscious and alert for a minute, responding appropriately to all of our questions. I am hopeful there has been no brain damage.

"He is asking for something to eat which is a wonderful sign. But he is also very sleepy and has fallen back asleep. We will feed him later. Also, he asked for you. In fact, he almost pleaded to see you and so we sent for you but, as I say, he has gone back to sleep and he will do that all today and likely tonight, but you can sit with him if you wish and he will sometimes awaken and it would probably be good if he saw you sitting there."

The doctor looked away. He wanted to let her react privately, in her head, to what he was telling her, advising her in fact. He was uncomfortable saying any of this to her but he knew how important her presence would be at the bedside as John regained full consciousness.

"Doctor Gilbere. I really do want to be there beside him." As if she could sense his unease at asking this of her she added quickly, "This is no chore for me. It's what I most want." And the tears flowed again, even against her wishes. Again, the doctor looked away.

Gently, he said, "Good. Well, let's go in then, shall we?"

But she wasn't as prepared for what she saw as she thought she'd be. John no longer had a neck. He was that swollen. Plus... there were so many hoses and pipes stuck into his body from the neck up that it was almost difficult to form a complete image of his facial features, such as they were.

Louise steeled herself not to cry again. It would have been all right had she cried. Perhaps even better than holding the flood in. For John's eyes were closed again and he seemed lost in a deep sleep. Her immediate fear was that he would not wake from this sleep. But as if sensing her anxiety Doctor Gilbere spoke, "The drugs are very powerful, and John is resting as we want him to, but he will waken periodically, for these drugs provide only a very fitful sleep. That, too, is what we want to see... him waking now and then so we can more accurately check for vital signs. It will be good for his eyes to see you here when he wakes. That kind of medicine is as powerful as any we have to aid his recovery." It was as if he knew quite a bit about the relationship John and Louise might provide for each other. How much had John told Doctor Gilbere Louise wondered.

"I must leave you both now. Nurses will be in and out of here all of the time. And I won't be far. I'm in the hospital most of the day today." All of a sudden he squeezed her hand, and looked directly into her eyes, and Louise thought she could see the faintest twinkle of a tear there. She knew then how hard this doctor was trying to save her husband's life, how much of himself he had invested in the continuing existence of one John Coliani.

When the doctor had left the room Louise was sorry that she hadn't grabbed him and hugged him the most expressive thank you she could muster but the energy simply wasn't there. She needed all of it just to keep from passing out with fear; the crying had been very draining.

It was enough of a chore right now to decide whether to stand by his bedside, or to sit in the chair in the corner. It took her a full four minutes or so just trying to find the answer to this when it occurred to her that it would likely be okay if she moved the chair closer to John's bedside and sat there holding his hand. So slowly did her mind function now as she became aware of the noises made by the various apparatus in the room, and in the background, coming now more to the foreground, John's laboured breathing.

She was not aware of falling off to sleep herself. But that's what she did. So she did not see the look on John's face when he opened his eyes and saw her sitting there, sleeping in the chair with her hand on the bed so close to his. In her own sleep she had lost her grip on his hand but their hands lay close together. John could see her hand on his bed and it was enough for him before he, too, fell fast asleep again, not really conscious enough yet to know whether he had only dreamt her there beside him.

"Well, someone's catching up on some sleep." These words made Louise stir some two hours after she first sat down beside the bed. It was a nurse gently waking Louise, who now opened her eyes with some embarrassment, rubbed them, and tried to stifle the yawn.

"Oh, I didn't mean to sleep like that but I guess I just couldn't help it."

"That's just fine, Mrs. Coliani. Don't you fret about it. We have all been watching you rest for a while now. Jealously. I wanted to join you!" She chuckled then. Louise could see a nametag on the RN uniform. "Mrs. Sandra Gaylord" was the name on the tag. She was a large lady, but instantly likeable.

"Actually, I wouldn't have wakened you even now except that we have to do some things for your husband now, and we are about to wake him, too. Did you know he has already awakened at least a couple of times and knows you're here?"

"No! Darn it! And me asleep! I wanted to be there for him when he woke."

"Oh, but you were. I was in the room for two of these wake-ups and I saw him smile at you the second time. That, believe me, is a very good sign. He is sleeping and not comatose. As the drug dosage lessens with the doctor's orders, he will sleep less. But rest was the first order of today for Mr. Coliani so the drug dosage has done its job well."

"When will he be out of danger?"

"When he is moved from ICU and no longer in critical care will be a good sign that he is out of immediate danger. I suspect that Doctor Gilbere and the rest of the team want to make sure that John's carotid artery isn't going to act up again before they release him into a recovery room.

"But the signs have been good. We're going to do some more checking now, and we are gong to have to ask you to wait in the waiting room for us to compete our procedures. Don't be concerned. These are normal protocols."

Louise began making for the door but her progress was arrested by the entry of two more ladies in uniform and a man in white she had not seen before, another doctor or a male nurse, she wasn't sure. Eventually she cleared the doorway and made her way to the waiting room. When she heard the beeping behind her coming from John's room she got very scared and was stopped dead in her footsteps but the male she hadn't recognized now came toward her on his way somewhere else.

The look of terror on her face made him pause and say, "Hi. I was John's anesthetist during surgery. Frank O'Connor. Myself and Doctor Gilbere are responsible for the drugs he's being given now to help him rest. I just dropped by now and he's doing fine. In fact so well, that I didn't need to hang around."

"What is that beeping in there now?"

"Oh, those noises often go off whenever equipment is adjusted or fiddled with. We don't even notice them but I suppose you folks who don't work in hospitals do. Not to worry. I just saw him and he's doing remarkably well. My recommendation at the team meeting this evening is going to be for release into a recovery room.

"Now that's only one opinion among quite a few on the team. And I don't want to get your hopes up and then dashed again if it doesn't quite happen like that but you look as if you yourself could use some encouragement."

Louise broke down again and was angry inside that she wept now uncontrollably in front of a perfect stranger who was trying to console her.

"Was it something I said?" he uttered quite mirthfully, when it appeared that she had regained control and a smile seemed trying to force its way onto her face. His joviality worked almost instantly, defusing her tension, her tears, and forcing that grin onto her face. Without warning she hugged this tall man she had never seen before, still sorry that she hadn't done the same to Doctor Gilbere.

"Are you the only lawyer in Ontario with real emotions?" he joked. He knew more about her than she knew about him obviously. She realized quickly that these people did their homework.

"I wouldn't talk," she joked back. "Many in your profession don't exactly wear their hearts on their sleeves." Where did she find the strength for this repartee, she suddenly found herself wondering.

"Too true. Too true. But we're changing. Holistic medicine and all that jazz. Or is it better public relations the better to ward you people off with your lawsuits every time we screw up? Anyway we're changing. Soon we are going to be taking mandatory courses in bedside manners again." And he laughed at his own words. But his strategy continued to have its effect on Louise. She was lightening up. He could see it in her face. The tears and the shaking had stopped. And he thanked heaven for his sense of humour which got him out of many a fragile moment such as this.

Doctor O'Connor went on, "And I'm even working on punctuality these days, which is why I am going to have to terminate this wonderful conversation with a sharp Toronto lawyer. But I am glad to meet you, Mrs. Coliani, and who knows, maybe you'll even defend me for a reasonable fee my insurance company can afford at my next malpractice trial?"

Louise smiled back at him. His levity was infectious. "There are some cases no lawyer can win I warn you." She could not believe she was enjoying this teasing, relishing the release from all of the dread and anxiety whose spell she had been under for so many hours.

"I'm sure we'll meet again before your husband is out of here." With these words he left her as he strode down the hall, a big lanky guy with arms swinging, and joyful exuberance in his gait. One of the nurses at the desk looked up and smiled at Louise. This nurse had been listening to the exchange between Louise and Doctor

O'Connor. It seemed as if she had almost been a part of the encounter. So Louise did not hesitate to ask,

"Where does he get this joy? This energy? This enthusiasm? He is like a spring breeze. Or what I remember about summer holidays on the last day of June."

"We ask ourselves the same question often. He's discussed often in the staff room, over coffee. His wife is dying of breast cancer and they are very much in love! They have two small kids."

Louise took this in, stunned by the news. "You just never know. That's amazing. He's amazing." But the nurse had to answer a phone and Louise walked on toward the waiting room where she found Brenda fast asleep on Wally's shoulder. Wally was skimming a magazine.

"Well, hello there," Wally said. "Are you surviving?"

"Barely. No, actually, I'm okay now. Tears are a tonic at times and God knows I've had many of those this morning, Wally. I see Brenda has taken the count. Why not take her home for some rest now?" At this Brenda woke up.

"Some friend I am, asleep here. What's the news?"

"Well, Brenda. You're as good a friend as I am a wife," and she was sorry she had blurted this out because it seemed to say more than she intended at this point. By way of self-correction, she quickly added: "I, too, fell asleep, with my head on John's bed. Apparently he woke up and saw me sleeping there and went back to sleep himself. Apparently, he even smiled. And the nurse said he's doing well. And the bleeding has stopped, and there doesn't seem to be any brain damage. And he may be moved out of intensive care this evening, and…"

The tears just burst all over her face when her voice broke, shifted gears and went into a loud sobbing. Her body was instantly shaking and Wally and Brenda were both quickly on their feet. Brenda put her arms tightly around Louise and was crying herself. Wally could only stand back and watch, as the tears came over his own face, as he realized that his friend John might just make it.

Louise finally convinced Wally and Brenda to go home. She

wanted to be alone anyway, trying to figure out what she wanted from life at this point. Of this, she was now quite sure. She was still very much in love with John Coliani. Her first order of business when she returned to Toronto – and she was anxious now about how long she could put that off – her job now seemed to be only that – a job – would be to fire her lawyer and to stop the whole divorce proceedings, no matter what John decided he wanted to do. Of this Louise was certain, if John were willing to get their marriage back togther, she certainly wanted the same thing. And she knew that her girls wanted the same thing. If nothing else came of this crisis in their lives, this was indeed a good thing – Louise discovered that she still loved her husband and she must have been insane to be thinking of spending the rest of her life without him. Hadn't she already had enough of the loneliness? Hadn't she already figured out that there was no one else she wanted to be with?

And when she went back into John's room and he was awake the first thing she told him after her hello, was "John, I really want to hug you but I am afraid to touch you with all of those contraptions sticking out of you. But I want my hug to say I miss you. I love you. I want to marry you again. I want this craziness of divorce proceedings to stop immediately. I will even give up my position in Toronto and move up here if you want me to. I just want to love you forever, be your wife again, and help you get better." And the tears flowed again. And from John's eyes the same tears of joy.

"But right now I do not want you to feel any pressure to decide anything. I just want you to get better. Don't say anything, John. I can wait for you to tell me if you want us to be married again."

And she knew she had told one hell of a lie in those words but knew as well that she had to say something like that to give John his space.

"Lou, I love you. I want you back. Wherever we live our lives." And he started crying again, and the doctor walked in now.

"I'm sorry. I will come back in a bit." And the doctor left.

"Louise, before this last emergency with my arteries, I had come to realize that when we were still together in Toronto, I worried more about my golf handicap than about being a husband to you. I took more pleasure from booze than I did from our marriage, from our own children. I no longer deserved either them or you. Maybe I had to come up North by myself to figure out what was important to me.

"I even prayed to God to help me to undo some of the damage I may have done to our girls by taking my own faith in God so for granted. What a stupid role model I have been to them, at a time when they are so impressionable."

"John, don't berate yourself like this."

"No, wait, Lou, let me finish, while I have the courage to tell you what I have to tell you, so that I can also admit these things to myself in the process. It's as if you are a witness to what I have to say to myself...

"I know that I never focused as much on being as good a husband and father as I ought to have. I know that there were times when I gave you the message that my buddies were more important that you were, that golf was more important than my family. And... it was. I was an asshole. I lost my way...

"I have always been too self-absorbed to be much good at loving..." And John could not talk now. He was sobbing. But Louise knew enough to say nothing. She just held his hand and let him regain his control.

"I was too damn interested in so many other things like spending money, buying toys, accumulating things, establishing a reputation as a good teacher, and my damn golf game. It is almost laughable now how important that stupid handicap was. If only that energy had gone more into my responsibilities as a father, as a role model. In my own confusion, I could not help the girls adopt the values you and I used to speak of when we were courting, Lou. Family fun. Caring for each other. Affirming each other. Believing in each other.

"I feel so badly, Lou, that I may well have pushed you into the arms of that guy..." And he could say no more, except, "I lost your love myself."

"John, you never lost my love. But I thought I'd lost yours. And that guy never meant anything to me, then or now. That's as honest as I can be. It was just a stupid mistake, made when I was... very tired, yes... confused, perhaps...stupid, for sure. I do not know to this day why I did that."

"It has never been a temptation since. It was not a temptation before that night. It just happened. And I am also the one with so damn much guilt because of it. If only we could just forgive each other and heal each other now. And get on with loving each other, and our girls, who are so very precious to both of us. And who need us together, of that I am quite sure."

"Lou, I want to be married to you again. Now. I will live anywhere with you, Toronto, Nairobi, here. I don't care. I want to try again."

And so they agreed to do exactly that. And Louise was John's best medicine and he hers for the rest of his stay in the hospital, just as the doctor had hoped.

And so John Coliani recovered. Twelve days later John Coliani was released from hospital, to his cottage on the shores of a lake where he continued his recovery from stab wounds both to the body and to his psyche when Louise had to return, four days after his release from hospital, to a law practice demanding her attention in Toronto. John could not, did not, wish to stay with his mother, for there at Emma's home, where John spent most of his childhood, his mother was preparing to get off the train from which her had husband had already disembarked.

John made a good recovery and that was good because he would need his strength for the following summer. He never did go back that year to teach at the Catholic high school since a supply teacher replaced him for the rest of what was left of the school year upon John's release from the hospital. And eventually the furor and publicity of what he had endured died down in the town so that he was able to go out to shop and do whatever he required without being treated as the main character in a significant news event.

The staring eventually abated. People whom he knew stopped asking him to tell the whole story over and over again, about how he had become involved in the first place. At first John could not get over the nerve of people, especially people he hardly knew wanting him to narrate the entire story from beginning to end. He knew he had probably pissed off quite a few people when he tired of their boldness, their curiosity, and began telling them he was trying to forget what had happened and chose not to speak of it anymore.

Even the police eventually stopped coming to his cottage and asking him again and again to go over every detail. It appeared that had long ago they had accepted that John's role in the story was merely that of someone in the wrong place at the wrong time. He knew from Wally that the investigation was far from over; the RCMP and the OPP had many staff working full time on this case. They wanted Jean-Guy Fong's principals and would do everything possible to apprehend them. They were prepared to work very hard for a long as it took. Barry McDevitt, whom John never saw again, did survive and was incarcerated somewhere awaiting trial. Being very valuable to the combined police forces, the location of his incarceration was unknown to most.

John spent most of that summer in his home town, with frequent trips to Toronto, and Louise came up every weekend with the girls, except that Nancy now had a summer job as grocery store cashier and could not always come up with her, and with Debbie, but as he regained his strength he also gained some new interests. These did not include golf. Walking, and more walking, seemed to preoccupy him, as did spending time with his mother, sometimes at her home, sometimes in her hospital room, where despite her wishes, she was often to be found that summer of 1997.

John and Louise talked often that summer. In fact, it was like a real honeymoon that summer, except when they were forced to deal with matters domestic not long after his release from hospital and immediately after her return to the practice of Toronto law. For their youngest daughter Debbie, now 14 years of age, had just failed her first year of high school. And their oldest daughter Nancy, 18 years of age, graduated from high school and announced that she was not going to accept either of the two offers of admission to attend university but instead, wanted to get a job, save some money, and do some traveling. Actually, she wanted to go traveling immediately but knew that her parents would not bankroll such aspirations.

Louise was hit very hard by the news concerning both her daughters. These were two very good little girls whose ships were, suddenly and without warning, about to sail into troubled waters. It was a shock to John as well. He knew what was going on? Debbie had always seemed to enjoy school, her teachers and the friends she had there. Now at the end of her Grade 9 year, came this report card on which more than one teacher had said about Debbie that she was not "working up to her potential".

While she had passed the courses in the first semester, albeit with marks quite a bit lower than they were used to seeing her get, both Louise and John half expected as much, what with the adjustment to high school, and the fact that her parents were talking a divorce, and the family "home" such as she had experienced it, was no more. But they were not prepared for her failing three out of four subjects in the second semester, and finding out that she had been skipping a great deal of school. Worst of all, Louise had discovered that letters sent home by the school pertaining to Debbie's frequent absences, and concerning her almost total lack of application, had been intercepted by Debbie herself and destroyed, so that Mom would not know the truth. This kind of behavior on Debbie's part was a complete mystery to Louise. Who was this child all of a sudden? How had she become capable of this kind of deceit? What was going wrong at school?

It was not that Louise was naive about her marital break-up's effects on children and school performance. She knew what to expect and was watching for signs in what she thought was a diligent manner. It was more that when it did happen she could not see it happening. Poor report cards in the first semester were one thing under the circumstances, but no report cards, no contact at all during second semester she did not notice in the least, being so preoccupied with many of the details of her professional and personal life. If she wasn't dealing with pressing problems at work, she was dealing with her own lawyer's letters to John, about whom she grew increasingly confused and agitated.

And John, the absent parent, woke up suddenly one summer day to the news that his oldest daughter did not choose to go to university. In addition to watching a dying mother, he now had two daughters to worry about. Luckily, he and Louise would be able to face parenting a little more together now.

John went immediately to Toronto, when he got the news about Debbie's school year. There were discussions at the Debbie's high school, and John and Louise spent hours talking with each other and with Debbie about what had gone wrong. Mostly Debbie cried and said how much she had been angry with Daddy. There was not much he could say. Both John and Louise knew that if they could be a family again, and they were working on that–Louise had begun discussions with Bags' law firm in Beach Bay–they could oversee Debbie's return to academic grace.

But it was with Nancy that John felt most depressed. His anxieties took over him totally, as he remembered all of those young people who had "taken a year off" between high school and university, never to go back to school. He was worried that this would happen to Nancy. He knew that university was not meant for every student, that there was nothing wrong with completing one's education in the workplace, that no definition of "school" should be limited to the four walls of a classroom, and that people often went to work, and then came back for more formal education later.

He was also quite familiar with the buzz about lifelong learning. As a teacher, he knew the need for upgrading in summer courses. But, hey, this was his own daughter now; he wasn't just counseling acceptance with the parents of one his students now. And he also knew his own daughter, or so he had thought until now.

She was bright; she was university material. She would not be happy with any sense of herself which was marked by a failure to fulfill her own learning potential. She would feel like she had failed every time she interacted with someone she knew who did not have her native intelligence but had yet stuck it out at school long enough to get a degree. Especially when someone of this stature, in Nancy's eyes, was in a position of authority over her. And it would hurt like hell when Nancy realized that no matter how hard she worked in any corporate enterprise, the person with the degree would have more opportunities than she ever would. Having this rubbed in her face throughout her twenties, thirties, and forties, would sustain this sense of her own failure. John wanted hurt to be avoided in Nancy's life, wanted her spared this pain, as any father does.

He tried to explain some of this to her but discovered a daughter with a mind of her own, a daughter he had been growing away from for some time and only this summer did he see this for the first time. A daughter who wanted to distance herself from the control of her life by her parents, even if she had never articulated this to either of them before, and perhaps not even to herself. It was not so much that she hated school; not even that she could not abide the idea of more formal education for herself. It was more that she wanted to make a decision about her own life which was completely her own decision. As much as educated people like himself could be expected to foresee this stage in the lives of their children, John was stunned to see it happening with his own daughter–it stung to feel her rejection of his input, what he saw as his loving attempt to watch out for her future.

Louise rallied more quickly and saw Nancy's gambit for what it was, an attempt to become more adult, and to decide her life for herself. Louise also realized that the more quicky she and John allowed this natural process to take its course, the easier it would be for Nancy to return to whatever formal education she chose to take up. The rebellion, if it could even be called that, would live only as long as there was opposition from her parents to her decision to quit school for now. She convinced John to accept the inevitable as gracefully as he could under the circumstances. Reluctantly, John tried his best to do just that and returned to his cottage still feeling like something of a failure as Nancy and Debbie's father.

And so it was while dealing with these aspects of family life together that John and Louise, put the house up for sale in Toronto. Louise resigned from her law firm, accepted a position in the Bags'

BEARE PARTS

law firm, registered Debbie in the Beach Bay high school for the fall, and received the news of the death of Emma Coliani, on August 21st, 1997.

It was very hot that August 24th morning. The church had been cool but not the cemetery. Humidity had its way with everyone. Beads of perspiration blossomed on more than one brow, but they were mixed with the tears on so many faces, it was hard to distinguish between them.

As John saw his Mom being carried to the grave side by the pallbearers he thought now of his last visits with his mom. There was the one in her kitchen when Louise had been back in Toronto, but having already told him what his own mother could not tell him– that she was dying. It wasn't until this time together in Emma's kitchen over a stracchiatella soup/salami sandwich lunch that day in late June that John finally blurted it out: "Mom, Louise has told me about you. About your health." He had a hurt look on his face that his mother recognized for what it was.

Emma walked to him and threw her arms around him and said, "Oh, John. I couldn't tell you myself. I'm sorry. But I couldn't do it. You had so much to deal with these past months that I didn't want you to hear about this until you had to. And until lately, it hasn't been that much to bear. Until lately. Now… well. My son, I want to join your Papa." And she was crying now in his arms.

John realized how glad he now was that he had been in his home town this past year, closer to his Mom than he'd been in a long time, spending much more time with her this past year than he had been able to spend with her for many a year. "Things do work out for their own reasons," he had thought to himself with his mother in his arms that not so long ago morning in June.

Now this funereal morning at grave side, as he remembered that morning, he wished he could have just a bit of it back, that particular morning, to hug her once again. And the realization that this was not to be, ever again, brought on the sobbing.

Louise squeezed his hand hard which only made him feel ever sorrier about his loss. His mind went then to that morning he went up to see her at the hospital a couple of weeks before the end and, getting out of the elevator, had heard the moans of pain coming from what he had thought was another woman's room only to discover that the moans were those of his own Mom, semi-conscious now, from the heavy sedation, or the cancer, he was unable to tell. But he knew then that he wished it was over for her now. He would be able to say good-bye now if it meant the end of her suffering.

It had to end soon for her, it just had to. All of July and the first weeks of August had been one long purgatory of suffering for his mother, and while not the same kind or degree of suffering, for all of those who loved her, John, Louise, Nancy, Debbie... everyone who had anything to do with this beautiful, loving, Italian Canadian wife, mother, mother-in-law, Nanna, friend, neighbour. Many were those who came to the hospital in July to say their goodbyes.

"Do you want me to bake and bring you a blueberry pie, Mom," he whispered in her ear one day upon entering her room, knowing full well this had usually made her laugh, especially since they both knew he couldn't bake anything, let alone a pie. But this particular time, she merely opened her eyes and smiled a half-smile for him, her signal to him that she was glad he had come again. But she was gone again very quickly into her drug-induced space where he could not follow. The last few visits, she did not even seem to know he was there. And John had sat quietly holding her hand by times, knowing that he would soon have her no more but wished it would happen sooner rather than later.

And this morning at the grave side he wondered whether his Mom had now joined his Dad. He knew that the bones of his Dad were likely all that was left right here beside the hole in the ground dug for his Mom's coffin. But somehow he hoped that resurrection was not limited to a resuscitation of the physical body but meant some other kind of continuation, in some way he could not understand. He just couldn't accept that this was the end of his Mom.

Some such hope had certainly been his Mom's hope. She had told him as much... that she hoped her husband, John's Dad, was somehow waiting for her... that she would soon join him. John remembered that conversation this morning and wondered if his Mom had her wish now. These were the thoughts flitting through his head– memories.

Louise held John's hand but not merely to comfort her husband. It was as much to comfort herself. For her own thoughts were much aggrieved. She, too, had loved her mother-in-law, knowing well the extent of her loss. And while Louise loved her parents, it was wonderful how in marrying John she had gained a whole new set of parents. She had cried hard at John's father's funeral but this time, although she was crying, she too was glad it was over.

Emma had always let Louise know how much she loved her. And when John and Louise had split up, Emma had continued to be that loving mother figure for Louise, and a Nanna for her daughters. Emma had taken no sides, and it must have been difficult for her, Louise realized this morning–after all, John was her own flesh and blood. Louise was so very grateful for Emma.

It was for this reason that the first person she told, even before her own parents, about the partnership she was buying into, in John's hometown, was her beloved mother-in-law, Emma Coliani. They had both cried tears of joy that Canada Day when she told Emma that she and John would be getting back together again, that she would be working in Beach Bay so they could be a family again. Emma had said, "Oh, Lou, now I can join John's Dad in peace, knowing you both are going to be just fine. You have made me so happy today. I don't even feel so sick today," and she started to laugh and cry at the same time. Louise remembered that laugher now as one of the last times she had seen Emma laugh.

Nancy and Debbie were able to stare straight faced ahead of them for as long as their own Daddy and Mommy were not sobbing. But when their own parents sniffled, or worse, when Dad outright sobbed, it was impossible for Nancy and Debbie not to follow. But somehow they had got through the church service and were now getting through their time at the grave while everyone was saying goodbye to, and praying for, Nanna, whose coffin was just now being lowered into the earth.

Nancy, 18 going on 30, could not get over the finality of it all. She just kept thinking about not ever being able to laugh with her Nanna again. Debbie thought similar thoughts but most of all she was taken with seeing her Mom and Dad standing side by side, hand in hand. And somehow she knew she was going to be able to live with the loss of her Nanna, painful as though that might turn out to be, as long as she had her mother and dad again.

As they walked toward the car parked and waiting for their drive to the church basement reception, for friends and family, John stopped, looked back once more at the grave site, then whispered to Louise, "Thanks Lou, for being here with me today." And he sobbed when he hugged her to himself.

"Hey, teacher. I love you," she said. And John, Louise, Nancy and Debbie did a group hug before getting into the car. Emma would have been pleased. Who can say she wasn't?

also available from publishamerica
LEFT TO DIE
by Roman Garreis

Josh lives a horrific life. Abused, beaten, and betrayed by those who were to love and protect him, he can no longer bear the misery and hits the streets in search of hope, only to find that life on the street offers no reason for hope at all. His only false refuge is to sink deep into one of his delusions, which takes place in an opulent mansion. Inside, a beautiful paradise awaits with seemingly angelic benefactors who supply his physical needs and desires and nurture his intellectual talents—only to find they have turned him into an unwitting instrument of evil and a powerful weapon that misleads others along the path of death and insanity. Captured in this delusion, his mind keeps him between what he was running from and what he ran to, and there amongst the abusers and users, he is left to die as the strain of his inevitable fate from the drugs, prostitution, abuse and decay takes its toll.

Paperback, 142 pages
5.5" x 8.5"
ISBN 1-4241-9301-X

About the author:

Roman Garreis was born in Philadelphia, Pennsylvania, in 1957 and grew up on the South Side. His parents were divorced when he was five years old. His mother had a habit of moving to different neighborhoods which, along with the divorce and the coldness of city street life, left him detached and beaten down. At eighteen years old, Roman left his troubled life behind, and he now spends his time helping others to do the same.

available to all bookstores nationwide.
www.publishamerica.com

also available from publishamerica

GHOSTLY LOVE
A LOVER'S REVENGE
by J. Ferrell

Jacqueline Summersby finds herself stumbling on a house in the small town of Portsmith. A house that has haunted her dreams for as far back as she can remember. Dreams throughout her life that turn out to be glimpses of reality, releasing a hidden power locked deep inside her. A power used to save her most dear and loving friend, from the clutches of an angry spirit that has vowed to seek revenge on her soul. He tricks her with seduction and charm trying to win her heart, only to find that she has unlocked her hidden power putting an end to his wrath of evil.

Paperback, 231 pages
6" x 9"
ISBN 1-4137-9351-7

available to all bookstores nationwide.
www.publishamerica.com

also available from publishamerica
THE HORSEMAN
by Tom Alberti

Tom Blandini is a young rancher from Arizona who travels to El Paso, Texas, to buy four horses for breeding to build up his herd. His troubles begin almost immediately when he does not have enough money left to bring his horses back to Arizona by train. He makes a hasty decision to ride the horses the 300 miles back to his ranch south of Tucson. During the journey he must deal with an outlaw tracking him to kill him and steal his small herd. He also feels the brunt of a vicious storm that scatters his four horses. Tom's troubles turn worse when he encounters the notorious horse thief Chato Rosario and his bloodthirsty partner Blue Dog. His beautiful and impetuous wife Dominique sets out from their ranch with the help of their trusted foreman Rafael to help in her husband's return

Paperback, 185 pages
6" x 9"
ISBN 1-60474-906-7

About the author:

Tom Alberti was born in Chicago but, from an early age dreamed of owning and riding horses. When he was fifteen, his family moved to Phoenix, Arizona. At the time Phoenix was mostly small with an Old West environment. It was here Tom started riding horses and studying Western history.

available to all bookstores nationwide.
www.publishamerica.com

also available from publishamerica
GOD'S MOMENT
by Franklin Howard

God's Moment is a story of possible redemption, like *The Color Purple*. It'll make you laugh, think, and cry. It's a story that many will relate to and enjoy. It's about a beautiful and sexy African-American woman who happens to be an unwed mother. She seems to always choose her own happiness over her children's welfare. She does the unthinkable to her children. We also find out about her family and how they live life in the South during the Jim Crow era. There are a lot of funny and moving anecdotes in this book that will keep you wanting more. Will this woman's priorities change before it's too late or will she continue to only seek her own happiness? You'll want to know how her story ends.

franklin howard

Paperback, 119 pages
5.5" x 8.5"
ISBN 1-60610-371-7

About the author:

The author was born in 1964, in Memphis, Tennessee. He is a lifelong Memphis resident. He has a beautiful and loving wife, Sophia. Together they have two wonderful and extraordinary children, Brittany and Trey. He currently works for the Internal Revenue Service and really likes his job. He is a Christian. He has an exceptional relationship with his Lord and Savior, Jesus Christ. He says Jesus empowered him to write this book.

available to all bookstores nationwide.
www.publishamerica.com

Also available from PublishAmerica

CUT THE CLOTH
by Joseph W. Boothe

"*Cut the Cloth* is a challenging exhortation to decide what you want to do, set goals to succeed, and overcome fears that lead to failure. In his frank and unconventional style, Mr. Boothe shares timeless principles which would enable anyone with the conviction and courage to implement them to succeed. Whether you need 'a gentle shove to get going,' or a 'serious kick in the seat of the pants to get off dead center,' this is the book for you. Let the wisdom of the words of this book, written with sincere conviction and genuine concern, motivate you to new levels of accomplishment and success in life."

—*Jerome Hancock, Sr. Pastor Southside Nazarene Church, Chesterfield, Virginia*

Paperback, 73 pages
6" x 9"
ISBN 1-60474-890-7

About the author:

Joseph W. Boothe has been in business, sales and marketing for over thirty years. He has consulted small businesses to enhance their bottom line, increase productivity, strengthen employee relations, develop workflow systems and aid in the creation of marketing programs. His website, www.CutTheCloth.com, is a resource to assist individuals and businesses. Nurturing aspiring entrepreneurs is his mission. Mr. Boothe received his business degree from Lee College, now Lee University. He is married to his wife, Sharon, and has four children and six grandchildren.

Available to all bookstores nationwide.
www.publishamerica.com

Also available from PublishAmerica

THE UNALTERED CANVAS
by Vanessa Wheeler

In the yard of a man was a tragic murder. One that Jolie Summers had filmed like a true reporter. With her eyes firmly set on the throne of God she wiped her tears and began to embark on a life as an artist. But eyes spied her mad artist skills and took her life and turned it upside down. Could she gain her freedom? Or would she believe in their lives?

Paperback, 108 pages
5.5" x 8.5"
ISBN 1-60672-395-2

About the author:

The author, Vanessa Wheeler, was born in Fresno, California. She is currently working on her second novel. She loves her dogs, Christianity, art, politics, science, and psychology. She is a born-again Christian and hopes her characters reflect Christian imperfections to honor their bravery as believers.

Available to all bookstores nationwide.
www.publishamerica.com

Also available from PublishAmerica

SWIFT EAGLE'S ODYSSEY WITH THE BUFFALO

by Ken Eichler

Swift Eagle's Odyssey with the Buffalo is a sensitive story about a young Indian boy and a huge buffalo that saved the boy from a near drowning in a storm-swollen river and from some hungry wolves. The boy's parents sought help from the Great Spirit to save their boy from harm. Was it by chance that the buffalo was at the right place at the right time, or did the Great Spirit intervene to help the boy? While with the buffalo, Swift Eagle takes a sleep-induced magical journey to the domain of the Great Spirit. The buffalo in the story is from a herd of thousands that were near Swift Eagle's Cheyenne village. The boy's love for the buffalo is heartwarming as is his affection for his playmate Little Flower. You will feel you are at Swift Eagle's homecoming celebration.

Paperback, 59 pages
6" x 9"
ISBN 1-60474-199-6

About the author:

After graduating from high school, I enlisted in the US Navy and served four years (1948-1952). After my discharge from the Navy, I enrolled in the University of Southern California and graduated from the School of Engineering in 1957. I was employed by North American Aviation, Inc. and later by McDonnell Douglas Company (MDC). My principal assignments were in contract administration. I retired from MDC in 1995.

Available to all bookstores nationwide.
www.publishamerica.com

Also available from PublishAmerica

COMING AROUND
by Ginger Williams

Iris Corrigan and William Pendleton embark on more than just a one-week Caribbean cruise in this exotic, erotic, sometimes funny, and almost disastrous, second-time-around, modern-day romance. Both having lost loved ones, under completely different circumstances, however, find themselves alone onboard the cruise ship *Whimsical*, but not for long. William, determined to get more than a tan on this trip, has a lot to offer Iris, which she soon finds out. And Iris has the one thing William has always desired, but never had—a family. News from back home in Tennessee, events onboard the *Whimsical*, three tropical ports of call, hot days and even hotter nights, all add up to one life-altering week. From heartbreak and devastation to love and passion beyond their wildest hopes and dreams, Iris and William are coming around…in more ways than one.

Paperback, 242 pages
6" x 9"
ISBN 1-60441-821-4

About the author:

Ginger Williams lives in Franklin, Tennessee, with her husband Danny. Their three children and six perfect grandchildren live nearby. Whether it's riding their motorcycle on back country roads, dancing to the songs of their favorite rock 'n' roll band, or exploring their favorite Caribbean islands, they're always in motion.

Available to all bookstores nationwide.
www.publishamerica.com